"What are we doing?" Noah whispered, his lips brushing my ear. I shivered with delight and turned the handle. The door opened, and I pulled Noah inside.

"I'm giving you the tour," I replied in the same soft whisper. "I thought you might like to see where I take English."

"But I can't see anything." His backpack hit the floor with a soft thud. Then his hands were in my hair as he placed gentle kisses all over my face.

I pushed him against a wall. "Then I'll describe it for you." I nuzzled against his neck. "There's a big desk at the front of the room, and a bunch of smaller desks in the back." We kissed, and I melted into his warm embrace, overcome by the feeling of being so close to him. Then his lips moved to my neck and he began planting soft kisses there, a sensation I craved. He moved back, but as I leaned in to kiss him again, he pulled away.

"Something's wrong."

I thought he meant that someone was walking toward the classroom. I listened, expecting to hear approaching footsteps or voices in the hallway.

"We're alone," I assured him. "Everything's fine."

"No, we're not. Someone's here."

**Also available from
Mara Purnhagen
and Harlequin TEEN**

*One Hundred Candles
Past Midnight
Tagged*

beyond
the grave

mara purnhagen

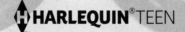
HARLEQUIN®TEEN

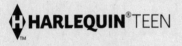

Recycling programs for this product may not exist in your area.

ISBN-13: 978-0-373-21031-2

BEYOND THE GRAVE

ACKNOWLEDGMENTS

A sincere thank you to the incredible people I'm lucky enough to know:

My editor, Tara Parsons, and the amazing people at Harlequin TEEN, with special thanks to Josie Freedman, Leonore Waldrip, and Natashya Wilson

Tina Wexler, world's greatest agent

Fireside Book Shop in Chagrin Falls, Ohio, with particular thanks to Lynn

John and Barbara Lohrstorfer

Rick Lohrstorfer and my fabulous cousins: Julie, Brooke, Kristen and Lisa Lohrstorfer

Sayrah Namaste, for offering insight

Marsaya Namaste, future author

Tina Smith Nonoyama, for remembering me

Dayton news anchor John Paul, for the technical insight

Bill and Mary Purnhagen

And finally, to the Craziest Kids in Cleveland (and best boys in the world): Henry, Quinn and Eli.

For spending over a decade putting up with thousands of bizarre, inane, and downright frustrating questions, this one is for Joe Purnhagen, who always has the answers I need.

one

I never should have sent my boyfriend to the electric chair. Watching Noah from a monitor in the next room, I felt awful for him. Frayed leather straps restrained his arms. Shackles held his legs in place and, even though his eyes were squeezed shut, I knew he was anxious and uncomfortable.

"Was it really necessary to restrain him?" I asked Shane.

"We're keeping it authentic," he replied.

Mr. Pate, the prison historian, scoffed. "Then you shoulda put the blindfold on him like I suggested."

I ignored him. We'd been Pate's guests at the Southern State Penitentiary for only three hours, but he'd already managed to completely offend me at least a hundred times. It wasn't just that he insisted on referring to me as "little lady," or that he was constantly snorting instead of blowing his nose into a tissue. What bugged me most was that he refused to leave us alone for even a second. He was openly suspicious of me and Shane and Noah, as if he thought we might try to steal something from the nearly barren building. As far as I could tell, the only things left in the abandoned prison were rusty metal bunk-bed frames and hungry rats.

And one antique electric chair.

"How much longer?" I asked Shane.

He glanced at his watch. "A few more minutes should do it."

On the monitor, Noah swallowed hard. Guilt flared through me and I fidgeted with my bracelet, the one Noah had given me on my birthday. I was the one who had convinced him to come along on this last-minute trip, even though four months ago I'd sworn off ever participating in another investigation. I reasoned that this was not a true investigation, but simply an outing to piece together needed footage. And it was Shane who organized the whole thing.

My family was semifamous because of my parents' work as paranormal investigators. Mom and Dad spent decades together debunking ghost stories and working under the theory that all hauntings were actually the effects of residual energy manifesting itself in different ways. Their career crossed over into book deals, DVDs and cable-TV specials and made all five of us—Mom, Dad, me, my older sister, Annalise, and our longtime cameraman, Shane—into dependable fixtures during Halloween TV marathons. I thought it would always be that way. It had never occurred to me that the Silver family would change the way we had—suddenly, and soaked in blood.

Four months earlier, Mom had been attacked in our home by a strange entity calling itself the Watcher. The head trauma she'd suffered had left her in a deep coma and doctors had warned us that even if she woke up, she might never be the same. I knew I had moved past the denial stage of grief, but there were still days when it didn't feel real. It had only been a week earlier that I had spotted a pair of her worn blue slippers tucked under a computer desk in the living room. I had thought of her sliding them on while she worked, and the way they looked as if they were simply waiting for her to return. I had left them where they were.

My injuries from that night had faded, but my memories had not. I often awoke in the middle of the night, my hand throbbing with a phantom pain. I had wallowed in guilt for months, convinced that everything was my fault, including the death of Marcus, the young man the Watcher had possessed. Mine was the last hand to touch him. Now that hand was scarred and Marcus was dead and I felt like a dull photocopy of the person I'd been before it had all happened, someone who was trying to hold on to anything familiar before it shattered into unrecognizable pieces. Because the truth was, I may have stopped the Watcher, but I wasn't sure if I had destroyed it. I doubted if such a thing *could* be destroyed, and that thought was enough to make me tremble.

Since the attack, Dad spent most of his time at the care center where Mom had been transferred a month before. He slept on a cot in her room during the week, and came home on weekends. At first, he had said it was a temporary arrangement. But days folded into weeks, and Dad's computers remained turned off, his files untouched. We all noticed but no one knew what to say, not even Shane, who was like Dad's brother. I didn't know what would happen to the *Silver Spirits* franchise or the hours of video footage that sat, unedited, in our living room.

It was strange to wake up each morning to a quiet house, but even stranger was the absence of anyone sitting at a computer with earphones on, editing footage. There was something so unsettling and somber about those blank computer screens that I tried to avoid the living room completely. It was no longer the heart of our house; instead, it was more like a sort of graveyard, with the monitors serving as tombstones.

One evening, Shane pulled me aside. "I need to complete

the DVD your parents were working on before everything happened," he told me after dinner at Trisha's apartment. Since their engagement, Shane and Trisha had insisted on hosting a Sunday-night supper every week. I liked it, not just because it gave me a chance to see Noah, but because it provided a rare opportunity to be with Dad, as well.

"Edit the footage," I told Shane. "Dad won't care if you come over and use the computers."

"I need more than that." Shane downed the last of his red wine—ever since he'd met Trisha, he had given up beer with dinner for a good Cabernet—and looked at me. "I need to go back to that old prison we visited last year. The video I took didn't come out right. I have to redo it."

"So redo it."

"We were supposed to film a reenactment scene. I need Noah to fill in." He glanced over at Trisha as she set a peach cobbler on the table, then turned back to me. "I need you to convince Noah to help me with this one. He said he'd go only if you were okay with it."

I refused. There was no way I was dragging my wonderful new boyfriend, the guy who had stood with me during my darkest days and was still by my side, to an old prison where people reported hearing the wails of dying inmates. We'd been through too much, and I wasn't eager to throw myself again into anything even resembling a paranormal investigation for a long, long time—if ever—and there was nothing Shane could say that would change my mind.

But Trisha could. "I know you've been through so much, Charlotte, and the last thing on your mind is stepping into a strange situation," she said. "But it means the world to Shane. He thinks that if he can complete this DVD, he'll be doing something for your mom, something she would be proud of." She lowered her voice. "And he doesn't want to worry you, but the production company needs the DVD completed before Halloween. Your family is under contract, but Shane doesn't want your dad to have to deal with it right now."

The practical importance of fulfilling a contract was one of the business aspects of my family's work that I was actually familiar with. Growing up I had witnessed my parents pulling all-nighters to get their work turned in. The house would fill with the scent of coffee, Mom and Dad would wear the same baggy sweatpants for days on end, tensions would rise and then, finally, the work would be completed and we would all go out to a fancy dinner to celebrate.

I missed those dinners.

"No pressure," Trisha said. "But please think about it, okay?"

And I did think about it. I thought about how Shane had been a constant presence in my life, how he would do anything for me. Now I had a chance to do something for him—and for the rest of my family.

Mom had always been in charge of the finances. I didn't know how much money we earned from DVDs, but I knew it was the most vital source of our livelihood. And while I was sure my parents had a savings account and we weren't drowning in debt—they were frugal people whose only indulgence was state-of-the-art equipment—I also knew that Mom's medical bills would be staggering, even with decent insurance. Meeting a deadline meant earning a paycheck, one I was sure we would need.

But I wasn't entirely comfortable with walking into an abandoned prison, and I suspected that Trisha had no clue that her youngest son would be an integral part of the investigation. I called Beth, my mom's friend and owner of a shop called Potion, to get her advice. I trusted her and her knowledge about the Watcher.

"Do you think we'll be in danger if we do this?" I asked her. Part of me hoped she would say yes, that the Watcher was asleep for the moment but if I did this he'd wake up. I didn't really believe that, though, and if I was truly concerned about rousing a demon, I wouldn't be conducting my secret late-night experiments on the floor of my bedroom. I realized that I *needed* Beth to tell me that everything was okay. Because if it wasn't, I had been putting myself in danger for weeks.

"I honestly believe that you subdued him for a good long while," she'd assured me. Her voice had a soothing, confident quality that acted like a bandage wrapped around my nervous mind, despite the fact that she had said *subdued*. Not destroyed or vanquished or incinerated. "This work is a part of your life," Beth continued. "The longer you stay away from it, the more scared of it you may become. Don't let the fear chase you, Charlotte. This could be a good thing for you."

A good thing for me would be to have my mom home, safe and recovering. I could almost hear her voice reciting words she'd spoken ever since I could remember:

Don't let fear guide you, Charlotte. Don't let it make your decisions for you.

In the end, I agreed, which was how I had ended up listening to the tired tales of Mr. Wilbur Pate, whose father and grandfather had worked as prison guards at the penitentiary.

I watched the monitor closely for any signs that Noah was in distress. He was alone in the execution chamber, with only a tripod camera stationed in front of him, but it was creepy to think that he sat in a chair in which hundreds of lives had come to their violent ends. I twisted my bracelet, feeling the cool black stones that circled my wrist, and turned to Shane. "We have enough footage," I said. "Please. Let him out of there."

"One more minute."

I narrowed my eyes. "In one more minute, I'm calling your fiancée."

The threat worked. Shane hurried out of the room, appearing a second later on the screen. I knew he was trying to recreate the execution of a young man, and that with his brown hair and medium build, Noah fit the description, but I wished we had spent a little money and hired an actor. Noah didn't mind, though. "It's initiation," he told me. "I'll feel like I'm a real member of the team."

I didn't have it in me to tell him that there was no more team. Once Mom had been hurt, it was over. But finishing the final DVD was important, and it only required Noah's presence for a few hours on a Sunday afternoon.

Shane released Noah from the chair and returned to the viewing area with him.

"Noah!" I flung my arms around him, careful to avoid touching his neck, and planted a kiss on his cheek. He cleared his throat and stepped back.

"That was intense," he said, keeping one arm around me.

Mr. Pate snorted, and I cringed when he loudly swallowed. "You was only in there for ten minutes. Anyone can sit in an ol' chair for ten minutes."

"Really?" I challenged. "Could *you* do it for ten minutes?"

Pate moved his mouth like a cow chewing his cud. "I do believe I could, little lady."

While Shane strapped Pate in the chair, I turned to Noah. "Was it terrible?"

He ran a hand through his hair. "I can think of better ways to spend an afternoon."

I tried not to look at the little bruise on Noah's neck. It was the size of a thumbprint, and midnight-black in color, almost like the stones on my bracelet. I knew how he'd gotten it, but I didn't understand why, after more than four months, it still remained. The other bruises had faded after a couple weeks, but this one refused to disappear.

"He's strapped in as tight as I could get it," Shane announced when he returned from the execution chamber.

"Good," I muttered. Maybe a few minutes in the chair would strip away some of the tough-guy veneer Mr. Pate had been shoving in our faces. When we'd arrived, he had slapped Shane on the shoulder so hard that he'd stumbled a little.

"We could just leave," Noah suggested. "Let him spend the night here."

"Be nice." Shane adjusted the color on the monitor. "He's doing me a favor by letting us in here."

"I think he's getting more out of it than we are," I said. "I mean, how often does he get to lead people through his empty building and bore them with stories about his grandfather shooting a rowdy inmate to death?"

Noah shook his head. "That was bad. Did he really have to imitate a death rattle?"

"Look." Shane pointed to the monitor. Pate was squirming and flexing his fingers.

I scoffed. "It's only been three minutes."

Noah peered over my shoulder at the screen, which sent a warm, tingly wave over me. "Ten bucks says he won't make it a full five minutes."

"I'll give him six," Shane said, his eyes on the monitor.

"You're both wrong," I announced. "He'll be screaming like a baby in thirty seconds."

Exactly twenty-nine seconds later, Pate was thrashing his head from side to side and straining his arms against the straps. I actually felt a pang of pity for him.

So did Shane. He rushed into the execution chamber and quickly released Pate from the chair.

"Looks like you win the bet," Noah said. "I owe you ten dollars."

I smiled at him. "Take me out for pizza and we'll call it even."

The door opened. Shane was holding up Pate, who panted as if he'd just participated in a marathon. "I heard voices," he gasped. Shane helped him to a folding chair, and I handed him a bottle of lukewarm water. He gulped it down noisily.

"There were voices. I heard them."

"Try to breathe normally," Shane instructed.

"They were real! You have to believe me!"

"Of course we believe you," I said. "Tell us what the voices said."

Pate's face burned bright red. He wiped at his forehead with the back of his hand. "They were whispering to me. They said no. Then they said *out*." He groaned. "They want us to leave!" He scrambled to his feet, knocking over the metal chair. "I'm getting out of here."

"We need a few minutes to take down our equipment," Shane said. We were in no rush. The debunker in me thought that Pate had probably overheard the wind. When the four of us had first entered the execution chamber, I had noticed small cracks in the concrete bricks. When I'd put my hand over one of them I'd felt a trickle of cool air. It wouldn't take much for a freaked-out imagination to interpret the whistle of wind as a voice. Besides, Pate had heard only two words, and simple ones at that. If he'd heard a sentence, I might reconsider the possibility that irate inmates were demanding his immediate departure.

Pate was still red and sweaty. "I never experienced nothin' in this place before," he said, his voice shaky. "I heard the stories but that's all they were. And then your family—" he pointed a chubby finger at me "—they come in here last year and now there's voices telling me to get out."

Noah stepped in front of Pate. "You might want to reconsider pointing at her like that." His voice was low and deadly serious, almost a growl. I'd never heard him sound like that, as if he was ready to punch someone.

"Okay, okay." Shane put his hand on Noah's shoulder. "Sorry, Mr. Pate. I know you've had a bad experience. We'll hurry up and be out of here in five minutes."

Noah stared hard until Pate looked away. "Five minutes," he mumbled. "I'll wait outside." He lumbered off, his heavy footsteps echoing through the hallway.

We automatically began the task of taking everything down. I knew Shane was upset by Noah's outburst—he considered it unprofessional to display a temper to anyone outside of the team—but he said nothing.

As Noah took down the tripod in the execution chamber, I asked him what was wrong. "I don't think I've ever seen you so angry," I said.

"I've had enough of that guy." He shook his head. "Let's get this done and get out of here."

We worked quickly to finish the job. It wasn't fast enough, though, because Pate began bellowing at us from inside the front door. "Hurry up or I'm locking y'all inside!"

Shane handed me a case of cable and the small monitor. "Why don't you head out so he knows we're making progress?"

"Sure." I lugged the equipment down the dark halls. The prison didn't scare me, but there was something undeniably creepy about the walls, which were moldy and covered with satanic-themed graffiti. I was happy to reach the front doors and step outside into the bright August afternoon. From the outside, the prison resembled an ancient mansion, complete with stone walls and narrow turrets. A barbed-wire fence enclosed the back of the property, but in the front, a graceful wrought-iron gate greeted visitors. The delicate curves of the iron provided an ironic contrast to what lay behind them.

Pate leaned against a wall and watched me as I slid open the van door and carefully placed the monitor and cables inside. I took my time, hoping Pate would get bored or that Shane and Noah would join me. Neither happened. Instead, Pate ambled over and peered inside the van.

"Fancy," he remarked. It was clear by his tone that "fancy" was not a compliment.

"The others will be here in a minute." I touched my bracelet and tried to push back the discomfort I felt at having Pate stand so close to me. He was still breathing hard and obviously did not use mouthwash. Or deodorant.

"Never shoulda let you people in here," Pate said. I kept my eyes down and pretended I was securing the monitor. "Everything was just fine. Never heard no voices before. But you roused 'em up, didn't you? You and all that fancy equipment."

He moved closer to me and I stepped to the side. "Nothing was roused up, sir." I kept my voice quiet and tried not to further agitate him.

"Don't you tell me lies, girl." I felt his finger jab me in the shoulder and I winced. Where were Noah and Shane? I was two seconds away from kicking this guy in the crotch.

"Mr. Pate, I'm very sorry you thought you heard something in there," I began.

"I don't *think,* girl. I *know.* Just like I know you got something to do with all this. Your family's cursed, and a curse attracts the spirits."

A drop of spittle landed on my cheek when he said "spirits." I felt my rage grow like a heat inside my chest and gripped the van's bumper.

"And another thing." He poked me again. Before he could say anything else, Noah was there, shoving Pate with both hands.

"Don't touch her!" he yelled.

Pate stumbled backward and landed on the pavement. Shane ran out of the building, his cameras left behind on the front steps. The wide wooden door of the prison was open, but it slowly began to close. As Shane pulled Noah off Pate, who was kicking his legs wildly as he lay on the ground, the door slammed shut, creating a cracking sound that reverberated in the air. Noah and Shane froze and looked at me. Pate scrambled to get on his feet.

The noise hung in the air, an echo that wouldn't die. I became dizzy and had trouble breathing. I tried to say Noah's name, but I couldn't. Black dots swam in front of my eyes, the world around me began to go dark, and the last thing I remembered before passing out was the sensation of falling—and of Noah catching me before I hit the ground.

two

For our final dinner together before Annalise returned to college, I displayed my culinary talents by throwing a bunch of stuff into a bowl. It had been almost a full week since the visit to Pate's prison, a week I had tried to fill by spending time with my sister, texting Avery at college and struggling to find moments for Noah and me.

"Is that parsley?" Annalise wrinkled her nose. "You're putting parsley in the salad?"

"It's green, isn't it?" I tossed in chopped walnuts, apple wedges and sliced carrots. If it had been sitting in the crisper drawer of the fridge, it was now part of my experimental dish.

A timer went off, and Annalise opened the oven to inspect her lasagna. "A couple more minutes, I think."

"I'm impressed, you know." I opened a bag of store-bought rolls. "I never knew you could cook."

"Mills and I took a couple's cooking class together last semester."

I liked my sister's boyfriend. He'd been so kind to me after Mom's injury, often staying up with me as I'd sat next to her hospital bed. We had talked a lot over the past few months, and he was starting to feel like family.

Annalise frowned as I arranged the rolls on a plate and shoved them into the microwave. "Maybe we should pop those in the oven," she suggested.

"No time." I pointed to the clock. "Everyone will be here soon."

Our guest list for the evening included Shane, Trisha and Noah. It occurred to me that out of the group, Dad would be the only one who had no idea that I had been having panic attacks.

Four months had passed since I'd witnessed the attack on my parents. Four months, one week and three days. And during that time I'd experienced six panic attacks, each one brought on by the sound of something cracking, each one jamming my mind with the agonizing echo of a metal fire poker smashing my mother's skull.

The first one had occurred when I was at home by myself. The second time, I'd been grocery shopping with Noah. A little kid had bumped into a display of canned vegetables, and the sound of the cans crashing had caused me to double over. Noah had practically carried me to the car, leaving our shopping cart behind as he'd whispered, "Please be okay, please be okay."

I understood the cause of the panic attacks, but I had no idea how to stop them. Annalise thought it was a classic case of post-traumatic stress syndrome. She consulted her former roommate, a psychology major, through daily emails and forced me to participate in annoying mental health exercises. I complained about it constantly to my best friend.

"She's your sister," Avery said as we sat in her room one day, organizing the things she was going to take with her to college. "She feels helpless and wants to do something for you.

Let her. She'll feel better and maybe she'll find something that helps you, too."

"I had to draw a picture of sadness for her."

She wrinkled her nose. "Okay, that's bad. What'd you draw?"

"A crying clown."

We burst into giggles. It felt good to laugh, especially with Avery. She was going to be leaving soon for college, and I couldn't bear to think about saying goodbye. It would be another absence to adjust to. We planned to call and email and stay in close touch, but I knew it was easy to make promises like that. Once she started school and her busy new life, would she have time for our long-distance friendship?

Satisfied that my salad was complete, I pulled the steaming rolls from the microwave. Dad walked into the kitchen and clapped his hands together. "Smells great!" I winced at his forced enthusiasm. Without Mom, he was miserable, but he tried to keep up a positive front for everyone. It had to be exhausting to pretend so much.

"It's all Annalise," I said, knowing that I was pretending, too.

My sister smiled. "Charlotte made the salad."

I couldn't tell if she was trying to warn Dad or give me credit for helping with dinner.

"Shane called," Dad said. "They're running a few minutes behind. Trisha got a call from Ryan as they were leaving."

Ryan was Trisha's oldest son. He was serving in Afghanistan, and a call from him was a big deal. She hadn't seen him in over a year, but he was finally coming back this summer. So was Jeff, Trisha's other son, who was also serving in the military. Trisha was planning her wedding to Shane around her sons' return so that all three of her kids would be there for the big event. "I don't care if it rains or snows or the reception hall catches fire," she told us. "As long as I have Shane and my boys there, it will be perfect."

Also as long as Mom was there, I wanted to add. It couldn't be perfect without her. But the doctors had warned us that she might never wake up. Then they spoke to Dad in hushed voices, advising him of the "options." I knew what that word meant—it meant pulling out the feeding tube and wires that kept Mom alive. It meant giving up and letting her die.

Dad said no. After Mom was transferred to the long-term care facility, he had to endure more kind yet firm speeches from a new team of doctors. They somehow convinced him that if Mom didn't show any brain activity within the next six months, they would need to "reevaluate the options." Six months, and there would be no options left. It was a death sentence, like pleasant words wrapped in shiny paper. Mom had until January to get better, even if it was only minor improvement.

For now, our lives were on hold, and that included the wedding. Shane had promised me that. "She'll be there no matter what," he'd said after the engagement was announced. "We won't have the ceremony without her."

It was a promise I was going to make him keep, although I wondered what he meant by "no matter what." At first, I thought he meant that she would be there even if we had to push her in a wheelchair. But maybe not. Maybe Shane didn't think she would come out of the coma. Maybe he thought Mom would be there in spirit, not in person.

"You haven't given up on her, have you?" I asked him.

The question earned me a look of sad shock. "No," he said, pulling me into a hug. "I have not given up. And don't you give up, either. Keep hoping. It's all we can do."

Maybe it was all *he* could do, but I had other plans. Despite my fear of accidentally triggering the Watcher, I was determined to help my mom. I was the reason, the *main* reason why she was lying in a hospital bed, which meant that I had to try my best to get her out of it.

Annalise checked on her lasagna and turned the heat down on the oven. "I can keep this warm until they get here. Any idea how long that will be?"

"Soon." Dad peered at my salad. "This is very colorful, Charlotte."

He sounded apprehensive, but I knew he would like it. Annalise had given me a foolproof job. How could I mess up salad?

"Have you guys given any more thought to your living arrangements?" Annalise asked. She tried to sound casual, but I could hear the worry in her voice.

"I thought we'd settled all that," Dad said. "Shane will be staying here with Charlotte while I'm gone. In fact, he's moving out of his apartment next week."

Annalise busied herself with selecting a salad dressing from the fridge. Her lack of response made it clear that she was not happy with Dad's decision, a decision he had made weeks ago but one my sister was hoping could be reversed through persistent questions.

It had begun after Mom was transferred to the long-term care facility near Charleston. It was the best place for her to heal and recover, but the distance meant that Dad would need to commute over an hour each way. He decided that he wanted to stay with Mom in her room during the week. Annalise would be able to visit often, as well, and promised that when Dad wasn't there, she would be.

Then there was me. My plans for the future had changed overnight. I deferred acceptance to college and instead decided to take courses at the local community college. I talked with an admissions officer, who told me as long as I got C's in my classes, the credits would transfer. I was staying home for at least one more year and filling my schedule with the basics: English 101, Calculus 101, Biology 102. I reasoned that my schedule would let me begin at a university as a sophomore and I could take the interesting electives there. Dad didn't protest too much when I told him my new college plan. He barely said anything at all.

Annalise, however, had a lot to say. "You can't stop living!" she cried when I told her about my revised educational plan. "Mom would want you to move forward."

"I *am* moving forward." I appreciated my sister's concern, even if it seemed a tad too dramatic, but she was beginning to border on the controlling. I was eighteen now. I didn't need permission from her to live at home. I changed my tactic. "Dad needs me," I said. "I can take care of the house. Do you really want him to be stressed about that?"

She backed down. "No. No, that's not what I want." She sighed. "I worry, though. Dad's so withdrawn and you're having panic attacks and if you need me I'll be hours away."

"You'll be a phone call away."

"It's not the same."

It wasn't, but it was all we had for now. I did not want to move to Charleston, which was Annalise's first suggestion. So much had happened in such a short amount of time that I decided I would not willingly make any more changes for a while, so when my sister came up with the idea that we should sell the house and relocate to a town closer to the treatment facility, I bristled. So did Dad, and I wondered if it was for the same reason: moving toward Mom meant that we were giving up on her ever getting better. And she had to get better. Although doctors couldn't tell us when, or how, or anything other than that she was stable, we believed that she was strong enough to come out of it.

"Charlotte and I have no plans to move," Dad told Annalise now. He looked over at me, and I nodded to show that, yes, I absolutely agreed with him. I wasn't going anywhere. My sister leaned against the fridge and folded her arms across her chest.

"But this can't be healthy, living in the same place you were attacked." Her eyes filled with tears. "Mom wouldn't want this. She wouldn't want you to live like this."

Dad averted his gaze. I knew it was difficult for him to look at her. Annalise looked so much like our mother. They shared the same clear eyes, the same wavy black hair. It was probably harder for him to look at his oldest daughter than it was to look at Mom, pale and motionless in her hospital bed.

"This is her home," Dad finally said. "This is where we're going to bring her when she recovers. I'm not leaving."

I nodded. "Neither am I."

The doorbell rang, and a moment later Shane's voice boomed from the foyer. "We're here!"

We turned to greet our guests with the happy smiles we'd all perfected. I didn't have to fake mine so much when I saw Noah. While everyone else helped bring food to the table, Noah and I hung behind. "You look great," he whispered.

I looked down at my jeans and white T-shirt. "I'm not wearing anything special." Except the bracelet. I always wore that.

"Doesn't matter. You still look great."

"If you really want to flatter me, you'll try my salad."

He kissed my ear, sending a little shiver down my back. "I'm sure it's fantastic."

Dinner was filled with bright conversation about Trisha's phone call with her son, Annalise's upcoming semester and the courses she would be taking, and how Noah would be starting school as a senior in a few weeks. I watched as everyone sampled my cuisine, taking careful bites and picking out the random unwanted fruit or vegetable. Noah ate three servings, so I was happy.

Trisha also talked about the wedding. "I know we don't have a firm date yet, but I want everything to be in order," she said. "When we have a date that accommodates everyone, I want to move forward with lightning speed."

I looked at Shane, who nodded. He was keeping his promise.

After everyone left, Dad retreated to the living room to watch TV while Annalise and I washed the dishes. "How do you do it?" she asked. My hands were immersed in soapy water and at first, I had no idea what she was talking about.

"I use the scrubber sponge." I rinsed a plate and handed it to Annalise to dry. We had a dishwasher, but I actually liked washing dishes sometimes. The warm, bubbly water and simple repetition of the chore relaxed me.

"I'm not talking about dishes." Annalise sighed. "I mean, how do you live in this house? How do you pass by the dining room every single day and not think about what happened there? I wasn't even here, and I think about it constantly."

"I do think about it." I held a fork to the light so I could make sure I had thoroughly cleaned it, then dumped it back into the hot water for one more rinse. "But if I didn't live here, I'd still think about it. At least here, I can face it. I'm not running from anything, and I think Mom would be proud of that." Again, I could almost hear her voice: *Don't let fear make your decisions for you.*

"Maybe." Annalise had been drying the same plate for a while now, rubbing it slowly with the dish towel. I put my hand on hers and she looked up, startled. "I don't want to leave tomorrow," she whispered. "If I go, I don't know how I'll be able to come back here again."

"You can come back with Mom." I hoped she believed me. I wasn't sure I trusted my own words, but if Annalise did, maybe they could be real.

"At least you'll be able to drive yourself to school," she said as she put away the small stack of clean plates.

"You're not mad about that, are you?" My eighteenth birthday in June had almost completely escaped my mind, the first time I could ever remember not being excited about the day. In fact, when I'd realized it was coming up, I'd cried. It was the first birthday without Mom, and after enduring the torture of graduation without her face in the crowd, I was not ready to tackle another milestone so soon.

Annalise had stepped in and made a sugary pink cake, Trisha had brought over a dozen fat balloons, and Noah had given me the bracelet from Potion. I wasn't expecting anything from Dad, as he was spending most of his time either asleep or sitting at Mom's bedside, but he'd surprised me by leading me out of the house and handing me the keys to his car. His gorgeous, shiny silver BMW, the one that I wasn't allowed to wash, much less drive. But with a quick kiss on my cheek, Dad had announced that it was time I had my own form of transportation. He'd dropped the keys into my hand, told me to drive safely, and was back inside the house before I could squeal with joy.

"I've already told you a hundred times," Annalise said. "I'm not mad about the car. I'm glad you can finally drive yourself around." She wiped at the wet silverware.

"Then what is it? I know something's bothering you."

She glanced toward the living room. The lights were off, with only the blue glow from the TV illuminating the room. "He loved that car. It was a gift from Mom. Why wouldn't he want to keep it for himself?"

I didn't know. He had bought a new car the following week, a little black hybrid.

"He needs time," I said quietly. "We all do."

"I know." Annalise put the silverware away. When she turned back around, her eyes were filled with tears. "I worry about you. Both of you."

I gave my sister a hug. "Well, I worry about you."

She sniffed and pulled away. "I'll manage. I have school and my friends and Mills."

"And I have school and my friends and Noah," I reminded her.

"But you also have—" she looked around the room "—*this*. You're stuck here, where she was hurt. I can remove myself from it. You can't."

What I couldn't make Annalise understand was that I did not want to remove myself from it. Yes, the house held horrible memories, but also good ones, and I couldn't separate the two. My life was formed by both, and I wasn't willing to let any of it go.

"I'm going to call you every day," I told Annalise. "And you'd better answer the phone."

She hugged me again. "I promise."

Later, after I was sure that Dad was asleep in his room and Annalise was asleep in hers, I pulled out the box I kept under my bed. Hidden beneath a bunch of wrinkled T-shirts were a few pieces of equipment my parents had used in their paranormal investigations. I turned on the EMF reader first and set it on my nightstand. Then I checked the battery on the digital recorder. Finally, I brought out my thermal imaging camera and turned it on.

"Is anyone here?" I whispered. In my parents' show, they always called out in a loud, clear voice, but that was to ensure the sound quality of the program. For my purposes, I only needed to be loud enough for the sensitive recorder to pick up my voice. "Can you hear me?"

I waited, as I had nearly every night for weeks. Only one light shone on the EMF reader, the one signaling that it was on.

"I need to know if someone's here."

I had been doing this for so long it felt like a sacred ritual. After I could no longer bear the daily visits to Mom's bedside, I decided that I could do something else to help her, something more powerful than my somber hand-holding. And even though nothing had happened yet, I still believed that I was helping her. I held on to the possibility that the answers I needed could be discovered if only I tried hard enough. Mom had suffered serious injury because of a paranormal entity. With her doctors at a loss for how to help her, I had to find a way they wouldn't dream of. If the cause of her suffering was paranormal, couldn't the cure be paranormal, as well?

My work was done in secret and in the dark. Not even Noah knew about it. After what had happened, it would freak everyone out. It freaked me out, at first. What if I contacted the Watcher or something like it? I wasn't even sure that the thing that had attacked my family was gone. Not even Beth, who knew more about the paranormal than anyone I'd ever met, could tell me that I was safe. She could only say that for now the Watcher was subdued, which made me think of it as being held back, but still struggling to escape.

Something had been after me and I'd stopped it, but that didn't mean it couldn't find a way back. It was my worst fear, and a solid reason to stay away from trying to make contact with the paranormal, but my fear was eclipsed by a powerful need to help Mom.

I waited, watching the lights on the meter and wanting so much for all of them to light up, but they didn't, and I felt defeated because I knew I was just a desperate girl whispering in the dark and asking for something I might never get. But there was still a voice inside me, quiet and insistent, telling me to try one more time. I clutched the EMF reader more tightly in my hand. "Please."

And something happened. Two things, right at the same time. Three lights on the meter lit up just as my cell phone buzzed on the nightstand. I ignored the phone and stared at the meter, willing it to light up again. Then I heard the tinkle of chimes from my phone alerting me to the fact that someone had left a message.

I stood up and, still holding the EMF reader, grabbed my phone, never once taking my eyes off the lights. I flipped open the phone and listened to Noah's voice.

"Hey. I thought you might still be up. Call me if you are, okay?"

Four lights flickered this time, and I took out the digital recorder and began speaking. "Is anyone here with me?"

It was how we always began an EVP session. The goal was to ask simple questions, wait for a few silent seconds, and then play back the recording to determine if it had captured an electronic voice phenomenon.

"Can you help me?" The EMF reader was showing only two lights now. I asked a few more questions, and by the time I was done, all signs of activity had vanished. Still, I was happy that after months of trying, it appeared that I had finally reached something.

After attaching headphones to the recorder, I sat back down on the floor and listened to what I had captured.

My first few questions seemed to go unanswered. The highly sensitive device picked up the sound of my own breathing, but not much else. I had been expecting more, even if it was an undecipherable voice, but on the tape I was already asking my final question.

"Can you help me?"

And then, after a few seconds, a high-pitched whisper responded.

I am trying.

three

Annalise returned to Charleston the next morning. She engulfed me in a firm hug and blinked back tears, then turned away before I could see her cry. I watched her car pull away, waving until it turned the corner and disappeared, and then walked down the hill to Avery's house. I pulled out my key, unlocked the front door and stepped inside. A low whimper greeted me from the top of the stairs.

"It's just me, Dante," I called. When Avery's little dog didn't appear right away, I sighed and trudged upstairs to find him. He always hid in the same place: underneath Avery's empty bed.

It had taken only moments for the airy pink room I had spent so much time in to transform into something completely different. Gone were the delicate silver picture frames that used to dot Avery's dresser. The closet held several dangling hangers and a single formal dress from Homecoming. Even the bookshelf had been stripped of all but a few titles. It wasn't her room anymore, I thought. It was the space that used to be her room.

I had helped her pack the week before, pulling clothes out of her dresser and stacking books she thought she'd need.

"This should be enough, right?" Avery had surveyed the half-dozen plastic storage bins that sat on her bedroom floor. They'd reminded me of oversize building blocks. "I mean, I'll be back over Labor Day weekend if I need anything."

"I don't know," I'd said. "I don't think they have stores in Ohio. You might be in trouble with only—" I pried open the lid closest to me "—twenty pairs of shoes? Wow."

"I need those." Avery swatted at my hand. "Besides, it took a lot of work to get them all into one bin, so don't mess anything up."

I wished that I could mess everything up. I wished I could make Avery stay here instead of driving off to Ohio for college. I wished I could keep at least some things in my life the same instead of sitting back and watching one more person slip away.

Avery sat on the floor, labeling her bins with a squeaky black marker. "That's it," she said. "Last one." We were quiet for a moment, both of us staring at the containers. Half her life and most of her room was packed inside them. They would be stuffed into the back of her mom's car and travel six hundred miles north. Six hundred miles away from me.

"Part of me wishes I wasn't going," she said. I looked up, surprised. "I mean, what if I have a crazy roommate? What if the classes are completely over my head? I thought I was ready for this, but now that's it's almost here…" Her voice trailed off.

I fought the urge to say that her concerns were totally justified and that she should stay home and take the year off. Instead, I forced a smile. "It's going to be great," I said. "You have nothing to worry about. And you won't be alone."

The day Avery announced her college choice was also the

day that Jared revealed that he had been accepted to the same school. He and Avery would be in different dorms, but they would be able to see each other every day.

"You won't be alone, either," Avery reminded me. "And with Shane and Trisha getting married, Noah will be like family."

"So I'm dating a relative? Nice."

"That's not what I meant." Avery pushed a bin off to the side. "He'll be around more. You can spend time with him."

"Yeah, but it's time spent with everyone else, too. I want more *alone* time with him."

I couldn't remember the last time we'd gone out to dinner, just the two of us. Even the simplest moments, like making sandwiches in the kitchen, turned into a group event. Shane would show up or Dad would wander in or Trisha would require my opinion on wedding favors, and whatever conversation Noah and I had been having stalled.

Dante had trotted into the room. He ignored me and immediately went to Avery and curled up in her lap. "What's going to happen to him?" I asked.

"He's going to have a rough adjustment." Avery scratched behind Dante's ears. "Unless I can convince my very best friend to stop by once in a while and check on him?"

"He hates me." And I wasn't too fond of him. We'd reached a strange understanding: he acted as if I didn't exist and I pretended not to notice.

"He doesn't hate you," Avery said. "And once I leave, he'll be lonely. Mom will be at work all the time, so it'd be nice if you came by to walk him, you know?"

"I didn't think Dante took walks," I said. "I thought he ran around in a hamster wheel."

"Funny." She looked at me with wide eyes. "Please? For me?"

"That pleading look doesn't work on me." I shook my head. "But you're my best friend, so yes, I'll do it."

She clapped her hands together, startling Dante. "But if he bites me it's over," I said. "Got that, Dante? I bite back."

Now I was in the empty room, crouched on my hands and knees in an effort to coax Dante out from beneath the bed. "Come on," I urged. "One little walk. I promised Avery, okay? Do it for her."

The mention of his owner's name caused Dante's ears to prick up. Finally, he emerged. I gently scooped him up and took him downstairs, where his powder-blue leash dangled from a hook by the front door.

"It's nice outside," I told him. "You'll see."

He gave me an unconvinced look. I was sure he blamed me for Avery leaving, and now he was resigned to putting up with the brief walks and random treats I offered him. It wasn't much of a consolation prize.

Outside, it was warm but not too hot yet. I slipped on my sunglasses and began walking up the hill, Dante trotting in front of me. The neighborhood slumbered in typical Sunday-morning mode. I let Dante determine our slow pace, which gave me the opportunity to gaze at the houses that made up my familiar street. Each house followed the same nonthreatening neutral color palette. Personal touches included a few cement lawn ornaments or decorative rocks or a basket of flowers.

I liked our neighborhood, even if I didn't feel as if I completely belonged here. I didn't know any of my neighbors by name. There was Lady Who Always Sat on Her Porch Talking on Her Cell Phone, Man Who Washed His Car Three Times a Week and Family With Screaming Twin Boys. I wondered who I was to them. Girl Who Walked Best Friend's Dog? No, they probably knew my face from what had happened inside our house months earlier. Girl Whose Mother Was Attacked.

When we were halfway up the hill, Dante came to an abrupt stop. He sniffed the air, then whimpered.

"What is it? You smell a bigger dog? A squirrel?" He was looking at the street. "Don't worry," I assured him. "I won't let a squirrel get you."

Dante responded by crouching down. His eyes were still focused on the street, trained toward the top of the hill, but I didn't see anything unusual.

"Come on, there's nothing there." I tugged at the leash, and Dante whimpered again. "I can see my house from here. If you walk with me, we'll stop there and I'll give you a treat."

As I was debating whether to drag him up the hill or carry him, a car came into view. Sunlight glared off the windshield, so I couldn't see the driver. The car crawled forward slowly, as if the driver was searching for a particular address and was afraid he'd go too far and miss it. The car stopped in front of my house. A camera emerged from the side window and the driver snapped some pictures.

I angrily scooped up Dante and stomped up the hill. If some guy was going to take pictures of my house, I wanted to know who he was and what he wanted. But as I got closer to the burgundy-colored vehicle, its driver noticed me. Suddenly, the car lurched forward and sped past me. Dante burrowed in my arms as I watched the car reach the bottom of the street, turn around too quickly and speed back up the hill. Its tires squealed as it flew past me. The darkly tinted windows made it impossible to see anything inside, and the space where the license plate should have been was occupied by a paper temporary tag.

It took only a second for the car to vanish. I stood there, petting Dante's coarse fur in an effort to calm him down. He was shaking as I carried him into my house and placed him gingerly on a kitchen chair while I searched the fridge for a treat that he would like. My own hands were shaking a little as I sifted through the drawer where we kept the cold cuts. What was going on? Maybe it was a curious fan, but if so, would he have sped away as soon as he saw me?

It's not the Watcher, I told myself. He's not driving around in a car. Calm down.

"Oh, good. There you are." Dad walked into the kitchen and tossed a pile of mail onto the counter. He saw the plastic deli bag I'd retrieved from the fridge. "Making a sandwich?"

"Sort of. But it's not for me." I motioned toward Dante, who was still curled up in a quivering ball of rattled nerves. "He got scared by a car," I explained. There was no reason to tell Dad anything. He had enough to worry about, and if the demented driver was simply an embarrassed fan, I would be causing him unnecessary stress.

Dad sat in a chair across from Dante while I placed a pile of smoked turkey on a napkin. "So, I've decided to go see Mom," he said. "I'm leaving in an hour. Can you be ready by then?"

A trip to see Mom took hours. We wouldn't return until close to midnight. "I start school tomorrow, remember?"

Dad nodded. "Right. Of course. Your first day of college."

He had forgotten. I placed the meat in front of Dante, who sniffed at it, then began to lick it. "I guess I could go. If you think we can be back by dinner."

There was no way that would happen, and we both knew it, but I didn't want Dad to think I was trying to get out of the visit. We were quiet, both of us watching Dante eat as if it were the most interesting event in the world.

"When was the last time you saw her?" Dad asked.

The question felt like a shove to the chest. I knew it was

coming, but I wasn't prepared. "Couple weeks ago. I went with Annalise."

It had been a brief visit, one that my sister had insisted on. While she made a consistent effort to see Mom twice a week, I often found reasons why I couldn't go. During the first month after she had been hurt, I went to the hospital every day. I spent hours in her room, feeling the rhythm of the machines that kept her alive. Her heart monitor was a drum, softly tapping out a beat. Nurses checked her vitals every hour. They would smile at me before reaching for Mom's limp wrist. She was so pale, so still. She would look exactly the same if we laid her in a coffin, I thought.

Days passed, then weeks. The hopeful doctors decided that they'd done all they could and said Mom would be better off in a long-term care facility. Long-term. The suggestion behind the word terrified me. Would she remain in this motionless state for months? Years? Forever? The doctors didn't know. She had survived the critical first twenty-four hours. Only time would tell, they said. Head trauma took time to heal. But no one could tell us how much time. And after months of minuscule success—her finger twitched once when I held her hand—a part of me gave up.

How long can a person cling to hope before it becomes too much? I wanted to remember Mom as the laughing, determined person she had been, not the helpless body she had become. Seeing her lying in the crisp white bed, the monitors beeping steadily, reminded me that she was not the person I had always known. It hurt. And I was tired of hurting. I wouldn't give up on her, but it was easier to hold on to hope when I didn't have to look at her.

"I know it can be difficult," Dad said, his voice soft. "But I also know that it matters. Us being there matters. I believe that."

Did he? Before the attack, Dad had never trusted anything that wasn't based purely in science. When had he transformed? I almost wished that he hadn't. Everyone was changing without me.

"I'll go next time," I said. "I promise."

"I'm going to hold you to that." Dad crossed the room and kissed my forehead. "See you tomorrow, Charlotte."

"Have a good trip, Dad."

After he left, I flipped through the mail. A thick white envelope had already been opened. I checked the return address. It was from the insurance company. I stole a glance at the bill enclosed and gasped when I saw the amount due. Dad's car didn't cost that much. I resolved to assist Shane more. The looming DVD deadline had to be met.

Dante finished scarfing down his turkey and I walked him back down the hill. Avery's mom was away for the weekend, so I made sure Dante had fresh water and added some kibble to his dish. Then I took him upstairs and put him on Avery's bed. He liked to be petted as he fell asleep, a job I hated at first but now found somewhat soothing. As the little dog drifted off into sleep, I looked around at the bare room. Avery had left behind so little. Just pink walls and a depressed pet.

I pulled my cell phone out of my pocket and dialed her number. It went straight to voice mail, but I didn't leave a message. Before I allowed myself to plunge deeper into pity, I called Noah. He picked up on the second ring, and before he even said a word, I felt better.

"Rough day?" he asked.

"You could say that." I told him all about the strange burgundy car. Noah was one of the few people I trusted completely, and he was the only one who knew my biggest secret: I had seen the other side, and that brief experience had triggered the Watcher.

"If you see it again, you let me know, okay?" Noah shifted into protective mode, something he seemed to do a lot lately.

"I will." I looked out Avery's window. There wasn't much of a view, just the side yard and part of her neighbor's house. "What about you?" I asked. "How was your day?"

"Interesting. I spoke to Jeff."

"Your brother?" Noah didn't talk about his older brothers much. I knew that they had both left home as soon as they'd graduated high school and enlisted in the army. Noah rarely saw them.

"Yeah. He called from someplace near Kandahar. I don't think I'm supposed to know that, though." He chuckled. "Everything with him is always so top secret."

"What did you guys talk about?"

He paused. "Our dad."

Noah had mentioned his father to me only once. He had left the family when Noah was very young and moved to parts unknown, randomly contacting his sons with a card every few years. The last time his father had reached out was with a postcard, sent a week after Noah's eleventh birthday.

"Why did Jeff want to talk about your dad?" I asked cautiously.

"Because he found Jeff." He sighed. "He Googled him, can you believe that? Found out about Jeff being in the army and got in touch with him. Jeff was always his favorite."

"Wow." I wasn't sure what to say. Noah's voice didn't reveal any clear emotion, but I knew he must be struggling with this new development.

"I'll tell you something," he said, and I could hear a fierce determination in his words. "I'll never be that guy. I'll never have to search for my kids on a computer, and they won't ever have to search for me."

"You're not him," I said. "You could never be like that."

Noah didn't respond. His silence was a sign that he was angrily mulling things over. "I could come over," I offered. "We could hang out."

"Sorry, I have some things to do. Thanks, though."

It was rare for Noah to not want to get together. He was really upset, and I felt helpless. I didn't know how to make him feel better, and I hated the idea of him sitting alone with his angry thoughts.

"Maybe later, then. I can swing by for a few—"

"No," he interrupted. I was taken aback by the force of his refusal, but then he softened. "I appreciate the offer, Charlotte, I do. But I want to be alone, and I have a ton of work to do tonight. I'll call you later, okay?"

"Sure. Okay."

We hung up. I remained sitting on Avery's bed, watching Dante and twisting my bracelet around my wrist. I knew Noah wasn't mad at me, and there was nothing I could really do for him except give him the space he needed. But he was holding back with me, not telling me what he was feeling or what he was doing, exactly.

Dante whined in his sleep and I reached over to give him a reassuring pat. "Everything's fine," I told him. "I'm not going anywhere."

After all, I thought, there was no place to go. I was settling into limbo, but as long as everyone else was there with me, I would be fine.

I hoped.

four

Like any normal person, I dreaded the first day at a new school. I told myself that this time was different because it was college, but I still felt the uncomfortably familiar clenching of my stomach as I parked the car, glanced over the campus map and gathered up my purse and backpack. I was marching into unfamiliar territory. Again. When was it going to get easier? I could picture myself at eighty, pushing a metal walker across the floral carpeting of a nursing home for the first time and feeling the exact same way I did now.

Better sleep would have helped my nervous mood. I had gone to bed early the night before after spending an exasperating hour working with my secret stash of equipment. My attempts to contact something had been unsuccessful, though, so I'd given up and gone to bed, only to be awakened at two in the morning by a strange sound coming from downstairs.

I had listened to the rumbling noise for a while before figuring out that it was Shane, who could snore loud enough to drown out power tools. If Shane was spending the night on our sofa, it meant that Dad had decided to stay with Mom.

Shane had made me an omelet when I'd woken up. I'd told

him about the burgundy car from the day before, and he'd listened with serious interest. "I'll keep an eye out," he'd promised. "You let me know if you see it again, okay?"

"Absolutely." I'd remembered the medical bill from yesterday. "Are you working on the DVD today?"

"That's the plan."

"Need help?"

He'd beamed. "That would be great."

I'd finished my breakfast and headed out for the first day of school. Now I was on campus, trying to locate the Yerian Building on a wrinkled map so I could make it on time for my first class of the day. My first college class, I mentally corrected as I hurried across the crowded walkways. It wasn't that I was in a rush to get to English 101, but the late-August sun, combined with South Carolina's thick humidity, was already causing my T-shirt to cling to my back. I hoped the classrooms were equipped with intense air-conditioning.

I was in luck. As soon as I pushed through the glass door of the Yerian Building, I felt air so cold I was sure the school sponsored a penguin breeding program.

The building's lobby reminded me of a decent hotel. Clusters of beige sofas surrounded wide coffee tables and potted plants too green to be real. I pretended to look for Room 107, but in reality, I was stealthily checking out the other students.

An interesting mix of people roamed the large lobby. Silver-haired women mingled with tattooed guys. A boy about my age nodded as he talked to a man who was old enough to be his grandfather. There were more than a few pregnant women and fortysomething guys. There was no one type, I realized. Everyone was so different that everyone was normal. Including me.

My stomach began to unclench. This was good, I decided. No obnoxious frat boys, no glittery cliques. I could be whoever I wanted to be. It was a clean slate, devoid of rumors or speculation or pity.

Then I spotted a girl near the back of the lobby, gazing out the tall windows. I wouldn't have noticed her at all, but she was dressed head to toe in sky-blue. She turned her face slightly, and I immediately recognized her.

"Bliss!" My voice echoed throughout the two-story room. A few people turned their heads, and I blushed. I strode over to the windows, trying to appear confident instead of completely mortified.

"Charlotte, hi." Bliss fidgeted with her purse—a tiny satchel also sky-blue in color—and cleared her throat. "What are you doing here?"

Bliss Reynolds and I did not share a positive history. We'd both spent the previous school year as seniors at Lincoln High School, where she'd worked hard as the school news anchor and I'd edited her stories with Noah. She viewed me as a constant threat to her position as lead anchor, while I saw her as merely annoying. When her grandfather had died in March and she was out of school for a week, I had taken over her job. It wasn't something I'd wanted to do, but our teacher had insisted. Despite my best efforts to be mediocre, I had won rave reviews from the student body—and jealous anger from Bliss. I had thought she would never let it go, but Bliss had proved to be a better person than I'd given her credit for. After my mother's injury, she'd stayed late every day to make sure my work got done. And when I'd returned to school two weeks later, she was nothing but nice to me. I almost missed her snarky comments. Almost.

"I'm taking classes here this year," I told her now. It was crazy how happy I was to see a former classmate, even if it was one I didn't get along with well.

"Me, too." She snapped the clasp on her purse. "I was supposed to go out of state, but then my grandfather died, and my mom needs me right now. I'm helping her out and earning some credits here so they'll transfer next semester, maybe."

I nodded. "Same with me. Although I'll probably be here all year."

"Oh." Bliss smiled hesitantly. "So, is it a long commute for you?"

"Not really. You?"

"Not at all. We live over on Woodlyn. It's my grandfather's house, actually." She got a kind of faraway look in her eyes. "We still have all his garden gnomes in the front yard, even though my mom hates them."

I thought of Mom's blue slippers sitting under the computer desk. Would she ever wear them again? Or would they remain there forever, a curious monument to remind us of how she used to be?

Bliss and I chatted a little longer. "Maybe we could have lunch sometime," I suggested. "That is, if the cafeteria here isn't like the one at Lincoln."

She laughed. "I already checked it out. Not sure about the hot food, but they have an impressive salad bar."

"Sounds good. We should do that sometime."

"Sure."

I waited for her to suggest a day we could meet, but she didn't say anything more. She was being polite, I realized, but had no intention of actually hanging out with me.

"It was nice to see you, Bliss."

She nodded. "See you around, Charlotte."

We went in opposite directions to our classrooms. I was right on time for my first class, which I enjoyed simply because all I had to do was sit back, listen to the lecture and take notes. It wasn't high school. There were no late passes or slamming lockers or people whispering rumors to each other about who did what behind the bleachers last Friday. I had entered into a drama-free zone, where everyone was too occupied with real, adult life to worry about the eighteen-year-old girl sitting in the middle of the room. I was wonderfully anonymous, and as long as I completed my work and didn't bother anyone, I would stay that way.

The only person who knew me was Bliss, and I guessed she was as alone here as I was. And maybe she was reluctant to be friends with a former high school classmate she barely knew, but that could change. I really did want to have lunch with her. Noah was at school every day until three-thirty and Dad was usually with Mom. It would be good not to have to eat alone every single day.

Class ended and I shut my notebook. My momentary good mood had faded with the thought of Dad sitting by Mom's bedside. He was still asking me when I was going to visit. It would need to be soon—I was running out of valid excuses.

I was typing a quick text to Avery—*survived first class, will check on Dante later*—when I became aware that someone else was still in the classroom. I glanced to my left, where a tall, lanky guy was gathering up his books. He appeared to be about twenty and was dressed in khaki pants and a white T-shirt. He looked up, and our eyes met.

"Hey." His voice was deep but friendly. I nodded, put my phone away and checked my schedule.

"Need help?" the guy asked. "Finding your next class, I mean."

"No, thanks." I held up my schedule. "There's a very informative map on the back of this thing."

"Yeah, well, if you need anything…" His voice trailed off. Was this guy hitting on me? Avery had told me all about the perils a freshman coed faced. She said the upper classmen referred to them as "fresh meat." Luckily, she had Jared by her side at every party, so she didn't have to worry too much about being a target for drunk and disorderly frat boys.

"I'm good," I assured the guy. "Thanks anyways."

He nodded and walked out of the room. I waited a moment before following. As I approached the door, something on the floor caught my eye. It was a business card. A very familiar one. I knelt down and picked it up. *Potion* was typed across the cream-colored front in swirly purple letters.

"Weird." Potion was a store I knew well, but it was located about an hour away. It seemed strange that Beth's business card had found its way here, to my classroom.

I flipped the card over, hoping to find a message, but it was blank. Had the too-helpful guy dropped it? Or did it belong to someone else? It was an odd coincidence.

When I returned home after my day of classes, I found Trisha sitting at the kitchen counter with over a dozen plates arranged in front of her. On each plate sat a single piece of cake.

"I was planning on having an apple," I said, pulling up a stool. "But this looks good, too."

Trisha gave me a weary smile. "I'm trying to decide on the wedding cake." She glanced toward the living room and raised her voice. "But someone is refusing to help me even though it's his wedding, too!"

I heard a chair push back. Shane appeared in the doorway a moment later. "I told you, I'm not a cake person. Whatever you decide will be fine with me."

"We're supposed to be doing this together!" Trisha seemed genuinely upset. "We need to make a decision."

I hated to see Trisha stressed, and not just because she was Noah's mother and Shane's fiancée. She had been a comforting presence in my life after the attack, handling everything we were too numb to remember. She had answered our phone—which never seemed to stop ringing—responded to an avalanche of email messages, and still found time to make dinner for everyone. She had stepped in long after the initial wave of concerned friends and neighbors had returned to their lives, leaving behind half-eaten casseroles and promises to check in on us.

When Shane had announced that he had proposed and Trisha held out her hand to reveal a single sparkly diamond, it was the first time in months that everyone in my family felt a real moment of happiness. Annalise and I hugged her, Dad shook Shane's hand, and we all sipped champagne from coffee mugs because we didn't have wineglasses. The wedding preparations had begun the very next day, with Trisha bringing over a stack of thick bridal magazines that she and Annalise flipped through, circling everything they thought was pretty or elegant or festive.

Noah had rolled his eyes. "She's gone insane," he'd told me as we watched a movie in the next room. "She's already picked out my cummerbund."

I had giggled, and he had pointed a finger at me. "She's picking out a dress for you, so don't laugh."

Terrifying visions of puffy taffeta had filled my mind as I heard Annalise squeal over a veil. I had stopped giggling.

I understood Trisha's enthusiasm—she had eloped with Noah's father at age eighteen wearing jeans and a T-shirt—but I didn't understand the rush to get everything done. They had months and months before the big day, a date picked because it would coincide with Ryan's leave from the army, but also because it would allow time for Mom to heal.

I turned my attention back to the slabs of wedding cake. "How about this? Trish and I will narrow the cakes down to three. Then you can pick your favorite."

Shane beamed. "Great! That okay with you, hon?"

Trisha considered it, then nodded. "Yes. Yes, that would work."

Shane gave me a thumbs-up and went back to editing footage.

"Where's my dad?" I asked Trisha.

She handed me a fork. "Taking a nap. Shane is supposed to wake him before dinner."

I wanted to tell him all about my first day at school, but it could wait.

"So, I think we should take a bite from each piece and rate them on a scale of one to ten." Trish pulled out a notepad. "I'll keep score."

We spent the next half hour stuffing ourselves with the sweet samples. We agreed that the slices covered with fondant were out. They looked nice, but neither one of us could stomach the fondant, which was a tasteless, rubbery skin stretched across a thin layer of frosting. We also agreed to eliminate chocolate and anything with a fruity filling. Finally we had it down to three samples and called Shane in to taste.

Trisha watched her fiancée with anxious eyes. She had a favorite and was hoping it would be his, as well. Shane took his time, and I couldn't decide if he was torturing us or really trying to take the task seriously. He put down his fork.

"This one." He held up the remains of a white slice.

Trisha squealed. "That's my favorite, too!" She jumped up from her chair and hugged him, then grabbed her phone to call the bakery.

Shane smiled at me. "Thanks, kid. I owe you one."

"Yeah, well, I owe you about a thousand." I looked at the kitchen clock. It was after three. "Will you tell Trish I'll pick up Noah from school?" I grabbed my keys and purse off the counter. "We'll see you for dinner and maybe we can work on the DVD afterwards."

"Sounds good. Do you have a minute, though? I need to talk to you about something."

I glanced at the clock again. "Sure. I have a minute." I sat back down and braced myself for an onslaught of wedding details.

"I got a call today," Shane began. "You remember Pate?"

"The prison guy?"

"Yeah. His lawyer contacted me. Seems our favorite prison historian is suffering from emotional distress since our visit and is demanding compensation."

"Great. A lawsuit." It had happened before, and usually didn't go anywhere. People thought we were loaded and they were looking for easy money. "Can't we threaten to sue him for menacing me?"

Shane nodded. "That's my plan. I'm hoping to put an end to this before it gets off the ground." He paused. "I haven't mentioned any of this to your dad."

"Good. He doesn't need the stress."

"There's something else, Charlotte. Pate claims that there's been damage done to the prison since we visited. He says he saw our van in the area last night."

"He's lying!"

"Yeah, I know. But he's not letting go. Promise me you won't go anywhere near the place."

"No problem," I said, getting up from the table. "I have no intention to ever return there."

"Noah's been talking about it, though. If he wants to swing by there, talk him out of it, okay?"

"Of course." I thought Shane had misinterpreted something. There was no way Noah would want to drive an hour to gaze at the creepy old prison. "Do you think that burgundy car I saw had something to do with Pate?"

He nodded. "Yeah, I do. Maybe he hired a private investigator."

"What a creep."

Shane followed me to the front door. "Drive carefully." He planted a quick kiss on my forehead.

As I got into my car, I thought about how Shane would make a great dad. Then I wondered if that was going to happen. Trisha already had three sons. Would she want another one? I shook my head and backed out of the driveway. It was too much change to digest.

I was able to get to Lincoln High before the final bell rang, which meant traffic wasn't crazy yet. I parked across the street and stood next to my car. Ripples of heat danced on the street. The final bell rang from within the school building, and almost immediately, students flooded the parking lot. I watched them, the way they walked in groups and laughed. It made me a little envious. I had been one of them a few months earlier. This place had belonged to me. Now I was an alumnus, a word that made me sound older than I felt.

After a few minutes I spotted Noah. He was talking to a boy I recognized from last year's AV class. Noah pointed to one of the back doors and the boy nodded. They were probably planning on taking footage the next day for the school news, and Noah was explaining where he wanted the camera.

As Noah was talking, another boy rushed past him, toward the bus line. His huge backpack knocked into Noah's shoulder. Noah stumbled slightly, then reached out and grabbed the boy by his backpack.

"What's your problem?" Noah yelled so loudly that I could hear him from across the street. People stopped and turned to look. The boy, who seemed like a typical nervous freshman, glanced around, confused.

"I'm late for my bus," he stammered.

"So you thought it would be okay to knock into people?" Noah was now gripping the front of the boy's shirt.

"I'm sorry."

A teacher rushed over. "What's going on?" she demanded.

Noah released the boy. "Nothing. He's late for his bus."

The boy ran for the bus line. Noah said something to his AV partner, then began walking in my direction. He hadn't seen me yet. I watched him, thinking that he looked different somehow. His face was lined with anger. And there was something else, something that wasn't right, but I couldn't identify it. He looked around.

"Noah!" I waved. "Over here!"

He saw me and smiled. Just like that, the anger disappeared. He looked perfectly normal as he strode toward me.

"Hey!" He kissed me softly. "I'm glad you're here."

"What happened back there?"

"Back where?" He looked over his shoulder. "Something happened?"

I was completely confused. "You almost got into a fight."

He frowned. "That was nothing."

"You were yelling." The only other times I had heard Noah yell was when my family was being attacked and when Pate had gotten in my face. He was one of the most laid-back guys I'd ever met, someone who was comfortable with who he was. He didn't take unintentional bumps personally, and he definitely didn't become enraged over them.

Until now.

He opened the passenger door. "Let's get out of here. It's too hot."

I got in and turned on the ignition. A lukewarm gust of air-conditioning blew at my face. I sat there, letting a long stream of cars drive past.

"You okay?" Noah asked.

"I don't like seeing you so angry over something so stupid," I said. "It's not like you."

"Charlotte, it was no big deal. I wasn't even that mad."

"You seemed mad. I thought you were going to punch that kid."

Noah laughed. "I wasn't going to do anything. I think you read too much into what you saw. Seriously, it was nothing." He took my hand in his. "You know me. I'm not that way."

Maybe he was right. Maybe I'd seen it wrong. There were so many people wandering around. But my instincts told me that wasn't it. I glanced at the bruise on Noah's neck, the constant reminder that he had been touched by evil. Had some of that evil seeped through him? It seemed ridiculous, but it was an idea I couldn't get past.

I reined myself in before I could concoct any more wild concepts. This was Noah. Getting frustrated by a clumsy kid was not evil. It was human. Still, I hated to see him riled up, and I didn't like the way he was dismissing the incident as if it was nothing.

"I heard you yell. I could hear you all the way across the street."

He kissed my hand. "I did yell, you're right. I was irritated is all. It's been a long day and that kid's backpack must've weighed a hundred pounds. It really hurt my shoulder." He pulled the neck of his T-shirt down a little to reveal a red mark forming on his skin. "Great," he muttered. "That's gonna bruise."

I automatically looked at his neck again.

"Does it hurt?" My concern over his outburst had morphed into concern over his shoulder.

"It's sore." He smiled. "But I know how you can make it better."

I returned his smile. "We have two hours until dinner. Where do you want to go?"

"You decide."

I wanted to be alone with Noah. Someplace cool, with lots of shade, but quiet, as well. An oasis away from everyone else.

"I know a place," I said as I put the car in Drive. "It's crowded, but no one will say a word to us. It's perfect."

five

On the evening of my eighteenth birthday I sat behind the wheel of my car, the big present that wasn't quite new but just as nice, while Noah sat in the passenger seat. We watched the June sun as it sank behind the trees, Noah's arm draped over my shoulder. After the final sliver of sun had melted into a dark puddle over the hill, he reached into his pocket and pulled out a silver box wrapped in white ribbon.

"Happy birthday," he said.

I kissed his cheek and reached for the box, but he stopped me. "Before you open your gift, I need to tell you the story behind it."

I sat back against the soft leather of the seat and waited. Noah seemed nervous, as if he was afraid he might use the wrong words.

"I heard a story once. I think my dad told it to me, but I can't be sure," he began, then shook his head. "Doesn't matter. A long time ago, there was a group of Apache warriors. They were attacked by a military settlement. Most of the Apaches were killed right away, but there were a few survivors." He shifted in his seat. "And instead of letting themselves be captured or killed by others, these survivors chose to jump off a cliff."

"This isn't exactly a happy story," I said.

"No, it's not." Noah offered me a rueful smile. "But there's a point, I promise." He looked at the box in his hands. "Everyone who had loved the warriors—their family and friends—spent a month mourning the loss. And their grief was so real and so pure that God preserved their tears inside special stones." He placed the box in my hand. "For you."

I untied the ribbon and took off the lid and there, sitting in a pillow of tissue paper, was a circle of shiny black stones. I picked up the bracelet, marveling at how each stone was different from the others. They were not perfectly round. Each held its own strange shape, but they were silky smooth under my fingers. "I love it."

"They're called Apache tears. And the best part—" Noah gently took the bracelet from me. He flicked on the overhead light in the car and held the bracelet up to the light. I could look through the stones, to the very heart of each one, where I could see a single clear tear. "It's a promise," Noah said as he fastened the bracelet around my wrist. "I will never make you cry."

I felt my eyes water. "I think that's a promise you may have just broken."

He laughed. "Okay, then. How about this? I will never be the source of unhappy tears. Only good ones."

And we kissed under the dim light for what seemed like hours. His mouth was warm and his hands even warmer as they circled my back and pressed me closer to him. We were breathing in sync, I realized with happiness. I wondered if we could keep it up forever.

Now I touched the bracelet lightly as Noah and I headed toward a familiar place so that we could be alone.

"We're here," I announced.

I had always loved cemeteries. Whereas some people automatically associated the places with rotting corpses and despairing ghosts, I saw them as quiet, peaceful islands slipped inside the forgotten corners of every busy city.

I knew from listening to my dad's lectures that for centuries, cemeteries were used as parks. Pathways were constructed to be wide enough for horse-drawn carriages to move through, and families would often picnic next to the stones of their deceased relatives. It was considered respectful to lay flowers before the grave and then stay a while to enjoy the afternoon. Now people assumed you were a morbid freak if you mentioned spending a few hours in the company of the dead.

Noah didn't think that way. When I suggested we spend our precious alone time at a tiny local cemetery, he'd cheerfully agreed. We'd both been there months before and knew the caretaker, Mr. Kitsman. After parking the car we went to his house and rang the bell, but he wasn't home, so we crossed his backyard and climbed the dozen stone steps that led to the entrance. Just beyond a weathered iron gate, surrounded by slouching trees, were a couple dozen old headstones, their names and dates almost unreadable. But I knew their names.

Noah spread out his jacket on the grass and sat down. I sat with my back to his chest. "You make a nice chair." I sighed happily.

He kissed the top of my head. "You make a nice everything."

I settled into him. I could feel his heart beating beneath his shirt. We talked about our days and I told him about seeing Bliss.

"Is that good or bad?"

"Good, actually. I like knowing at least one other person there."

Noah ran his hand over the back of my head, letting his fingers sift slowly through my hair. I closed my eyes, relaxing at the sensation. We were removed from noisy traffic and hectic wedding plans and crowded school campuses. It was just him and me, and I felt certain I could spend the night like this, warm and calm.

We talked about school and how Mr. Morley had asked Noah to train a new group of freshman boys about to maintain the cameras. Noah mentioned that his computer needed to be replaced soon and that his mom was hinting that she might get him a car before the wedding.

"Which would be great, because then you wouldn't have to work as my chauffeur all the time."

"I like being your chauffeur," I said. "It's nice to be needed."

He buried his face in my hair. "I need you for other things."

I laughed. "A new car would be great. As long as you don't drive out to the old prison."

Noah froze. "What are you talking about?" He pulled away so he could look me in the eyes. "Why would I go back to the prison?"

"It's something Shane said." I told him about Pate's potential lawsuit and how Pate was claiming he'd spotted the van and that someone had damaged the interior of the prison.

"I don't know how he can say that the inside was damaged," I said. "It was pretty bad to begin with. But he thinks one of us is behind it." I nudged him. "So where were you on Saturday night?" I asked jokingly.

But Noah didn't respond right away. "I don't know," he said softly. He pulled away from me even more and ran a hand through his hair. "I mean, I was at home, but I woke up at three in the morning. I was standing in the living room."

"You were sleepwalking? Has that ever happened before?"

"No, not that I remember." He looked down at the ground. "I keep waking up feeling exhausted, like I haven't slept at all."

I felt a rush of concern and placed my hand on his arm. "When did this start happening?"

"A few nights after...you know."

Noah and I never talked about the night we were attacked. We saw the same things: my dad thrown across the room, my mother struck on the head so hard she nearly died. He had tried to help, but the thing that called itself the Watcher had grabbed Noah by the throat and lifted him from the floor.

The permanent bruise, the sleepwalking—what had the Watcher done to Noah? Again, I made myself stop. A little sleepwalking wasn't a catastrophe. His interrupted rest was probably the result of stress, not demonic possession. I was looking for problems that didn't exist. In fact, I decided, the only real problem was me. The past year had been crazy. Maybe I'd gotten used to drama. Maybe my instincts were not as sharp because I had seen too much.

"What can I do to help?" I asked.

"I don't know." He wrapped his arms around me. "Just stay here with me for a little while."

We listened to the birds and the distant traffic. I put my ear to his chest so I could hear his heart beating. I wondered if my heart was thumping in time to his. It felt like it.

"Any more panic attacks?" he asked, breaking the comfortable silence.

"Not since the prison." I sighed. "Pate was so rattled. He was sure I'd caused something to happen."

Noah squeezed me. "It wasn't your fault."

"What if he was right? I've caused other things to happen."

Noah turned toward me. "None of it was your fault. You didn't choose it."

That was true, but it didn't mean much. I might not have chosen what had happened to my family, but it had still happened because of me. I could not escape that one terrible, simple truth. I didn't contradict Noah, though. We'd had this discussion before, and I knew he worried about me. I didn't want to add to that worry, so I stayed quiet and enjoyed our moment together.

"I'm sorry about earlier," he said.

"Earlier?"

"The guy at school. I shouldn't have let him get to me."

"No, you shouldn't have."

There was no excuse for his sudden aggression. But this was Noah. He was allowed to make a mistake. I didn't want to dwell on his odd outburst. He was sorry, and that's what mattered most.

"We have to get back soon," I murmured. "Everyone's waiting for us."

"Let them wait." Noah kissed me softly. "There are more important things."

THERE WERE MORE important things. And the most important one was to help my mom. That night, after Dad had retreated to his room, I reached under my bed and pulled out the box of paranormal supplies I kept there. I would not give up, I vowed. I could make something happen if I invested my energy and concentrated hard enough. As I retrieved the tools I wanted to use, my bracelet clinked against them. I carefully unclasped it and set it on my nightstand.

I was turning on the K2 EMF reader when my cell phone buzzed. It was Annalise.

"You're up late," I said, glancing at the bedside clock. It was past midnight.

"I figured you'd be up." My sister yawned. "I wanted to hear all about your first day at college."

I filled her in quickly, having regurgitated the boring details to Dad and Shane and Trisha over dinner earlier. Then I had endured endless wedding talk, a topic that I was beyond being sick of. I'd wondered how Trisha could even make all these plans and decisions when no date had been set. I couldn't listen to one more conversation about the pros and cons of blowing bubbles instead of throwing confetti at the happy couple after they recited their vows.

While I talked to Annalise, I kept my eyes on the EMF reader. One green light showed that it was operational, and I was hoping at least one more would illuminate. I thought I saw a second light flicker.

"Sounds nice," Annalise said. "So, have you been to see Mom yet?"

So that's why she was really calling. I should have known it was a trap. "Not yet."

"But you'll go soon, right? You promised."

"Yes, I'll go soon."

Annalise picked up on the irritation in my voice. "I'm not trying to nag," she said. "But I think it would be good—for both of you."

It would also be good for both of us if I could get back to work. True spiritual help might be waiting for the right time to intercede, and chatting about school with my sister was holding me back from finding a possible answer.

"I said I would and I meant it." I was tired of the conversation.

"Okay. You promised, and that's enough for me. I'll let you go. Good night, Charlotte."

"'Night, Annalise."

I returned to the EMF reader, convinced that I had seen a second light blink. I stared at the gray box, focused on seeing another bulb come to life.

And it happened.

A second green light, followed by the yellow and orange. Then the last red light was glowing, and I knew I was not alone.

I fumbled for my digital recorder, desperate to make contact. "Hello? Is anyone here? Can you hear me?" I was talking faster than I should have. I knew I was supposed to pause after asking each question so that if something was there, it would have a chance to respond. I took a deep breath, held the recorder away from me and started over.

"My name is Charlotte. I need help. Can you help me?"

This time, I waited a few seconds before continuing. The lights were still on, although the red light flickered a little. "Can you help my mom?"

Can she be helped? I almost asked, but I didn't, because I wouldn't be able to bear the wrong answer.

Another minute passed. The lights went out, leaving only a single green bulb shining. Whatever had been with me was now gone. I turned off the EMF reader, rewound my digital recorder and hit Play. I held the recorder to my ear and kept my breath still.

Can you help me? my voice asked.

And the reply, soft but clear even though it was enveloped in static: *I will keep trying.*

six

Bliss was right: our school had a great salad bar. It covered one side of the huge cafeteria and boasted three kinds of lettuce, ten dressings and every kind of topping you could possibly want, including strips of smoked turkey and chunks of imitation crabmeat. I piled hard-boiled eggs, croutons and red onions on top of a heap of romaine, drenched it with a generous ladleful of ranch dressing, then sat across from Bliss at the table she'd chosen for us.

It was the second week of September, and I was finally comfortable with my new routine. I attended two morning classes, came home for lunch and to walk Dante, then met up with Noah after school. When Dad was away at the care facility, I helped Shane with the DVD project, offering my opinion on scenes and searching our computer files for the original footage we'd taken a year earlier. We were more than halfway done.

I'd even worked out a simple schedule with Avery. I texted her after English class, she texted after her Communications class, and we took turns calling every other night around nine. It wasn't so bad. I knew all about her roommate's love of German techno music and how the dorm always smelled like onions and how Jared had decided to become vegan.

"I love him, but every time I have a hamburger, he gives me a look," she complained. "He can eat what he wants, so why can't I eat what I want without feeling guilty?"

Despite their differences in diet, they were still going strong, and I was happy for them.

And Avery knew all about Trisha's wedding plans and my classes and my walks with Dante, which I actually enjoyed, even if I was constantly on the lookout for the burgundy car. Nothing had changed so much that it couldn't be put back the way it was, and for that I was grateful.

I was also grateful that my late-night project was finally having some success. Encouraged by the two clear sentences I had recorded, I knew I had found positive energy. The helpful, non-evil kind that might bring me a step closer to making Mom better.

Every night I spent an hour reaching out, and so far, I had captured five distinct EVPs, all of them assuring me, *I will keep trying.* The voice sounded female to me, and while most of the recordings were faint and garbled, it was enough for now to know that something was listening to me—and trying to respond.

Happy that I was being helpful, I was able to concentrate more on my classes. My good mood carried me through the week, when I ran into Bliss outside the cafeteria and convinced her to have lunch with me. She hesitated at first, but finally gave in. I was determined to make her comfortable, to erase any of the suspicions she'd had about me in high school.

"This is fantastic," I said as I stuffed a forkful of ranch-soaked goodness into my mouth.

Bliss smiled and took a dainty bite of her own salad, which consisted of lettuce and a few sliced cucumbers.

I pointed my fork in her direction. "No dressing? How can you eat plain lettuce like that?"

"I like it this way," she said. "Trust me. When you spend your entire elementary-school years being called Big Juicy you learn to enjoy things plain."

I almost choked on a slice of hard-boiled egg. "They called you Big Juicy?"

Bliss shook her head. "It's stupid, I know. I was a chunky kid, and one day in the fourth grade I made the unforgivable mistake of ordering a double cheeseburger at lunch, which wasn't even on the menu. The nickname stuck."

"That's terrible."

"Yeah, I was traumatized. But my grandfather was also heavy, and when I told him what had happened, we went on a diet together. We both lost weight. It was nice, actually."

"Sounds like he was very supportive of you."

Bliss stared at her salad for a moment. "He was."

I didn't know if that was my cue to say something encouraging, like, "I'm sure he still is." I wasn't good at sentiments like that, mainly because I didn't believe that the dead lingered behind in order to watch over their loved ones. The silence between Bliss and I stretched for longer than was comfortable as I struggled to come up with something to say.

"Well," I began, "I'm sure he would be very proud...."

My awkward attempt at optimism was cut off by a loud crash.

I froze. My vision began to swirl, and my chest tightened. Bliss was looking past me, at the source of the noise.

"Someone dropped a bunch of lunch trays," she said. "They're cleaning it up."

I heard her voice, but it sounded as if she was far away. I was dizzy and having trouble breathing.

"You okay?" Bliss sounded concerned.

I couldn't answer her. *Not here,* I thought. *Oh please, not here and not now.* I felt that I should be able to control this. I knew why it was happening, so why couldn't I stop it? That logical part of my brain was overridden by something else, though, something with a stronger pull. Because that was how it truly felt: as if I was being pulled down into something dark, something awful, and I needed to get out. I needed to escape from this room, which had no oxygen, and away from these people. I had to go somewhere, anywhere else.

"Charlotte?"

By now I was hyperventilating. "Don't," I gasped. "Don't let them see me." The dizziness claimed me and my head hit the table. Wet salad stuck to my cheek and I didn't care. I wasn't sure what I'd said to Bliss or what it meant, but I knew I had to get out of that room. In a flash, Bliss was at my side, propping me up.

"Charlotte? You need to talk to me or I'm going to have to call an ambulance."

"No." I struggled to sit up, but I was still having trouble breathing. "Please, get me out of here."

I heard a male voice close by. "She okay?"

"Yeah." Bliss was struggling to lift me from my seat. "It's just her period. Those cramps can be brutal."

"Whoa." The guy scurried away.

"Listen to me," Bliss said into my ear. "I'm going to get you outside, but I need you to breathe, okay? Listen to me. Breathe in, breathe out."

I focused on her voice. I made myself breathe when she directed me to do so, and within minutes, I was feeling less dizzy. Also, I realized with confusion, I was outside.

"What happened?" I held a vague memory of the cafeteria, but my mind was blurry. I had no idea how much time had passed, but Bliss and I were both sitting in the grass outside.

My back was pressed against a tree. Bliss was across from me, dabbing a damp paper towel to my forehead.

"I think you had a panic attack." She squeezed excess water from the paper towel before pressing it against the back of my neck. "First one?"

"No," I admitted. "Not even close. How did you know what was happening?"

"My mom used to have them all the time. It took me a minute to catch on with you, though. Do you know what caused it?"

"The sound of the trays crashing."

I told Bliss about my previous panic attacks and how they always occurred after a loud, sudden noise. The first one had happened when I was alone. I had spent a long day at the hospital with my mom and was exhausted, so when I got home I had curled up on the couch to watch a little TV. I was slowly flipping through the channels, hoping to find a decent rerun, when an action movie filled the screen. Men in business suits chased a girl through a warehouse. She stumbled, the men surrounded her, and she looked up as a board came smashing down on her body.

The scene cut to a commercial, leaving the girl's fate uncertain, but I was already sliding into panic mode. I immediately felt dizzy and nauseous. I bent over, trying to breathe but also trying to keep myself from throwing up all over the sofa.

I wasn't sure what was happening to me. My first thought was that I was sick, like food-poisoning sick, but when my vision began to blur, I knew it was something else. Later, when I typed in my symptoms on the computer, I figured out that I had experienced tunnel vision, a painfully common aspect of panic attacks.

The sharper the sound, the more quickly I felt dragged back

to that shattering moment when I'd witnessed my mother's attack.

"So that's how it is," I said. "For the rest of my life, I'll be reduced to a shaking mess anytime someone drops something."

"That's not true. You can fix this, Charlotte."

"I don't know how."

"Well, I do." She placed the paper towel on the grass. "I helped my mom through it. And now I'm going to help you."

"What happened to your mom?" I asked. "I mean, what caused her to start having them?"

Bliss picked at the paper towel. "She had just loaded groceries into her car and was about to back out of the parking lot when a man tried to carjack her. The doors were locked so he couldn't get in, but she was terrified. She couldn't drive for months, and anytime she tried, she'd melt down." Bliss gave me a wry smile. "That's why I learned to drive when I was thirteen."

I almost laughed. "I can't picture you breaking the rules and driving around town at thirteen."

"Yeah, well, I did. Someone had to take her to work every day."

"How did she overcome it?"

"It took time. Time and help."

I shook my head. "I'm not going to see a psychiatrist."

"And I'm not going to make you. But you need to confront the root of the problem, Charlotte. Look it in the eyes."

"Her eyes are closed," I whispered. I said the words without thinking. It was a shock to me—the trigger may have been an abrupt sound, but the real problem was my mom.

And my fear about losing her.

Bliss took my hand. "First, let me tell you that these episodes are harmless. They won't kill you. So the next time it happens, tell yourself that it's only panic, and it's not fatal."

"Sure." I appreciated Bliss's desire to help me, but even if she had experience with the same kind of problem, it wasn't the same. She hadn't seen what I had seen.

"Charlotte." Bliss touched my arm. "Charlotte, you can make this better. But in order to do that, I think you have to go see your mom."

Everyone was telling me the same thing: go see Mom. Did they really think one visit would help me? I looked past Bliss, at the people rushing to class. If they glanced over, they would simply see two girls sitting on the grass, talking. It was so nice not to be noticed, I thought.

Then I saw someone across the green expanse of lawn. He was looking directly at me. It was the guy from my English class, the one I had chatted with briefly. I frowned, and he turned and walked away, his backpack slung over one shoulder.

"Still here?"

I blinked. "Yes. I'm still here." I tried to smile. "Thanks for getting me out of the cafeteria, Bliss. I appreciate it."

"Did you hear me before? About visiting your mom?"

"Yeah."

"So?"

I had to make a decision. No more stalling, no more excuses. I squeezed Bliss's hand.

"Okay," I said. "I'll go. I promise."

I HAD ANOTHER promise to keep first. With Dad away at the care facility for the night, Shane and I would have hours of uninterrupted time to work on the DVD. After changing into a pair of comfy plaid pajama pants, I settled into one of our workstations, prepared to tackle our project.

My family never used a living room as space for a nice sofa and coffee table. Instead, the room was reserved for our many computers, filing cabinets and boxes of data. It was essentially a massive home office.

Three computers were already on when I sat down next to Shane, ready to work. "The good news is that the A-roll is done," Shane said. "But we need to throw down the B-roll."

Slipping into the familiar tech language was as comfortable to me as my pajama pants. When we worked on a DVD, the audio had to be completed first. Then the raw video clips were trimmed and placed within a timeline. It was an intricate puzzle, one I loved piecing together.

"We're using footage taken at the penitentiary last year, but we need to splice it with some of the shots we got with Pate." Shane held up two memory cards. "Your choice—old stuff or new?"

I reached for the new card. Watching scenes featuring Mom was not something I was sure I could handle. The clips came up on my monitor, and I realized the amount of work we had to do. One afternoon at Pate's had resulted in a thousand different clips, each one needing to be sorted through and pruned down to about ten minutes of video.

"What's our deadline again?"

Shane had more than three times the video I had. "Less than a month. It's doable, but we need to get going."

"Got it." I opened a clip of Noah first. The reenactment scene would come toward the end, and I wanted to see how much we had. I smiled when his face appeared on the screen. The project wouldn't be so bad if I could spend most of the time watching my boyfriend. In fact, I wished he was with us now. He knew how to edit better than most people. I suggested it to Shane.

"I asked him, but he's busy tonight. Some school project."

He was probably taping a football game for AV class. His teacher had put Noah in charge of training all the new students, which basically meant taking them to different sporting events and making sure they didn't break the cameras.

We continued to work for a while. Shane turned on some music, but I begged him to turn it off as soon as I heard the heavy guitar intro. "Can't you play something from the last decade?"

"This is classic rock. It's classic for a reason."

"It's dead-guy rock."

"Blasphemy!" Shane put a hand over his heart. "I have impeccable taste in music. It's why Trish put me in charge of the wedding playlist."

"Please don't make her regret it."

"That's the same thing she said! Trust me, it's going to rock."

Over the next hour, we made some real progress. Shane had put together an outline, which made it easier to choose clips and discard the ones I knew we wouldn't use. I fell into a nice rhythm as I marked in-points and out-points, then dragged the video into our timeline. I liked getting lost in the work. Thoughts of school and concerns over Noah were replaced with a focus on lighting and where we could splice in effects.

"Can you show me the hallway?" Shane asked. I was so absorbed in my work that I was barely aware of his presence.

"Sure." I clicked on a segment.

Shane wheeled his chair closer. "Crap. That might be a problem." He showed me original shots of the hallway. Compared to the more recent shots, there was a definite difference. The graffiti had doubled, and some of it would need to be blurred out if the show was going to air on television.

"I can't believe Pate thinks we're the problem, when obviously people have been sneaking in for over a year," I said.

"And coming up with inventive new ways to describe bodily functions," Shane added.

Something on the opposite wall caught my eye, and I opened a clip that showed it more clearly. In tall, lopsided black letters was a single sentence that stretched from one end of the hallway to the other: *The gate is now open.* Beneath it, a shaky arrow pointed toward the execution chamber.

"Was that there last year?" I asked.

Shane checked his footage. "Nope. That's new."

"The gate is now open," I whispered. On the surface, it sounded so simple and nonthreatening. But it bothered me. I studied the still image, trying to pinpoint what it was about the line that made me shiver a little. How had I not seen those words during our recent visit? We had walked down that hallway several times, and the huge letters would have been difficult to miss.

I closed the clip and returned to my work, but the sentence lingered in my mind. It was probably nothing. Meaningless graffiti scrawled in the middle of the night was not my concern. But every time I dragged through the new footage, it was there, and I couldn't shake the feeling that it was not supposed to be there.

Or maybe we weren't supposed to have gone there.

seven

The next day I signed in at the nurse's station. I concentrated on the white walls and speckled floor, afraid that if I allowed myself to really take in the surroundings, I might not be able to breathe. I hated this place. They tried to make it seem more homey by decorating the hallways with brass-framed pictures of the quiet countryside and a few shiny oak tables, but the antiseptic smell that drenched the air and the perpetual beeping of a hundred machines working to keep people alive provided a constant reminder that this was a sad, sick place.

After I had made my decision to finally fulfill the promises I had made to Dad and Annalise and even Bliss, I knew I had to act quickly, before I thought about it too much and changed my mind. I had called Noah and asked him to come with me, but he was swamped with schoolwork.

"I wish I could be there for you," he'd said. "But Morley has me taping a game tonight. I'm training two freshmen."

I didn't think the AV teacher had ever asked Noah to give up a Saturday night before, but I didn't press it. Visiting Mom was something I needed to do on my own, without Noah present to serve as my emotional crutch. We made plans to see each other on Sunday, and I grabbed my keys and wrote a note to Dad about where I was going.

"It's nice to see your mother get so many visitors," said the nurse behind the counter.

"I'm glad." I handed back the sign-in roster.

"In fact, there's someone in there with her right now."

"Really?" I was surprised. No one had told me they would be visiting today.

The nurse examined the roster. "Yes. His name is Mills Davidson. He signed in an hour ago."

"Mills is here?" I had spoken with Annalise earlier. Why hadn't she mentioned it?

There was a flash of confusion in the nurse's eyes. "He's on the approved visitor list."

"Yes, he's family. I'm just surprised that he didn't say anything to me about coming today."

"He's been here several times this week. In fact, he's here every other day, always at the start of my shift. He's a nice boy, isn't he?"

Mills was not a boy, I thought. He was older than the nurse. I thanked her and walked down the hallway, still puzzling over the nurse's words. I had no idea that Mills made the hour-long trip to visit Mom so often. It seemed like something Annalise would mention to me. And why was he coming here without my sister?

I opened the door to Mom's room. A young man was sitting next to her bed, holding her pale hand in his. He looked up at me, immediately letting go, and I realized he was the guy from my English class.

"Who are you?"

He stood up. "Charlotte."

"Are you following me?" I took a step closer. "Tell me who you are or I'm calling security."

"Please don't." He looked anxious. "I only wanted to help. There was no other way for me to see her."

"Why do you need to see my mother?" Could he be an overzealous fan? Or maybe someone sent by Pate?

"It's my job. To help her, I mean." He grabbed his jacket from a chair and pulled a small card from the pocket. "Here," he said, handing me the card. "She can answer your questions."

I took the card but didn't look at it. The guy brushed past me, but paused at the door. "Your mom's getting better, no matter what they tell you. Believe that."

I listened to the sound of his footsteps as he left, then crossed the room to the window, which overlooked the parking lot. I gazed out at the tops of all the cars, and waited. I saw the guy hurrying outside, weaving his way around the cars until he came to his vehicle. I was half expecting him to drive away in a burgundy car, but he opened the door of a black sedan instead.

I turned over the card he had given me, even though I already knew what it said.

After all, I had one exactly like it tucked inside my purse.

I DROVE WAY too fast, prompting more than one driver to honk his horn and flash me the finger. I didn't care. I had to get to Potion immediately. My visit to Mom's room had been cut short, obviously. I had spent a few minutes at her bedside, making sure that none of the tubes she was connected to had been removed. I paged the nurse, just to make sure. Then I held her hand for a brief moment and, unable to look at her still face any longer, fled the building and slid into my car.

Normally it would have taken me more than an hour to reach the store, but my speeding got me there in 45 minutes. I parked on the street, jumped out of the car and pushed open

Potion's front doors so hard that the bell above the frame seemed to shriek in protest.

There was no one in the main room. Gentle music pulsed from the ceiling speakers, urging me to relax. But I was too wound up, too angry. I walked swiftly to the back room. Beth was there, dipping a tea bag into a mug.

"Charlotte." She didn't seem surprised to see me. "Would you like some tea?"

"What I'd really like is some answers. Have any of those?"

Beth sat down at the round table in the center of the room. "Have a seat."

Although I wanted to remain standing, I reluctantly pulled out a chair. Beth's calm demeanor annoyed me. I was seething mad and she was acting like she had been expecting me. I wanted her to apologize profusely for sending a guy to spy on me at school and sneak into the hospital to see my mom. Instead, she sipped her tea as if she'd done nothing wrong.

"I'm happy that you went to visit your mother. She needs you right now, more than you know."

"How did you know—" I shook my head. "Right. You know everything. Your spy does quality work."

"He's not a spy." Beth stared into her mug. "I'm sorry you're so angry, Charlotte. It wasn't my intention to upset you. Please understand that I'm only trying to help."

My anger diminished slightly. I knew Beth. She had been kind to me and my entire family. Of course she wasn't intentionally doing something to rattle me. But why all the secrecy? Suddenly I knew. Her way of helping me meant protecting me from news I might not be able to handle.

"Something's happened, hasn't it? Something bad."

She shook her head. "Not exactly, but we have reason to believe something may happen. We need to be ready."

"We? Who's we?"

The bell above the front door jingled. Fast footsteps approached the back room, and the guy from my English class burst in. "She's on her way here—" He saw me and stopped.

Beth introduced us. "Charlotte, I'd like you to meet Michael."

"I think he already knows me," I snapped, my anger resurfacing for a moment. "But I don't know him." I glared.

"Are we going to tell her now?" Michael asked Beth. "I thought you said we should wait a while longer."

Before I could protest about being talked about when I was sitting right here, Beth turned to me. "I'd really like it if you would have some tea," she said. "It's very calming, and what I'm about to tell you might not be easy to take." She nodded toward Michael, who retrieved two ceramic mugs and poured the steaming, amber-colored liquid into them. "Here," Beth urged. "Take one sip, and I'll tell you everything."

I eyed the mug in front of me with suspicion. "Is it drugged or something?"

Behind me, Michael scoffed. "It's just herbal tea."

Beth was asking me to have faith in her. She wanted me to show that I trusted her. I sighed and took a sip of the bland, hot water.

"Now, then." Beth sat back in her chair. "Let's start at the beginning."

I ALREADY KNEW some of the beginning, knowledge earned the hard way after the attack on my family. There was an entity called the Watcher, something like a demon but not confined to an underground realm, if such a place even existed. Beth had told me that a Watcher was something that had once been human but had lived such a despicable life that the soul could not move on. It also could not remain on earth, so it was confined in between, in a place that was not a place, where it could observe life on both sides of the curtain separating life from death. When someone pushed back that curtain and glimpsed the other side, the Watcher was pulled forward, driven by an enraged need to punish those who did not stay on their side.

There were many Watchers—no one had any idea how many—and they searched for a person to inhabit, someone susceptible to their control. When a Watcher came after me, it used the body of Marcus, a young man who had been working as an assistant to a self-proclaimed demonologist. I had seen Marcus die. Some might say that it was by my hand he had perished. And my hand still showed the scars, a swirl of lines that blended with the others on my palm. But I felt the truth: I had not killed Marcus. The Watcher had done that. I had removed the Watcher, but I hadn't killed it, either, because a Watcher couldn't die. It was a soul. A dark, broken soul, but a soul nonetheless.

I listened patiently as Beth recounted a history I was already familiar with. "But there is something else you should know about," she said.

Fear crept into my stomach. "Something worse than the Watcher?"

"No." I had been listening to Beth so intently that I had forgotten Michael was behind me, standing against a wall. Now he came over and sat down beside Beth. "There's nothing worse than a Watcher. This is something better."

"Okay." I looked to Beth for confirmation. I didn't know Michael, and so much of this demented-soul-on-the-rampage stuff was hard for me to digest. Yes, I'd seen it happen and knew it was real, but the theories behind it were just that: theories. Everything we knew, every technique we had employed to protect ourselves had been based on semi-educated guesses. We needed a dose of solid science. I was hoping that was the "something better" Beth was getting ready to tell me about.

"The universe works on a balance principle," Beth started. I leaned forward a little. This was good. This was a scientific theory. We could use this.

She explained that every time a Watcher came into power, so did its opposite. "A Protector," Beth said. "Something with positive strength to combat the negative energy of the Watcher."

"Oh." I should have been more excited, but this news wasn't what I had hoped for. I wanted information about a fantastic new piece of equipment, like a laser gun or something that we could use to blast this thing into oblivion. "So a good spirit takes over the body of someone and battles it out with the Watcher?"

Michael laughed, but Beth took my question seriously. "No, that's one of the differences between them." She explained that possession was a trick used only by negative energy. Positive energy simply added its strength to a person. And the stronger a Watcher became, the stronger the Protector became.

"So where was this great Protector when my mom was hurt?" I wanted to know.

Michael and Beth exchanged a quick glance. "There was a situation," Michael said.

"He was detained by forces far beyond his control," Beth added.

"So this Protector guy isn't too reliable." I turned to Michael. "Is that why you're here? To keep an eye on me until the real help arrives?"

"No," he replied, his voice hard. "That's not why I'm here."

My cell phone buzzed. I didn't care who it was—I needed to get out of the room for a minute. Without saying anything to Beth or Michael, I jumped up and answered the call out in the main room, surrounded by racks of bright dresses and shelves practically bursting with candles and incense.

"Hi, Annalise."

"Hey! Did you visit Mom?"

Great. I had walked out of one uncomfortable conversation and into another. "Yes, I saw her today."

"And?"

"And she's the same. No major progress."

"Oh. But it was a good trip, right? Did you talk with her doctors?"

I tried to sum up my micro-visit with a few details. I talked with the nurse, I said. I sat with Mom for a while. Then I left but would return soon. My promise had been kept, so now she and Dad could back off a little. I knew she had expected that I would experience something deeper, something that would inspire hope. And maybe if finding Michael in Mom's room hadn't rattled me so much, it would have been better.

But I doubted it.

"I have to go," I told my sister. "I'll call you later, okay?"

"Sure. Okay." Her disappointment was clear.

I hung up and returned to the back room. Beth and Michael were deep in a conversation that stopped the moment I walked in.

"Why did you say that you could help my mom?" I asked Michael. "The nurse said that you visit all the time. What's that about?"

"That was my idea," Beth said. "And we can talk about it later. For now, we need to get back to discussing the Protector. I don't think you understand what this means."

I remained standing. "You're right. I don't understand."

"This is a good thing, Charlotte," Beth said. "We have power now. We can be ready when the Watcher returns."

When it returns. Not *if.* Beth's choice of wording did not slip by me. "Something has happened, right? That's why Double-O-Seven has been hanging around?"

Michael crossed his arms. "I've been helping your mom. Feel free to thank me."

Beth rubbed at her temples. "I was hoping this would go much more smoothly."

She sighed. "Let's try it again. Charlotte, meet Michael." She looked me in the eyes.

"He's the Protector."

eight

"So he's like a guardian angel-slash-bodyguard kind of thing?"

"That about sums it up," I told Avery. "Except that he's also a healer."

The first person I'd called after my wild windstorm of a day was my best friend. I was lucky to catch her when she was on a break from classes, and we had spent the past hour chatting while I lounged on my bed.

At first, I only wanted to hear about normal stuff, such as what she thought about her professors and her dorm room and the weekend parties. Avery downplayed college life, telling me that she mainly had TAs instead of professors and the dorm bathroom where she had to shower was always crowded. I knew she was trying to make sure I didn't feel like I was missing out on too much.

"So what's the best part?" I asked. "There's got to be something you love."

She paused. "Honestly? The best part is the freedom. I mean, I have a schedule and responsibilities, but it's all up to me. No one's asking me for a hall pass."

"I think that's the most underrated part about graduating

from high school," I said. "Once they hand you that diploma, you get to go through life without ever asking anyone again for a slip of paper to use the bathroom."

"That's true." She laughed. "And I love not having a curfew. Last night Jared and I drove out to the country to look at the stars. It was so nice we stayed to watch the sun come up."

"Sounds wonderful." And it did. I wished Noah and I could do that, just take off without having to check in with anyone and go wherever we wanted.

After I caught her up on my classes and Noah, I told her about my strange, brief visit to see Mom and my even stranger meeting with Michael. "And you know the real reason this guy is at my school?"

"I thought he was there to keep an eye on you."

"Yeah, but there's more." I sat up on my bed. "One way to permanently confine the thing that's out to get me is to learn its true name. Michael is doing research. He thinks the original person was an inmate at the asylum we visited last year."

"That makes sense, since that's where everything began," Avery said. "What does Noah think about all this?"

"I haven't had a chance to tell him yet," I admitted.

My gut instinct was screaming at me not to tell him. I hated keeping anything from him, but lately I got the sense that he was holding back from me, as well. He was always so busy, but never very clear on what he was doing besides general "work."

At first I had thought he needed a break from the perpetual drama that was my life. I had bothered him too much with stories about mystery cars and panic attacks. Then I worried that it was something deeper than that. I couldn't explain it, but I felt like Noah was changing somehow, that he was gradually shifting into a new, more tense personality. I only caught glimpses of it, and he was fine and happy when we were alone together, but something was off, and I could not escape one idea that gnawed at me, the one that whispered to me late at night when I couldn't sleep—that Noah had been forever changed by his encounter with the Watcher.

Had evil left its mark on my boyfriend?

"I don't know what he'll think," I said to Avery. "Relieved, maybe? I know he worries about me."

"Yeah, he does. And this extra protection power sounds good, but why do you need it now? I mean, do they really think you're in immediate danger? Because if you are—"

I cut her off. "I'm not," I insisted, although I wasn't sure how much truth that statement held. I had left Potion shortly after learning that Michael had basically been assigned to me and my mom. My brain was buzzing with information overload, and I needed some time to understand everything.

Also, I felt more than a little guilty over the way I had treated Michael, who had been working overtime for weeks. He spent half his day following me around, then went to the long-term care facility to work on healing techniques with my mom. And I had treated him like dirt the second we'd met. Why would he want to help me when I'd been such an angry, whiny brat? Beth had wisely suggested that we meet on Monday, just Michael and I, to talk things out.

"We're going to the mall," I told Avery.

"You hate the mall."

"It was his idea. I guess he wanted to make sure we were somewhere public in case I flipped out on him again."

"Charlotte, if things get too heavy, you'll let me know, right? Jared and I can drive back in a day."

"Thanks. But I don't even know completely what's going on, so don't worry yet, okay?"

If things got bad again, I didn't want Avery or Jared any-

where near me. I couldn't risk the chance of them getting hurt.

"Can I make a suggestion?" she asked. "Wait until you have
all the information before you say anything to Noah."

"That's a good idea." He didn't need the stress, not on top
of his crazy new class workload and his troubles with insomnia
and sleepwalking, which he constantly assured me were not
that bad. I would tell him everything, but only when I knew
everything. I felt relieved that Avery had given me a sort of
permission to stay quiet. It eased my guilty conscience.

I got off the phone with Avery and remained on my bed,
mulling everything over. Sometimes it felt like my brain was
one of those lottery machines on TV, and all my thoughts
were a different little ball, popping haphazardly in the air until
one was sucked up to the top. But as soon as I pinned down
one of my thoughts, another one popped up next to it, a line
of random thoughts in no particular order.

Something was bothering me, something I couldn't quite
articulate to myself. My main worries—my mom, Noah and
the possible return of the Watcher—were connected by something. I was sure of it.

Feeling restless, I went downstairs. Shane and Trisha were
off comparing floral arrangements, Noah was working on yet
another school project for AV class and Dad was at the store. I
needed to get out of the house, but I wasn't sure where I could
go. As I plucked my car keys from the front table and slipped
on a pair of shoes, I thought of something. Within minutes,
I was headed in a new direction. I hoped it would lead me to
practical answers.

AN ARMY OF GNOMES greeted me when I pulled up to Bliss's
house. At first glance, the mass of red and green caps looked
like an overgrown field of crazy Christmas-colored mush-

rooms. I rang the doorbell and tried to ignore the slightly creepy sensation that the hundreds of tiny ceramic eyes induced.

"Charlotte?" Bliss looked confused. "What are you doing here? How did you know where I live?"

"You mentioned the street on the first day of school," I reminded her. "And you said the front lawn had a lot of—" I glanced behind me. "These."

"Oh. Right." She stood in the partially open doorway. "I'm not trying to be rude, but why are you here? Are you okay?"

"Sort of not okay. Can I come in?"

Bliss stepped out onto the front porch, shutting the door behind her. "I wasn't expecting company. The house is kind of cluttered right now."

"Maybe we could go somewhere?" I hated to sound desperate, but I truly thought that Bliss might be able to help me. She seemed unconvinced, though, as if maybe I had strange ulterior motives for dropping by unannounced.

"Let me grab my purse," she said finally. "We can get coffee or something. Wait here."

She slipped back into the house, opening the door as little as possible. A minute later she returned.

"I counted fifty-three," I told her, waving my hand over the yard at the little stone men.

"That means a few more have been stolen." We got into my car. "Not that I mind. We used to have over a hundred."

"That's a lot of gnomes."

She laughed. "When I was younger I thought they came to life at night. I was convinced they would break into the house and attack me in my sleep."

"I would probably think the same thing," I admitted. "How did you sleep at night?" I headed for Giuseppe's. It was close, and I figured we could talk over their famous cannolis and iced tea.

"My grandfather told me that they did come to life at night, but they would stay away from the house if I fed them. So after dinner, I would put the leftovers outside. The food was always gone the next morning."

We arrived at Giuseppe's. "Where did the food go?"

Bliss smiled. "My neighborhood is home to some of the fattest raccoons around."

Inside, the restaurant was wonderfully empty. It was after lunch but before dinner, so we had our choice of booths. Craving sugar, I ordered a cannoli but couldn't convince Bliss to do the same. She sipped on unsweetened iced tea while I tried to figure out what I wanted to say and how I wanted to say it.

Bliss beat me to it. "So, you wanted to talk?"

"Yes. I hope that doesn't seem too weird."

"Well, we spent our senior year basically hating one another despite the fact that we hardly knew anything about each other. So, yes, maybe you showing up at my house is a little strange."

Her voice held no malice. She was simply stating facts. I appreciated that. In fact, I respected it. High school was behind us. Whatever petty problems had once existed there now remained there, forgotten along with the locker combinations and the lunch schedule.

"I need advice," I began. "Advice from someone removed from my situation."

"You mean an outsider." She stared at the red plastic tumbler in front of her. "Because that's what I am, right? An outsider."

"In a way..."

"In every way." Bliss sighed. "I've lived here my whole life, but I've never fit in. Do you know what that's like? To know people since kindergarten, and for them to never accept you?"

"No," I said. "But that's because I'm a different kind of outsider. I've lived here longer than I've lived anywhere, and I've only been here for a year."

This brought a small smile to her face. "So we're both outsiders. Just a different breed, I guess." She swirled a straw through her tea. "Maybe that's why we clashed. We're too much alike."

"Maybe." It wasn't as if I had set out to hate her, though. She had disliked me from the moment I had stepped into the AV room. She had never trusted me. And now here I was, asking for that trust, and all I could think was that, despite our conflicted history, it felt right to be here.

"So." Bliss looked at me. "You brought me here so I could give you advice."

I set down my fork next to the untouched cannoli. "You know about the panic attacks."

She leaned forward. "Did seeing your mom help?"

"No. I don't know, I didn't stay long. Something happened while I was at the hospital." I wasn't sure how to explain everything. Bliss knew nothing about the events that had shaped my life over the past year. She was, as she had pointed out, an outsider. Her knowledge of what had happened to my mom was gained from reading the same news stories that everyone else had read or seen, a story that had been crafted to protect my family and friends. A demented fan had attacked us, we claimed, not a demonic force.

"You obviously want to tell me something important," Bliss said, filling the silence that I had allowed to form. "I'm here and I've got time. So start talking."

There was a time when Bliss's inherent bossiness would

have annoyed me. But now I appreciated her no-nonsense approach to things. If you have something to say, say it.

So I did.

I didn't start at the beginning, which for me was the summer before, when my family had entered the Courtyard Café in Charleston together—and had left with something else entirely. Instead, I started my story with the New Year's party. She had been there, sitting with me and some of our classmates around a hundred candles. She had been at the school when so many strange things had occurred. She knew who was responsible for those happenings—before prom the truth had been revealed—and she had read the scattered news reports about my mom. But she didn't know the truth, and that's what I needed her to understand, so I told her everything, including all the details about the Watcher and what, exactly, had happened to my mom.

She listened, her brow furrowed. I kept my voice low, even though the restaurant remained empty and the waitress only came by to check on us once. It felt good to release my words, to tell my story to someone for the first time. Once I got started it was difficult to stop. I even told her about my late-night attempts at making contact with something, and how that had finally happened a few weeks earlier.

"You're actually communicating with an entity?" Bliss asked.

"Yes. I'm not sure what—or who—it is, but I have a recorder full of EVPs."

"Charlotte, are you sure that's a good idea? After everything you've told me, it seems dangerous to mess with this stuff. As in, really dangerous."

"But maybe not. If there's even a chance it could help my mom, I have to try. And now I have Michael, so I'm safer than I was before."

"Right." Bliss sat back. "The Protector."

I felt a flicker of panic. Did she not believe me? Had I just spilled all of my secrets to someone who thought I was crazy? I waited, trying to decipher her reaction to my story, but Bliss kept her face perfectly blank.

"So?" I braced myself for the imminent recommendation that I visit the nearest psych ward. "What do you think?"

"I think…" She seemed to be searching for the right words. "I think you've given me a lot to digest. And I'm still not sure why you came to me with all this."

I didn't have a response to that. Why *had* I come to Bliss? It had to be more than simply needing an "outsider" opinion.

"Charlotte." Bliss studied the glass in front of her, not meeting my eyes. "When I was in the eighth grade, some kids convinced me that there was a student in the boys' bathroom that needed help. I went in, and saw one of my teachers using the urinal."

The change in topic temporarily silenced me. "What?"

"In the ninth grade, everyone convinced me that Monday was Tacky Day," she continued. "I showed up wearing my grandfather's old pea-green suit coat. No one else was dressed that way. And in the tenth grade, I received an invitation to an exclusive party. It wasn't until I had been dropped off that I realized it was an abandoned house."

"That's terrible, but why are you telling me this?" I asked.

"Because." She looked up. "Because if this is a joke, I need you to tell me now so I can walk away with a little dignity. If this is some weird trick you're playing to see how I'll react, I'm begging you—don't. I've been through it before, Charlotte. Please don't do this to me again."

There was something achingly sad buried in her voice, something that made me want to scream at all the people who had tricked her before. How could I convince her that this was real?

."Bliss, I swear to you." I reached across the table and took her hands in mine. "I swear on my mother that this is real. And I swear that I am not the kind of person who would ever, ever play a prank to hurt someone."

I realized in that moment why I had come to Bliss. She had helped me through my panic attack without hesitation. She was a person who wanted to help, who wanted to do the right thing, even if it was for someone she didn't entirely trust.

Finally, she looked at me. "Okay. I believe you, Charlotte. I do. And I want to help, but I'm not sure how."

"Start by telling me what you think about all of this."

She pulled her hands gently away from mine. "I think I have a theory."

"About the Watcher?" Or about my mental stability, I wanted to add, because clearly, Bliss thought I was a freak show.

"You said you wanted advice. But you didn't say what kind of advice, which makes me think you don't even know."

I shrugged. She had me. I didn't know what I wanted, except maybe some clarity and a few reassuring words. The waitress came by our table, refilled our drinks and left the bill on the table. I reached for it before Bliss could.

"It's okay to be confused by all of this," Bliss said after the waitress left. "You have a lot going on right now, and none of it falls under the category of minor personal issues."

I chuckled. "Yeah. Leave it to me to have only big, dramatic problems. I leave the small stuff to normal people."

"But what you're feeling right now *is* normal," she said. "Maybe your problems are unusual, but your reaction isn't. In fact, I'm impressed that you haven't curled up in a ball of depression or stayed home in the dark or something. You're pressing forward in your own way, and that takes guts."

The thought was oddly reassuring. I wasn't crazy—but the rest of my little world was. Somehow, I could deal with that. I took a bite of my cannoli, trying to savor the sweetness, but it tasted flat.

"Here's what worries me about all this," Bliss continued. She pushed her cup aside. "One, I don't like that you're dabbling with the other side. You may think you've contacted a friendly presence, but it could be a trap."

I had considered that, but the voice on the EVPs held none of the menace I had heard in the Watcher's voice, which had been an awful combination of male and female. It was definitely otherworldly, whereas the voice I had captured was simply female and slightly familiar. It wasn't the same at all.

"Two, this Watcher thing is obviously working hard to regain power. If it wasn't, Michael wouldn't be a Protector, right? I mean, he can only come into his powers if there is someone who needs protecting."

"Yes," I admitted. Michael was a regular superhero, custom-built for me. If the Watcher was gone or fading or not a threat, Michael would remain a normal guy.

"So I think you need to work with him to try to figure out the name of this Watcher. It seems to me that's the key to at least some of its strength."

So many cultures throughout the world thought one's true power rested in a person's name. By simply knowing that basic information, you had something to hold over them. I remembered living in an apartment complex when I was ten. The pool was constantly being shut down because someone was throwing cans of soda and garbage into it. One night, I looked out my window and saw the culprit, a boy named Tyler who lived upstairs. Before he could dump a leftover casserole into the water, I yelled at him from the half-open window. "Tyler, we know it's you! Knock it off!" The pool remained unpolluted from then on.

"Makes sense," I said. "I can spend time helping Michael with his research."

"You're not going to like number three," Bliss warned.

"Let me have it." So far, her advice had been solid. I was ready to listen to whatever she had to say.

"It sounds like Noah is having problems. From what you've mentioned, I would say that he might even be in trouble. As in, Watcher-related trouble."

My fingers immediately went to my bracelet. The dark, smooth stones always seemed to relax me, even if only a little bit.

"But it's Noah," I said softly. "He's not evil."

"Of course he's not evil." Bliss grabbed my hand, forcing me to let go of the bracelet. "Have you ever outright asked him what he felt that night? Have you asked him if he feels different now? Because I think you could help him, but it's one of those things you need to catch early."

"Like cancer." Saying it felt ridiculous, but Bliss nodded emphatically.

"Exactly. What if evil is a cancer that slowly spreads? What if Noah has been infected but you could stop it now?"

"I have no idea how to do that."

Bliss let go of my hand and sat back in her seat. "But you know people who do know how to stop it, Charlotte. And one of them is your Protector."

nine

"Tell me what you see."

I looked away from my computer and leaned over to check out the footage displayed on Shane's monitor. It was Sunday morning. Noah and I had plans to meet for lunch, but until then I was helping Shane. The DVD was more than halfway complete, and if we kept up the pace we would meet our deadline a few days early, which meant a contract completion payment would come sooner. Judging by the growing pile of medical bills stacked neatly on the hallway table, the check couldn't come soon enough.

I turned my attention to the monitor. "I see Pate strapped down in the electric chair." We had moved past the old footage and were splicing in the new. I was glad—seeing my mom's face on the screen was more difficult than I had thought it would be.

"Okay. Watch this." He went back to the beginning of the soundless 30-second clip. Pate glared directly into the camera, but his tough-guy veneer quickly vanished. He turned his head to the left, frowning. Within seconds, he was struggling to get out of the chair.

"Did you see that?" Shane asked. "He looked to the left, like he heard something coming from that direction."

"So? We determined there were cracks in the wall. The sound of the wind could have gotten his attention."

"The cracks were to the right. There's a room on the other side of the left wall."

"You think Pate actually heard something?"

Instead of answering, Shane pulled up another clip. I instantly recognized Noah strapped down in the same chair. "This was shot just a few minutes before Pate went in there," Shane said, as if I needed to be reminded.

It was a longer clip, about ten minutes. Noah sat in the chair, his legs and arms restrained. Shane had directed him to stay relaxed but look defeated, something Noah was able to pull off by keeping his head down and remaining still. It was a good image that would fit in nicely with the narration we had prerecorded.

After a few minutes of watching Noah sit still in the electric chair, I began to wonder why Shane wanted me to view the footage. I had watched it several times already, and there was nothing unusual about it.

"Here it comes," Shane murmured.

In a gesture that seemed to mimic Pate's, Noah suddenly turned his head toward the left. It was sudden, as if something had caught his attention.

As if he'd heard something.

"It's probably a coincidence." Even as I said it, I knew the words were not true. Both Noah and Pate had heard something coming from the left side of the room. "It's nothing," I said. "I asked Noah if anything weird had happened while he was in there, and he said no. And even if they did hear something, there's probably a natural explanation. Just because there's a room next door doesn't mean there aren't still cracks where the wind could flow through."

I was trying to convince myself, not Shane. Because the clips were way too similar. There was something unnatural about them, something I couldn't understand—and didn't *want* to understand.

Shane didn't push it, and we moved on to other footage. By noon, when Noah came over for our lunch date, Shane and I had finished another twenty minutes of the DVD and were pleased with our progress.

Noah arrived with a backpack slung over one shoulder. "Hey."

Seeing him brought an immediate smile to my face—and an immediate reminder of my concerns about the possibility that he had been damaged by the Watcher. "I thought we were going on a picnic."

"We are." He let the backpack fall off his shoulder and unzipped it. "I didn't have a basket, so we're using this instead." Inside his pack were sandwiches and plastic baggies full of fruit.

"You got in late last night," Shane said.

Noah shrugged. "The game went into overtime."

I hoped that his AV duties would end with the football season. It was taking up at least three evenings every week.

We said goodbye to Shane and drove to the community college. My previous trepidation about his behavior and sleepwalking seemed silly as we drove to my school. Noah was completely at ease as he chatted about his classes and an upcoming football game. Nothing was out of the ordinary. A truck cut me off as we approached the school, causing me to brake hard, but Noah simply shook his head. "Wouldn't it be nice if they denied driver's licenses to jerks?" he asked with a laugh.

A few days earlier, I had been the jerk behind the wheel as I had sped to Potion, so I figured it was a little karmic payback being tossed my way. I hadn't told Noah about Michael, who I was supposed to meet at the mall the next day. Avery was right—he didn't need to know until I had more facts. And I couldn't ignore my gut feeling that I shouldn't tell him yet. Until then, I would enjoy my Sunday afternoon with Noah.

The campus was fairly deserted, and we held hands as I gave him a brief tour. It was Noah's first trip to see the place where I spent so much of my day now, and I was pleased with his observations as we walked across campus. He liked the landscaping and the ample parking. He thought the buildings had a modern look to them. He even admired the one statue on campus, a bronze woman reading a book.

Noah spread out a blanket in a shady spot behind a cluster of buildings. "I feel like we haven't been alone together in so long," I said as I unwrapped a turkey sandwich.

"I know. I've missed you."

I tried to chew and smile at the same time, which I was sure looked less than elegant. "Me, too."

My conversation with Bliss and my concerns about Noah seemed to have taken place in another time, in another world. Being with him made all my fears evaporate.

His warm smile and clear green eyes were exactly the same, and there was nothing unsettling about his touch except for the fact that it thrilled me. If Noah really was infected with something evil, wouldn't I be the first person to detect it?

"Ryan called my mom last night," he said. We had finished our sandwiches and were moving on to my favorite dessert: oatmeal raisin cookies. "They were on the phone for a long time. I think something's up."

"Do you think it has something to do with Jeff?"

"No, that's just it. Mom kept whispering, like she wanted

to make sure I couldn't hear anything. Usually when she's on the phone with Ryan there's a lot of happy squealing."

"Maybe she was filling him in on Pate's lawsuit," I suggested. Shane had updated me the night before. Pate wasn't backing down, even claiming that there had been another break-in at the prison. He couldn't prove it was any of us, but he had a hunch. "Good thing you can't prove a hunch in a court of law," Shane had said. He was fighting back, but would need to inform my dad about it soon.

"Maybe. I don't think so, though." Noah frowned. "It was weird."

"Then it was probably wedding details." I shrugged. "Although, I don't understand why your mom is so intense about this. They don't even have a date yet. It'll be months, at least."

Maybe longer. Mom was stable but not showing signs of improvement, despite Michael's insistence that she was somehow getting better. And I knew Shane would keep his promise to me: Mom would be at the wedding no matter what.

Noah and I didn't discuss my mom very much. It wasn't that we avoided the conversation. It simply didn't come up, and I was good with that. Everyone else wanted to talk about it. I needed Noah to be the one person who didn't ask me the same sad questions, and he knew that. Like so many things between us, it was understood.

I finished my cookies and stretched out on the blanket.

"Tell me about your brothers."

"What do you want to know?"

"I can't picture them," I said. "I can't even picture you with them. To me, your family is just you and your mom."

"Sometimes it feels like that for me, too." He zipped up his backpack and lay down next to me so that we were facing one another. "I always said that Jeff and Ryan had two career choices—the military or professional wrestling. They were huge and strong and disciplined. I was the runt."

"You were the youngest," I pointed out. "Of course you were smaller."

"It wasn't just that." Noah explained that Jeff and Ryan were only a year apart, and most people thought they were twins. They had the same features, the same body type. They enjoyed sports and yelling. Noah, who was younger by four years, was the quiet one.

"They pounded on me all the time," he said. "They'd stuff me in a closet and tell me to wait until they came back because it was a test. I'd spend hours in the dark, scared but trying so hard to prove myself to them. It was always Mom who found me." He ran his fingers down my arm, causing me to shiver despite the warm afternoon sun.

"They were merciless at home. But if we were at school or in public, they were fierce about family."

He told me about an incident when he was in the eighth grade. A boy had been picking on him, calling him a nerd. When Noah told his brothers, they took action. After school let out one day, they showed up in the parking lot and asked Noah to point out his tormentor. Then they approached the boy.

"They told him that if he even looked at me the wrong way, they would take his teeth, turn them into a necklace and make him wear it." Noah continued to caress my arm. "That kid never bothered me again. No one did. I became off-limits, and it stayed that way, even after Jeff and Ryan graduated."

"Sounds like, in a weird way, they made sure you could be who you were without other people bothering you."

"Yeah." Noah chuckled. "But I don't know if they did it for me or if they were more concerned with protecting the family reputation or something. Either way, it was nice to move through high school without being afraid."

We lay on the blanket for a while, enjoying the sunshine and occasional breeze that passed through the trees. I was content. After a while, some more people began walking around, and I decided I wanted some privacy.

"Come on," I said, standing up. "I want to show you something."

I took Noah by the hand and led him to the Yerian Building, where I had two of my classes. One of the main doors was unlocked, and we slipped inside, where it was dark and cool. Sunlight spilled in from the side wall of windows, but with all the overhead lights turned off, it was surprisingly dim. I loved the feeling of being in a normally busy place when it was totally empty.

"This way." I kept my voice low, but it still seemed to echo off the high ceiling.

I led him away from the main room and down the hallway leading to my English classroom. The corridor was pitch-black and our feet barely made a sound on the carpet. I found the door and hoped it would be unlocked.

"What are we doing?" Noah whispered, his lips brushing my ear. I quivered with delight and turned the handle. The door opened, and I pulled Noah inside.

"I'm giving you the tour," I replied in the same soft whisper. "I thought you might like to see where I take English."

"But I can't see anything." His backpack hit the floor with a soft thud. Then his hands were in my hair as he placed gentle kisses all over my face.

I pushed him against a wall. "Then I'll describe it for you." I nuzzled against his neck. "There's a big desk at the front of the room, and a bunch of smaller desks in the back." We kissed, and I melted into his warm embrace, overcome by the feeling of being so close to him. Then his lips moved to my neck and he began planting soft kisses there, a sensation I craved. He moved his face close to mine, but as I leaned in to kiss him again, he pulled away.

"Something's wrong."

I thought he meant that someone was walking toward the classroom. I listened, expecting to hear approaching footsteps or voices in the hallway.

"We're alone," I assured him. "Everything's fine."

"No, we're not. Someone's in here." He reached out one arm, feeling along the wall for the switch. I blinked against the sudden glare of light. Noah's eyes were wide with panic as he scanned the room. He moved away from me, walking up and down the aisles, even crouching to look beneath the desks.

"I felt it," he said. "I felt like someone was in here."

The genuine confusion written on his face told me that he truly believed what he was saying, but there was no one with us. There was probably no one in the entire building.

Our brief moment of intimacy ruined, we decided to go back to my house. Noah apologized repeatedly for his para-noia, but I told him it was fine.

"Maybe the janitor was spying on us or something," I said. But I didn't believe it, and I didn't think he did, either. As I drove us back to my neighborhood, an uncomfortable thought formed in my mind: Noah's unnerving paranoia had occurred in the one place where Michael had spent time. Did he sense the lingering presence of the Protector? Or was it simply a coincidence?

"Sorry about that," he said as we pulled into my driveway. "I didn't feel like myself."

"It's okay," I said. "Don't worry about it."

I wished I could take my own advice.

ten

It was my first visit to the Four Trees Mall, and I was hoping it would be my last. I avoided huge shopping centers altogether, preferring to order anything I needed online, away from the noisy crowds and persistent salespeople. But Michael hadn't given me an option, so I was stuck sipping an orange-mango smoothie and sitting by a gaudy fountain littered with nickels.

I had arrived early and purchased my smoothie, which was really the only thing that made a trip like this worthwhile. Then I claimed a spot at the fountain so I could watch the entrance. People hurried past me, their bulging bags slapping against their legs. There was too much echo, I decided. All those voices bouncing off all that space. It had the potential to become Panic Attack Central. Was it always so crowded on a Monday afternoon?

I looked around. Plastic pumpkins and fluffy black spider-webs decorated most of the store windows, reminding shoppers that Halloween was only a month away. And in an effort to make sure the name rang true, there actually were four trees inside the mall. Four huge, two-story plastic trees. Everything about the place was fake. I glanced at the fountain, wondering if the water was real. Maybe it was some kind of synthetic, antibacterial syrup.

One thing the mall didn't have was a clock. I pulled out my cell phone and checked the time. Michael was officially five minutes late. Not that I minded. I was nervous about this strange meeting and the news Michael would deliver. Was I really in danger? Maybe a better question was, would I ever *not* be in danger? If the Watcher couldn't be destroyed, what hope did I have of ever living a relatively normal life? Like so many things lately, it was too depressing to think about.

My smoothie gone, I debated a quick trip to the food court for a refill. My day was wide open and I had nowhere else to be. I had attended classes for the day, noting that Michael was absent from our English course. Dante had been walked, which had been nice not only because of the cooler weather but also because I needed a little alone time to think. Noah was in school for another hour, maybe longer. He was staying late every day, working on projects that he never quite defined. Research, he said, but I had no idea what would take hours a day to explore.

His schedule had become increasingly strange lately. If he wasn't putting in overtime in AV class, he was at the public library, studying nonstop for nearly every class he was taking. I knew senior year could be tough, but Noah was being crushed under an avalanche of essays.

Despite her preoccupation with the wedding, even Trisha had noticed. "Is everything okay with you two?" she had asked me the night before. She had stopped by our house to see Shane. "I don't mean to pry, but Noah has seemed so...so down."

I assured her that everything was fine, and that Noah was simply dealing with a heavy course load at school. Trisha seemed to accept my explanation, but I knew she was concerned. I was, too. Every time I saw him, he looked exhausted. He was still waking up at strange hours outside his bedroom, but it wasn't something he liked to discuss with me. It had nothing to do with the Watcher, I told myself. Noah had escaped with minor injuries and a permanent bruise. The sleepwalking was a result of stress. Nothing more.

"Charlotte?"

Great. I had been so lost in my thoughts that I had stopped paying attention to the entrance. "Hi, Michael."

"Hey." He stood in front of me, dressed in brown cords and holding a paper shopping bag. "Mind if I sit down?"

I scooted over. "Sure."

"Thanks for meeting me here." He placed the bag at his feet. I noticed that he wore black Dr. Martens, which fit his overall look as a potential indie band guitar player. "I needed some new shirts, and I figured this would be a good place to talk."

"Really?" It was so loud—hardly the best place for an intense conversation.

"Yeah. I figure, the more noise, the less chance someone will eavesdrop. I guess I'm paranoid that way."

"No, that makes sense." I smiled. "A little bit of paranoia might be a good thing, considering that we're going to be talking about demons."

Something changed in his face, but I wasn't sure what. Had I said the wrong thing? "I mean, not demons, exactly, but close. We're here to talk about the Watcher, right?"

"Yes." He nodded. "Absolutely. But I thought we could talk about other things first."

"Oh." I had no idea what other subjects we could discuss when only one thing truly mattered.

"I'm your Protector," he said, "but I feel like we got off to a bad start. I was hoping we could start over."

"I'm sorry." I held on to my empty smoothie cup, feeling the cold seep through my fingers. "I wasn't nice to you. At all."

"I could've done better, too," he said. "It's my first assignment, and I kind of blew it."

"You were assigned to me?"

Michael stood up. "I'll explain. Let's walk around, though. I had one of those gigantic cinnamon buns, and I could use a little exercise."

I almost laughed. Michael could consume a dozen cinnamon buns and I doubted that it would affect his wiry frame. As we walked down one wing of the mall, Michael explained how being a Protector worked. First, he was chosen. No one knew why a particular person was chosen, but it was assumed that, like those cursed individuals who were taken over by a Watcher, a person who became a Protector possessed an important quality that made him or her a strong candidate. Once a Watcher came into power, so did a Protector, but he required something a Watcher did not: guidance.

"I didn't wake up one day with superpowers," Michael said. "But I did feel different."

"More protective?" I guessed.

He laughed. "Yeah, but it was more than that." He stopped suddenly in front of a candy store. He lowered his voice. "See that guy? The one in the green jacket?"

I casually turned my head until I spotted the middle-aged man he was referring to. "I see him. So?"

"So, he's boiling with rage right now."

I looked again. There was nothing about the man that screamed anger. He was talking on a cell phone, but he wasn't yelling or waving his arms around or anything. He seemed perfectly normal.

"How do you know?" I asked.

Michael didn't respond right away. We took a few steps closer to better watch the guy, but pretended we were interested in a poster outside the candy store so it wouldn't be obvious.

"That wasn't our agreement," the man said into his phone. "I can't change my plans now. It's too late for that."

"He doesn't sound that upset," I whispered.

"Wait," Michael whispered back.

It took only another moment for the man's face to lose its calm façade. Soon he was screaming into the phone as he paced in front of the candy store, drawing concerned looks from everyone around him. "You will not do this to me!" he shouted.

He didn't notice the alarmed stares from other shoppers— or the little boy running toward the candy store. I took a step forward, reaching out to grab the boy before he crashed into the angry man, but the child was too fast. He ran right into the man's legs.

The man stumbled, dropping his phone. The boy began to wail, and his mother came rushing forward, panicked. "What did you do to my son?" she screamed.

"He ran into me! Maybe you should keep an eye on your kid instead of letting him run wild!"

They screamed at each other as the child continued to cry. Both the frantic mother and enraged man were red in the face, and I felt sure that something bad was about to happen.

Then Michael stepped forward. He put one hand on the man's shoulder and his other hand on the woman. He spoke softly to them. It reminded me of the way I sometimes coaxed Dante into coming out from under Avery's bed. As I watched, the man's face softened and so did the woman's. Even the little boy, still crouched on the floor and clinging to his mother's leg, changed. I could almost see the anger evaporate. By the time mall security arrived, everything was fine.

"How did you do that?" I asked. The mother and the little boy had entered the candy store, and the man had walked away casually, as if nothing had happened. Two mall security guards stood looking around, confused.

Michael shrugged. "It's what I do."

We began walking in the other direction. "You stop people from killing each other?"

"I diffuse negative energy."

"How did you know that was going to happen?" I was pestering him with questions, but I didn't care. I wanted to know more about his powers and how we could use them.

"Basically, I'm drawn to it. I feel the anger, and I move toward it."

He paused in front of a clothing store and looked at the window display. "Wow. That kind of sucks, though, doesn't it? To be around anger all the time?"

"Sometimes." He chuckled. "You know where there's the most negative energy? Guess."

"Um. The post office?"

"Nope. Toy stores."

Michael explained that people were easily overwhelmed in toy stores. They entered with a specific goal, and left feeling frazzled. Even kids were susceptible to it. They went in wanting something badly, and if it wasn't there or deemed too expensive, their helpless anger practically consumed them.

"Sometimes it's so strong, I have to pull over and go inside, just to try to help a little." He shifted his shopping bag to his other arm. "It's awful. But it makes a difference, so that's good."

It *was* good, I thought. Michael's gift helped people. We needed more like him, people who could be sent to war-torn regions. If there were more Protectors in the world, there would be more peace. I was surprised by the admiration I felt for him. This was someone who changed things for the better.

And he had been assigned to me. With power that great, it seemed wrong that it should be wasted on an eighteen-year-old girl. But some distant authority had decided it was necessary. I shuddered a little. What did that say about the power of the Watcher? It spoke loudly about the force that I was up against when my designated protection was a guy who could calm down irate strangers with a simple touch. That was the least of Michael's abilities, I was sure. I wondered what he was like when he was at full power.

We walked around the mall, occasionally stopping to peer into storefront windows. He talked about growing up in northern Michigan, where the snow would sometimes reach the second floor of his house. "My younger brother and I kept sleds in our bedroom," he said. "Sometimes we would open the window and sled right down into the yard."

I told him about my family, even though he already knew a little. At one point, he noticed my bracelet.

"Are those Apache tears?"

"Yes." I touched the dark stones. "It was a birthday gift from my boyfriend."

"His name is Noah, right? Does he know about me?"

"Not yet," I admitted. "Why? Should I tell him?"

We were back at the fountain. "It's up to you, but if you don't mind waiting a little while longer, I'd appreciate it."

"I don't mind." I was relieved, actually. "Can I ask why?"

"I don't want him to see me as a threat," Michael explained. "A guy assigned to protect you? It might rub him the wrong way."

It *would* rub Noah the wrong way, I thought. He was very protective of me, a natural instinct since the attack. I didn't want him to feel that he had failed and now someone else was stepping in.

We kept walking. "Who's in charge of you?" I blurted out. The question sounded silly, but I was curious about the structure of things. Was there a council of wizened old men sitting around a table, assigning Protectors and discussing the problem of battling evil entities?

"It's complicated," he said. We had arrived at the food court, which was fairly empty. I treated myself to another smoothie, Michael bought a coffee, and we chose a table away from the thin crowds. "You've heard of Swiss bank accounts, right?"

I sipped my smoothie as Michael talked about families that had been affected by different Watchers. Some of the families were powerful or political, and they had established an account for the Protectors, money used for travel and living expenses. Small groups of people all over the world knew about it, and did what they could to help find Protectors. There was even a type of school out West somewhere, a place where potential Protectors could receive training and guidance.

"So, there's no single person in charge," Michael said. "It's more like different committees."

I was halfway through my drink and we still hadn't answered the most important question: why was Michael here now? I poked the bottom of my cup with a straw. Around us, the food court began filling up with people. School was out for the day, I realized.

"You're here for answers," Michael said finally. "And I haven't given you too many of those."

I didn't disagree. "What's going on? That's the only question that matters."

He looked away, off to the side where a group of boys stood ogling girls in line for pizza. I wondered if he was sensing anger and getting ready to deal with another outburst. His eyes seemed locked on one particular boy, who looked to be about fourteen and was dressed in baggy jeans and a baseball cap.

"What's going on is something that hasn't happened in a long time." He was talking to me, but Michael's gaze remained steady on the boy. "The Watcher who attacked you should have been subdued, sent back to its place of origin. Instead, we think it's close to finding a way back." He looked at me, and I thought about how familiar his brown eyes seemed. "It never happens that fast."

"How long does it usually take?"

"The last one we know of took over 300 years to return." He let the news sink in for a moment. "I was chosen to help you because we share a certain connection. It's not something I'm ready to talk about, so you're going to have to trust me on this."

"We're connected?" I was still struggling with the revelation that the thing I had encountered was not a regular, standard Watcher, but some sort of super-Watcher.

Michael stood up. "Excuse me for a minute."

Over by the pizza line, something was happening. Most of the kids had paired off, but the boy in the baseball cap was hanging behind. His head was down, but it was obvious he was watching the others. It was also obvious that he was holding something in his hand, something he was trying to keep concealed.

Michael wandered over slowly, as if he wasn't sure whether or not he wanted a slice of pizza. He was blocking the boy's view of the others, so the boy tried to walk around. Before he could, Michael put out his arm. His hand brushed against the boy, causing him to look up. Michael said something to him. The boy nodded and handed over the object he had been trying to hide. After a few more seconds of conversation, the boy walked away and Michael headed back to our table. He tossed the object into a trash can before he sat down.

"What was it?" I asked. "That thing you threw away."

"Oh, that." Michael downed the last of his coffee. "The kid had a camera and some very bad intentions. It was a problem that needed to be stopped before it went too far."

He met my gaze, and again, I was struck by his eyes. I knew those eyes, but I didn't understand *how* I knew them.

"Can you really stop the Watcher?"

He took my hand in his, and I immediately felt calmer. It was like relaxing in a warm bath, a sensation that surrounded me completely.

"I will do everything I can, Charlotte," he said. "I promise. I will not fail again."

eleven

I was still mulling over the possible meaning of Michael's promise—*I will not fail again*—when I arrived home. Maybe he was referring to the fact that he hadn't been there for us when Mom was attacked, but something about the way he said it made me think that wasn't the case, that there was more to it.

We had chatted a little more before leaving the mall. Michael had narrowed down a list of inmates who had served unusually long sentences at the prison, men who had died behind its cold bars. Finding the Watcher's real name would be like uncovering a weapon: it would not defeat the entity entirely, but it would definitely weaken him.

I walked through the front door of my house and was greeted by the scent of pot roast and the sound of happy voices coming from the kitchen. Dad, Shane and Trisha were gathered near the counter.

"Hey, guys!" I immediately went over to the Crock-Pot. "This smells great."

"It needs another hour," Trisha said.

It had been a while since Trisha had come over to make us dinner. "What's the special occasion?" I asked.

My question was answered with an awkward silence. The adults exchanged nervous looks at one another, as if silently asking who was going to say something first. Dad took a deep breath. "Let's go into the dining room."

This was not good. Something had happened. It had to be Mom. Something had happened to Mom. "No," I said, gripping the edge of the counter. "Tell me here."

"Okay." Shane stood next to Trisha and put one arm around her shoulder. "We have news."

Trisha nodded. "I spoke with my son Ryan yesterday," she began. "Both Ryan and Jeff were able to arrange leave at the same time. They're coming home next month."

I immediately relaxed my grip on the counter. "That's great news!"

"But that's not all." Trisha nodded at Shane, who cleared his throat.

"Yes, well, since Jeff and Ryan will be here, we've decided to go ahead with the wedding. We're getting married on October 15."

I stared at Shane, confused. October 15 was only three weeks away. Had there been an update on Mom? Would she be well enough by then? "I don't understand."

"We all wanted Mom to be there," Dad said. "But this is wonderful news. It was a major feat for Jeff and Ryan to plan leave together. They won't be able to do it again."

I couldn't look at the three of them, so I stared at my hands instead. "But Mom is supposed to be there."

Shane sighed. "I know. And Trisha knows, too, and we came up with a plan."

"A plan?" Maybe there *was* news. Maybe Michael's healing techniques had been having an effect and Mom would be with us. I felt a surge of hope, like a seed pushing through the dirt.

"We're saving a seat for her." Shane smiled. "We'll have a framed picture of her right in the front row, next to your dad. And we're videotaping the ceremony, of course, and we can take the video to her room and play it for her."

It was like someone had stomped on my hope. "That's your plan?"

Shane's face fell. "You don't like it."

No, I didn't like it. Not at all.

"I don't like you giving up on Mom. I don't like you breaking promises." My voice was getting louder. "And I don't like you choosing her over us! We're family!"

"Yes, you are." Shane kept his voice low and steady. "But so is Trisha. And I know your mom would approve. I wouldn't be doing this if I thought she wouldn't."

"I'm sorry you're hurt by this," Trisha said, stepping forward. She sounded genuinely apologetic, and her expression was pained. "Please remember that your mother is my friend, and I wouldn't do this if I thought for a second that she would be upset by it."

I wanted to believe her. I wanted to trust her words because they made sense. But it was too much.

"When she wakes up, everything will be different," I said softly.

"No, it won't. Some things will have changed, but change isn't always bad." She gave me a half smile. "Honestly, I think your mother would be furious if she woke up and discovered that we hadn't moved forward with our lives."

"Maybe." But where did that leave Dad? His life consisted of sitting at her bedside, reading books on theology. Deadlines had passed, speaking engagements canceled, projects left abandoned. Would Mom be furious with him, or was it the unspoken deal when you had been married for decades that life stopped when the other person wasn't there?

I retreated to my room, desperately craving some alone time. But Dad followed me upstairs, insisting that we talk.

"Both Shane and Trisha love you. You know that, right?"

I shrugged. Of course I knew. But I also knew that the people who loved you were often the ones who hurt you the most.

"They came to me first," Dad continued. "They asked for my blessing and said they wouldn't get married if I had a problem with it."

"So why didn't you tell them you had a problem with it? You could have stopped this."

Dad frowned. "Stop two people from being happy? Why would I want that, Charlotte? For that matter, why would you?"

Because we're not supposed to be moving on without Mom, I thought. Because Shane and Trisha can't celebrate the happiest day of their lives without her. Because we can't give up yet, and this stupid ceremony feels like we are.

"I don't want to stop anyone's happiness," I mumbled.

Dad patted my back. "Glad to hear it." He got up. "This is a good thing, Charlotte. It really is."

"Okay." I agreed because it was what he wanted to hear. It was what everyone wanted to hear.

Everyone but me.

BLISS AGREED TO MEET ME for lunch the next day. I suggested that we go somewhere off campus, but she refused.

"The cafeteria," she said in a way that did not allow argument. "One way to defeat your panic attacks is to return to a place where they occurred."

I knew she was right, but I dreaded going back to the crowded room. My stomach twisted all morning as I sat through my classes, barely aware of what my professors were saying. I tried not to think about returning to the cafeteria. After all, it wasn't the place that triggered the attacks, it was the sound. But I worried that the same thing would occur again. Someone could make a simple, clumsy mistake and I would fall back into the hyperventilating state I was getting much too familiar with.

My classes did not provide the distraction I was hoping for, and I found myself doodling in my notebook and drifting back to my meeting with Michael. It had gone well, I decided. He definitely gave off a big-brother vibe, which I liked. I wondered if it was part of Michael's powers. Maybe he had a way of making sure I felt totally nonthreatened around him. Maybe he was assigned to me because he was not my type and there was no chance of some weird sexual attraction. Or maybe we were connected, as he had said, and that connection was somehow a family thing. Could we be related?

I wanted to determine how I was connected to Michael. It seemed important. But it was a topic that made Michael uncomfortable. I didn't want to push the issue yet, but I needed to know. It could wait, though. There were more important things to resolve first.

By lunchtime, I was a mess. I couldn't remember why I had asked Bliss to have lunch with me. What was I trying to accomplish? Another panic attack? I stood outside the cafeteria entrance, desperately searching for a valid excuse not to go in.

After twenty minutes, Bliss emerged from the cafeteria. "There you are. I've been waiting." She was dressed in a lavender shirt and dark purple jeans. I focused on the perfectly matched colors.

"I know. I'm sorry, but I don't think I can go in there."

She took my hand. "I thought this might happen. So we're going to Plan B."

"What's Plan B?"

"We're going in, but only for a minute. We'll get our food to go, and eat outside. Okay?"

My knotted nerves protested, but I decided to try. It was a compromise, and I could handle compromise. "Five minutes," I said weakly.

We sailed through the lunch line. I grabbed foam containers without really looking at them, paid at the end of the line, and followed Bliss out of the jam-packed room. I kept my eyes on her purple clothes, and somehow that helped. By the time we got outside, I was breathing hard, but not melting down.

"That wasn't terrible," I said, surprised.

Bliss sat down in the grass. I sat across from her, happy to be out in the open and away from the noise of the college.

"One step at a time." Bliss opened a clear plastic container holding her plain salad. I lifted the top of my white foam box and discovered a cheeseburger and fries, which I wasn't really in the mood for. But this was a minicelebration, I decided. I'd made it through the cafeteria without needing to be carried out. A cheeseburger was an appropriate award.

"So," Bliss said as she speared a leaf of lettuce. "Tell me about the Protector."

"He's nice." I munched on some fries and tried to come up with something more specific. "Tall, lanky. Very, you know, protective."

And familiar, I thought. Something about his brown eyes. It was as if I'd seen them before, but I couldn't place them.

"What did you guys talk about?"

I described our meeting at the mall, and the way Michael had defused two potentially disastrous encounters. Bliss nodded as she sipped her mineral water.

"Sounds like he's the real thing," she said after I'd finished.

"I think so. It's weird, though." I ate a bite of my cheeseburger. "I have to trust this stranger with my life, basically."

"It takes time to build trust," Bliss said.

I agreed. "That's what Michael said, so we're meeting again tomorrow."

"Good. Where?"

"We're going to see my mom." I wasn't thrilled with the idea, but again, Michael hadn't given me a choice. He was in charge. I was supposed to trust him, a guy I barely knew. But it didn't feel as strange as I had thought it would. It was probably some sort of Protector power at work, but I did feel safe with him.

"Have you told anyone about Michael yet?" Bliss asked.

I polished off the last of my fries. "I told Avery and I told you."

"Two people you don't see every day."

"So?"

"So maybe it's time to start letting your family know."

I had considered it, but I wasn't really speaking to Shane or Trisha right now, and I barely saw Dad.

"I guess I could tell my sister."

"You should. I know you don't want people to freak out, but it'll be worse if you wait too long and something happens."

Bliss was right. I'd waited too long before, and the mistake had landed my parents in the hospital. I couldn't do that again, even if this situation was different.

"Can I ask you something?" I was done talking about my problems, and there was something I'd always wanted to ask her. "It's kind of personal."

Bliss smiled. "I think we're at the point where you can ask me kind of personal questions."

"Every time I see you, you're wearing a single color. Why is that?"

She looked down at her dark purple jeans. "I think it started with the queen of England."

I couldn't help laughing. "The what?"

"When I was younger, I read that the queen of England always dresses in a single bright color. That way, she's easy to spot in a crowd. When I decided to go into journalism, I thought it was a good idea. I need to stand out, right?"

"That makes sense."

"You don't think it's odd?"

I sensed her uncertainty, and was determined to boost her confidence. "I think you look great. I wish I was as color co-ordinated as you. And you're right—you do stand out. In a good way."

Bliss beamed. "Thanks, Charlotte."

We collected our trash and stood up. "I'm glad you're go-ing to talk to your sister," she said as we walked back toward our building. "But promise me you'll consider telling other people, too."

"I'll think about it, I really will." We stopped in front of the Yerian Building. Bliss had another class, but I was done for the day. "Thanks for all the advice," I said. "I appreciate it."

Bliss looked embarrassed. "That's what friends do. Give advice, share lunch…"

"Save people from public panic attacks," I finished. "You're a great friend. I mean that."

She stood straighter. "Well, I'm getting out of here be-fore this conversation becomes unbearably mushy. I don't do mushy. Or sappy."

"Got it. See you tomorrow, Bliss."

I walked to the parking lot, happy and determined to talk to Annalise. But when I called her from my parked car, it went straight to voice mail. Instead of hanging up, I left a brief message asking her to call me when she had a minute. I checked my dashboard clock. Noah had lunch, and there was a chance his phone was turned on, so I called him, too, hoping we could meet after he was done with school for the day. He picked up on the third ring.

"Charlotte? Everything okay?"

"Yeah, everything's great. I just had lunch with Bliss." I wished he hadn't immediately thought something was wrong. He was worrying about me, and I hadn't even given him something real to worry about. "I was wondering if we could meet after school?"

"Today?"

"Well, yeah. I could pick you up from school."

"Today doesn't work for me. I'm staying late today. Another video assignment for Morley."

"Oh." I was disappointed. My conversation with Bliss had fired me up, and I wanted to follow through before my enthusiasm deflated.

"But we could catch up later. How about after dinner?"

"Sure. That works."

"Great. I'm kind of in a rush, so I have to go. I'll see you later."

He hung up before I could say goodbye. I sat in my car, drumming my fingertips on the steering wheel. Something in Noah's voice bothered me. I watched other students cross the parking lot. My windows were up, but I could still hear the muffled cadence of their voices. It occurred to me that I hadn't heard any background noise when I'd spoken with Noah. It had been absolutely quiet. If I'd caught him at lunch, I should have heard something. The basic chaos of the cafeteria. People passing by his table. Something.

I drove home, still trying to dissect my brief call. I walked Dante, texted Avery and started a load of laundry. When I

checked the kitchen clock, it was nearly time for school to
end. I decided that I needed to see Noah, even if it was only
for a moment. Mr. Morley would understand if Noah took
a few minutes to see me. I just wanted to check on him. We
could discuss Michael when we had more time.

The parking lot of Lincoln High was filling up with students when I pulled in. The back doors were wide open, so I
slipped inside and went immediately to the AV room.

"Hi, Mr. Morley."

My former teacher smiled from behind his desk. "Charlotte! What a nice surprise. What brings one of my favorite
alumni back to these hallowed halls?"

"I just stopped by to see Noah. Does he have a minute?"

"Noah's not here."

"Oh. I really need to talk to him. Will he be back soon?"

"I wish. He was the best editor I had." Mr. Morley shuffled
some papers on his desk. "But Noah dropped the class a few
weeks ago."

"He what?"

"No idea why," Morley continued. "It was an easy A for
him, and it would have been nice for his college applications.
When you see him, tell him that I'd love to have him back,
even if it's not until next semester."

"I'll tell him," I said as I backed out of the room. "The next
time I see him, I'll definitely tell him."

I was stunned. Why would Noah lie to me? I returned to
my car, struggling to figure out how I would confront him.
I sat in the driver's seat, trying not to cry. Then I opened my
phone and dialed Annalise. When she answered, I had only
one question for her.

"Do you remember the Pink Rose?"

twelve

Five years earlier

The Pink Rose Bed-and-Breakfast tried hard to live up to its name. From the wallpaper to the curtains to the heavy rugs, pink roses bloomed on every surface. Annalise and I unpacked our suitcases in our room, which featured a lacy pink canopy bed and rosebud wallpaper.

"It's overkill, don't you think?" I had just checked the minuscule bathroom, where even the toilet paper was pink.

"Absolutely." Annnalise stretched out on the queen-size bed we would be sleeping in for the next three nights. "Especially since this place isn't technically named after the flower. It's named after the girl."

"What girl?"

"This girl." Mom stood in the doorway. She pointed to a framed portrait hanging above the nightstand. I walked closer to get a better look. The child in the painting looked to be about seven or eight. Light blond hair framed her soft face with big curls, and in her hands she held a bouquet of roses.

"Her name was Rose," Mom said. "She was seven when she died here in 1888. And she's the reason why we're here."

I only knew the basic facts behind our trip to Virginia. At thirteen, I wasn't as interested in why we were going someplace as I was in where we were going and how close it was to a beach. But this was going to be a brief trip. In three days we had to be in Colorado to work on a new project.

"So this is the ghost girl," I murmured, still staring at the portrait. Little Rose had bright blue eyes and very pink cheeks. She resembled a cherub more than a child. The artist had surrounded her head with strokes of white, giving the appearance of a faint halo.

Mom looked at the painting with me. "She died from pneumonia. Her family was devastated, and this house became a kind of shrine to their only child."

"I wouldn't really call this a house," Annalise said from the bed. "It's a Victorian mansion."

"And people really think they hear her laughing in the hallways?" That part of the story I could remember. Normally, it wasn't the kind of tale that my family would drive hundreds of miles out of the way to investigate. But one of Mom's college friends had stayed at the B and B a month earlier, and the experience had rattled her so badly that she had immediately contacted Mom. Quick research had uncovered dozens of stories exactly like the one Mom's friend had told: the spirit of a child roaming the hallways, giggling and calling out to the guests. No one had seen the girl, but the voice was perfectly clear, and more than one guest had awoken to a single rose placed just inside their locked door.

"Dad's interviewing the owner right now," Mom said. "Shane's getting the equipment ready. We'll start after dinner, okay?" She patted my back. "And if we finish early, I thought the three of us could do some shopping in town tomorrow."

Annalise yawned. "Do you really think we'll finish early? This place has, like, thirty eyewitness accounts. What if we find something?"

"We'll see." Mom rubbed at the back of her neck. "I believe there's something behind those accounts, but I don't know what we'll find."

Both my parents kept a cool, skeptical attitude toward every investigation, but I had overheard Mom say that she was actually excited about this one. Her college friend was a skeptic and would not have called Mom unless she thought it was worth the trip.

"Dad spoke with a local team," Mom said. "They checked the wiring, structure, everything. The house is solid and was modernized within the past ten years."

"And?"

"And the team heard a child's voice several times. They excluded any structural causes. Dad trusts these guys, so maybe this could be something truly unexplained."

"That would be a first, wouldn't it?"

Mom smiled. "Yes, it would. And after twenty years of doing this, I would definitely like to be there when something big happens." She began walking back to her room. "I'll see you girls downstairs in an hour for dinner."

Dinner was held in the very formal, very floral dining room. Annalise and I met the owner, Mrs. Hollings, who introduced herself as a direct descendant of the original owners—and the little ghost girl.

"We're a proud family," she said as we sipped our first course of lukewarm soup. I avoided looking across the table at Shane, who was trying hard not to gag on the strange mixture of pumpkin and potato purée.

Thankfully, Mrs. Hollings didn't notice. "And a family such as ours must preserve certain traditions." She dipped her spoon into the soup. "This recipe, for example, was passed down through four generations."

"Is that so?" Mom feigned interest, but she was as tired of Mrs. Hollings's endless stories as we were—and we still had the main course and dessert to get through. Mrs. Hollings had made a big point of telling us that she did not normally prepare an "evening meal" for guests, but we were special.

After the second course, which consisted of a piece of bony fish and rice that could only be described as crunchy, Mrs. Hollings began to discuss the property.

"My great-great grandfather built the place and it's always been in our family," she said. "I grew up tending the rose-bushes in the garden."

"It's so generous of you to open the home to guests and visitors," Mom said.

"Ah, well, I wasn't left with much of a choice." Mrs. Hollings smiled sadly. "A property this large brings with it many expenses, the least of which is the maintenance. I've had to invest nearly everything I have to keep the roof from collapsing."

"Tell us about the repairs and modifications," Dad urged. "Are there any original fixtures?"

It was a routine question when we conducted an investigation, but an important one, so Dad often asked it several times. People sometimes forgot work that had been done, and he needed to know as much as possible about the place. Too often, a shoddy electrical job resulted in occurrences that people interpreted as paranormal.

Mrs. Hollings didn't need much prodding to begin listing all the work the property had required. There had been a new roof within the last twenty years and updated plumbing. "You know," she said, "most of the rooms didn't have their own bathrooms, which was a licensing requirement for opening a bed-and-breakfast. We converted closets into the bathrooms."

She said this as if we would be surprised. Considering that the toilet, sink and shower all touched in our bathroom, I wasn't.

"Anything else?" Dad asked. "Even minor repairs?"

"Let's see. I had to replace a few pieces of ceiling in some of the rooms. And a few years ago several of the steps on the grand staircase needed to be replaced." She looked at Mom. "Your friend mentioned her encounter there, I assume?"

"She did, yes."

"What encounter?" Annalise asked. I noticed that she'd barely touched her dinner and wondered if, like both me and Shane, she'd simply buried her fish beneath the rice.

"Genna heard light footsteps on the staircase." Mom sipped her water. "It was unusual because it happened while she was on the stairs. She said it sounded like there was a child following her up the steps."

Mrs. Hollings nodded. "I hear that story often. Little Rose loves to follow the guests around. I think she wants to play, poor thing."

Fortunately, dessert was edible. It was a white coconut cake purchased from a local bakery, and we wolfed down our thick slices before Mrs. Hollings had a chance to pour the coffee. "Goodness," she remarked. "I'll have to order from them more often."

As the adults drank their coffee, Mrs. Hollings described her own experiences with Rose. "Having lived here my whole life, of course I've had many, many encounters."

"Just sound or something else?" Dad asked.

"Oh, I've seen her." Mrs. Hollings added more cream to her coffee. "She used to come into my bedroom late at night.

More than once I woke up to find her kneeling by my bed, watching me with those big blue eyes of hers."

"That must have been terrifying," I said.

"At first, yes. But then I realized she was only curious. This was her home first, after all."

The dessert course finally ended, and Mrs. Hollings excused herself for the night. "I'll retire to the guesthouse so I don't disturb your work," she said. "I'm so glad you're here, and I look forward to hearing about your experiences tomorrow at breakfast."

"Man, I hope she's not the one cooking it," Shane whispered.

I bit my lip so I wouldn't giggle. Mrs. Hollings left, and we immediately got to work. It was already past eight and I was tired from the day of traveling, but setting up for an investigation always invigorated me. This was the work I knew so well. As my parents endlessly reminded us, we were a team, and every year I was becoming a more important component of that team. The year before, when I'd turned twelve, Shane had finally taught me how to operate his cameras, whereas before my job had been to make sure they'd been put away in the proper cases and to maintain the equipment log.

Our investigation of the Pink Rose would focus on several key areas: the second floor, the grand staircase and the great room, which were all places where activity had been reported more than once.

"Stay as quiet as you can," Dad told us before we got started. "Nearly all of the reports have to do with sound. We won't do an EVP session until later. For now, we wait and listen."

Annalise smirked. "Another wild, late night for the Silvers."

Mom put her arm around Annalise's shoulder. "You can work with me this time. It'll be fun."

"Oh, yeah. Sitting quietly in the dark is always so much more fun when it's with your mom."

Annalise was going through a surly teenage phase. At least, that's what Mom and Dad thought. As long as she helped out, they didn't bug her too much about her sarcasm.

"Great. Charlotte, that means you're with me," Dad said. "We'll take the second floor. Shane, we good to go?"

"Yep. Everything's ready. You want me down here?"

Dad nodded. "The great room is close enough to the staircase. You should be able to keep an eye on both."

I followed Dad up the creaky stairs to the second floor. We turned off all the lights, and then watched the downstairs lights flick off one by one as Mom and Shane went through the rooms. The investigation had officially begun.

For the first hour, Dad and I sat silently in the middle of the second-floor hallway. All of the guest doors were open, and we had a good view of the downstairs entryway, as well. I wasn't afraid of the dark, especially not when Dad was so close by. Mom always said that there was nothing to fear at night that you shouldn't also fear during the day. So if you weren't scared of a place in the daytime, why should it terrify you a few hours later? It was the same place, and energy was energy. It didn't keep a clock or set hours.

After the second hour, the dark silence began to get to me. "Do you think anything will happen tonight?" I whispered.

"Probably not," Dad whispered back. "But your mom hopes so."

I hoped so, too. Our investigations had a certain rhythm to them, a structure that had melted into a solid routine. We came, we taped, we debunked. Then my parents edited the footage into a neat, fifty-minute episode that aired on cable a month later. I worried that it had become too boring. My parents seemed restless, and when that happened, we ended up moving halfway across the world for a few months. If the Pink Rose produced something unexplainable, it might rejuvenate my parents. Maybe they would even stay in one place for a while.

The second hour blended into the third hour, then the fourth. I felt sleepy and bored. My legs were lead, and I wanted to jump up and run up and down the hall a few times to wake them up. A clock downstairs chimed once.

Nothing was going to happen, I decided. All those stories were wrong. Little Rose did not scamper on the staircase or knock on doors or leave flowers in the rooms. She was dust in a coffin.

Dad shifted. I looked over and saw him checking his cameras. He wouldn't quit yet, but maybe he would let me go to bed. I was about to ask him if I could go to my room when we heard it.

"Hello?"

It was a child's voice, high-pitched and clear, sounding almost like a note of music. Dad and I both sat up, alert and fully awake. I knew better than to say anything, but I wanted to ask where the voice had come from. Was she at the end of the hallway or the bottom of the stairs? I wasn't sure.

Dad shattered the silence. "Hello?"

We waited. Less than a minute later, a little girl's voice responded. "Rose."

"Your name is Rose?" Dad stood up slowly. After hours of sitting down, his legs were shaky. Rose didn't answer right away. A light flickered from somewhere downstairs. Then I heard footsteps. Small and fast, they came up the staircase, then stopped short of the hallway. There was a soft giggle, followed by one more footstep.

"Rose?" Dad asked.

But there was no other sound except for the pounding in my chest.

BREAKFAST WAS WAITING for us the next morning. To everyone's relief, Mrs. Hollings had not been back to the kitchen since dinner. Instead, she had ordered croissants and coffee cake from the bakery. After a late night and nearly no sleep, we were happy with the buffet. I helped myself to three croissants and a glass of orange juice while Dad described our eventful evening to Mrs. Hollings.

"Everything lines up with the witness accounts," he said. "The entire team heard her voice and the footsteps on the staircase."

Mom, Shane and Annalise reported hearing the exact same things from their positions downstairs. I thought it was a little strange that Rose's presence had been so loud. It was captured on both the digital recorder and the video cameras, something that had never happened before. How strong was this little girl? Could her energy be strong enough to reach out and touch us? Or worse, hurt us? The idea wouldn't leave me, and even though I had gone to bed after four in the morning, I had barely slept.

"I thought you might meet Rose," Mrs. Hollings said, pouring coffee.

"Yes." Dad buttered a croissant. "The stories are nearly exact. Almost *too* exact."

Mrs. Hollings set down her porcelain cup. "I'm not sure I understand."

"We expected some activity," Dad said. "None of us were prepared for every reported occurrence to happen all at once, within the same hour."

"Well, it appears you were here on a good night." Mrs.

Hollings smiled, but it looked tense, as if she was forcing herself to do so. "Rose must like you."

Dad continued to eat his breakfast. Shane was attacking half the coffee cake, and Annalise looked like she was still half-asleep. Only Mom and Dad were fully awake and alert.

"It is interesting," Mom mused. "Usually there is some variation when people describe their paranormal experiences. But Patrick's right. What we heard last night fit in perfectly with other accounts."

Dad pretended to be absorbed with breakfast, but I knew he was paying close attention to everything that was being said. He didn't believe the Pink Rose was haunted, I realized. He had already decided that it was a hoax. But he needed Mom to figure it out for herself, so he was planting the first seeds of doubt and gauging Mrs. Hollings's reaction.

"I'm pleased that Rose made herself known to you," Mrs. Hollings said. "She does have certain habits, which may explain why so many of our guests report similar incidents."

"Yes, that may explain it." Mom had a faraway look in her eyes. It was a look I knew well. She was in a thoughtful mode, her debunker skills on high alert. "We'd like to look around today, take some pictures. Would that be all right with you?"

Our schedule for the day had been planned a week ahead of time, but asking for permission from Mrs. Hollings was an important formality. Always show respect, my parents taught me. You are in someone else's space, and your job is to make them comfortable with your presence. Something about the way Mrs. Hollings was eyeing us told me that we were on the verge of losing that respect. Dad had challenged her. It wasn't a confrontation, but now Mrs. Hollings wasn't happy. Her smile vanished, and she took her coffee to the guesthouse.

"If you found something that suggests a hoax, I'd love to be filled in," Mom said to Dad.

"I haven't found anything yet," he replied. "It's just a feeling."

Mom laughed. "Well, if it's a feeling, then case closed. We can go home now."

Annalise, who hadn't been paying attention, looked up. "We're leaving? Thank God."

"Your mother was being sarcastic." Dad finished his croissant. "But I do think we'll be leaving sooner than expected."

It was another challenge, but this time, it was directed at Mom. Instead of being angry, though, she lit up, eager for the chance to prove something. We spent the rest of the morning inspecting the wiring and lights, but found nothing out of the ordinary.

"It all comes back to the sound," Mom said. We were sitting on the bottom step together. Annalise had returned to bed and Shane was running tests in the basement with Dad.

"And the sounds always come from this area," I added. "The staircase and the hallway."

Mom nodded. Then she walked up the staircase slowly, pausing between each step. When she reached the top, she bounced on her heels a little, testing the floor.

"Do me a favor," she called down. "Walk up here, but run your hands along the wallpaper as you go."

I was used to odd requests, and I didn't question this one. I put both hands on the wall and let my hands run over the antique-looking wallpaper as I climbed the stairs. I knew I looked silly, like I was trying to massage the house, but about halfway up, my fingers ran into a something, a place where the wall abruptly gave way. I stopped and looked over at Mom, who was carefully inspecting the banister.

"I think there's a little hole here."

Mom came over and ran her hands over the space. "You're right. Someone covered up a hole with this wallpaper." She looked down the stairs. "Stand in front of me," she whispered. I pretended to admire the chandelier above us while Mom pulled back the wallpaper. There was a soft tearing sound, then Mom gasped. I worried that she had torn the paper too much.

"What is it?"

When I turned around, Mom was pressing the paper back into place. She sighed. "It's time to leave."

At first, Mrs. Hollings denied everything.

"There's been a mistake," she insisted. "I have nothing to do with any of this."

But the evidence was overwhelming. The hole in the wall was filled with a tiny recorder set on a loop. Every twenty-four hours, it played a little girl's voice, followed by the sound of footsteps. As the recorder required batteries, someone would have to peel back the carefully placed wallpaper to replace them every week or so. It was so simple.

Maybe that was why the scheme had worked: a few clear sounds, nothing too dramatic or obvious, and people fell for it. The sounds were especially powerful if you were on or near the staircase. And Mrs. Hollings could have easily left a single rose inside her guests' rooms in the middle of the night. The Pink Rose was not haunted. It was simply maintained by a woman desperate to keep up business.

"You don't understand!" she wailed when we began packing up our things. "I've put every cent into this place. I can't lose it! I have nowhere to go!"

Mom busied herself with coiling the different wires we used, her jaw clenched. I didn't know if she was more angry with Mrs. Hollings for the lies or with herself for wanting to believe them.

"Ever since the ghost stories began, I've been able to pay

my bills," Mrs. Hollings continued. "I was facing foreclosure! This was the only way."

Surprisingly, Dad was sympathetic. I thought he would gloat or get mad, but instead, he listened to her.

"I understand why you did it," Dad said. His voice was soft, a noticeable contrast to Mrs. Hollings's loud protests. "But it wasn't right. You could have told us before we came here, and saved everyone a lot of trouble."

"Rose is real! I've seen her!" Mrs. Hollings clutched at the lace collar of her dress. "But she doesn't always show up, and I needed something every night. You have to believe me!"

Dad said nothing. He finished his work and left the Pink Rose. Shane followed, shaking his head. Annalise was already in the van, probably napping in the backseat.

"Please don't ruin me," Mrs. Hollings begged. Mom and I stood in the foyer, ready to leave. "If people don't think that this place is haunted, I'll have to close in a few months." Her eyes were shiny with tears. "Please. You don't know what this means to me."

Mom frowned. "Yes, I think I do." She looked out the front door, where Dad was sitting behind the steering wheel of the car. She took my hand. "Goodbye, Mrs. Hollings. I wish you the best of luck."

In the end, we didn't do anything with the footage. We could have created an episode about the hoax, but no one had the heart to hurt an old woman trying to make a living. Mom said that if people wanted to believe it, that was their problem. She asked Mrs. Hollings not to advertise that the place was haunted in her brochures, and that was the end of it.

I thought.

Mom remained quiet and sullen for weeks. At our investigation in Colorado, she was detached, leaving interviews and even the DVD commentary to Dad. On our last night in Colorado, I found her sitting in the library of our hotel, a closed book in her lap.

"Mom?" I tiptoed into the room. "Are you awake?"

"Yes. Just thinking."

I sat on the floor in front of her chair and pulled my robe around me. "Thinking about what?"

She set her book on a small table. "Thinking about why people lie."

"Because they think they need to," I said. "They think a lie will protect them."

Mom smiled. "That's very well put, Charlotte. Very well put."

I beamed at her praise, but knew the answer wasn't enough to pull Mom out of her mood. I was confused, too. We had been tricked in the past, usually by people eager to prove that we weren't the scientific debunkers we claimed to be. Mom always discovered the truth, and instead of feeling betrayed, she accepted the findings as a victory. So why was this time different?

"You were hoping that this time, it would be real. Is that why you've been so upset?"

Mom looked at me with a strange mixture of surprise and sadness. "We've spent so long searching. I suppose I thought that for once, it would be nice to find something exactly the way people described it." She patted her chair and I went over to her. She hugged me. "Trust is a choice we make. And you can't trust everyone," she said. "But you can always trust your family."

I believed her.

thirteen

Protectors were not punctual. Maybe this did not apply to all Protectors, but the only one I knew was Michael, and he was late—again. I checked my phone for the tenth time, then crossed my arms and settled back into the scratchy waiting room chair. I was the only one around in the too-cheerful lobby of the long-term care facility. Mom's room was a quick elevator ride up two flights, but I wasn't going to see her until Michael arrived.

My call to Annalise the day before had not provided me with the reassurance I had been hoping for. She only vaguely remembered the Pink Rose, and her memories did not involve any of Mom's quiet fury. Basically, she had slept through most of it.

"Why are you bringing this up?" she'd asked. "Are you going back there?"

I wasn't ready to explain Noah's deception. I wasn't even ready to talk to Noah, who had canceled our plans at the last minute in a rushed voice mail. "Schoolwork," he'd said. "I promise I'll make it up to you."

How could he make it up to me? He had lied. I trusted him

more than anyone else, as if he was family, and he had lied to me for months. My heart was not broken—it was slashed into ribbons.

And now I was sitting impatiently in a taupe waiting room, hoping my tardy Protector would show up soon so I wouldn't have to go upstairs alone.

My cell phone buzzed, startling me. It was Michael.

"I'm running late," he said, sounding breathless. "Something came up. I'll be there in about two hours."

"What? That's crazy. I'm not waiting here for two hours."

"You're right. You're going to see your mom."

I sighed. "How do you know I'm not with her right now?"

"Because cell phones don't work in her room. Now go upstairs and wait for me."

His calm bossiness annoyed me and I wanted to tell him that he had no right to order me around, but he hung up before I could snap at him. Again, I thought this must be what it was like to have an older brother.

If Michael thought I was going to leap out of my chair and rush upstairs to do as I was told, he was wrong. I stayed where I was for a few minutes longer. Spending two whole hours in Mom's room was not what I had planned for the afternoon. Finally, I went to the elevator and pressed the button. I would go, I would stay as long as I could, and then I would get some lunch. I didn't have to spend the entire time waiting for Michael in that depressing room.

As I signed in at the nurse's station, I happened to see a desk calendar. September 28. A little more than three months separated Mom from a doctor-approved "option." The reminder terrified me, but it also forced me to walk down the wide hallway and push open the door to her room.

Once inside, I avoided looking directly at her bed. I went to the window first and gazed at the parking lot to look for

Michael's black sedan. Maybe this was a test, and he was sitting outside, waiting behind the wheel. But the parking lot was half-empty, and most of the cars were silver or blue or white.

To my right, monitors beeped and the ventilator whooshed, steady as waves. I turned away from the window, grabbed a nearby chair, and pulled it over to the bed, my eyes locked on the floor. "Hey, Mom."

This was so stupid. I had no idea what to say, and even if I had, it wasn't as if she could hear me. My words were wasted, they didn't matter. But if they didn't matter, I could say anything. I could read the newspaper aloud or tell jokes or recite nursery rhymes. Michael seemed to think that simply the sound of my voice could be helpful. And since I wasn't making wildly successful strides toward contacting help from the other side, maybe I needed to settle for this.

For now.

Because I wasn't done with my late-night experiment.

"So I know it's been a while," I said, letting my finger trail across her nightstand. "I started school and things have been busy."

My excuse sounded phony, even to me. "I haven't wanted to come. Everyone said I should, but…" I raised my head so that I was finally looking at my mother.

And then I gasped.

Shoving back my chair, I got up and stumbled backward until I was pressing against the wall. I mashed my hand repeatedly on the call button.

"You only have to hit the button once," a tired voice said from the wall.

"Please, I need help! Now!"

Footsteps rushed down the hallway. The two nurses who burst through the door found me standing by the window, shaking. I pointed a finger at my mom. "Her eyes! Her eyes are open!"

One nurse came over to me while the other took Mom's vitals. "I looked over and she was staring at me," I said. "She was just *staring*."

"It's okay, hon. Everything's fine." The nurse straightened the toppled chair and led me to it. "Have a seat. You've never seen this before?"

Satisfied with the vitals, the other nurse left the room. Mom's eyes were closed now.

"She was staring at me," I mumbled. The nurse handed me a cup of water. I held it but didn't drink.

"This happens sometimes," she explained. "It's a reflexive movement, and it's perfectly normal."

But Mom's eyes hadn't looked normal. She had the gaze of a corpse, hard and unseeing.

"I'm going to send in a doctor to talk to you, okay? He can explain it." She patted my shoulder. "Don't be scared. She's still your mom."

The nurse left, her shoes barely making a sound against the floor. I could hear her talking to the other nurse outside the door, but their conversation was muffled, their tone one of concern.

I was afraid to look at Mom again. I wrapped my arms around myself and concentrated on the beeping monitor. I tried to match my breathing to it, which actually helped calm me down a little. I tried to be logical. Reflexive movement meant progress. It meant that she was starting the long journey out of her coma. I felt a flicker of optimism. Maybe she would be coming home soon, after all.

The doctor arrived a few minutes later. I met him with a cautious smile and told him how Mom had opened her eyes. "So that's good, right?" I prodded. "She's getting better?"

He pried open Mom's eyes and pointed a small flashlight in them. Then he glanced at his chart, jotted something down, and turned to me.

"You're Charlotte?"

"Yes, I'm her daughter."

He nodded. "Has your father explained your mother's condition to you?"

"She's in a coma."

"Yes, but it's more than that. She has progressed to a vegetative state."

I perked up at hearing the word *progressed*. "So she's getting better?"

"Not exactly."

The doctor barely looked at me as he recited information as if he was reading from a medical textbook. Normally, he said, a person in a coma will come out of it after two to four weeks. After that point, the patient was considered to be in a persistent vegetative state. Sleep cycles, eye movement and even sneezing were not uncommon, but it didn't mean that Mom was improving.

"I wish I had better news for you," the doctor said. "The truth is, it's very rare for someone to recover completely after a head trauma like this. That doesn't mean you can't stay optimistic, but you need to know that even if she regains brain function, her recovery would be very slow." He closed his chart. "I'm sorry."

When Michael arrived more than an hour later, I was still sitting in the chair, staring at Mom's pale face.

"You all right?"

I wasn't. The doctor's monotone declaration of Mom's prognosis had shoved me deeper into a confused abyss. Mom was basically dead, Noah was lying to me, and the Watcher had not been permanently extracted from my life. My problems were mountains. Huge, Everest-sized mountains. And I doubted that Michael could truly help, even if he was equipped with super-Protector powers. Healing skills and the ability to defuse anger could only do so much. I needed a badass guy covered with armor and wielding a sharp ax. Lean Michael, with his corduroy pants and concerned expression, was not going to give me the backup I required.

"She's in a vegetative state," I told Michael. He crouched down next to my chair, but I didn't look at him. "She's never getting better. She's already dead."

"That's not true." He took my hand and squeezed it. "Head injuries can be unpredictable. The doctors don't know everything."

"And *you* don't know everything!" I yanked my hand from his grasp. "Seriously. What have you done to help her? Your job is to protect me and my mom, but you're always late and you haven't done a damn thing for either of us! So maybe we need a new Protector." I shook my head. "No offense, because I think you're a nice guy, but this whole thing was a colossal mistake."

I buried my head in my hands. I knew my words had stung, but I didn't care. My Protector was an utter failure. All he'd done since his mysterious arrival was confuse me. He had failed at the one job he had supposedly been sent to do, which was to keep both me and my mom safe.

"Are you done wallowing?"

The harshness of Michael's words made me look up. "Excuse me?"

"I kept hearing from Beth about how strong you were, how resilient." He stood next to Mom's bed. "You subdued the Watcher. You returned to your house after everything that happened. You kept going." He gave a short, bitter laugh. "And now look at you, curled up in a chair and whining."

"I'm not—"

"Yes, you are." He cut me off. "This is a fight we can win. This is a fight that matters, and you're accepting defeat. After everything you've been through, how could you possibly give up so completely? How could you be so weak?"

If he wanted to piss me off, he had succeeded. I stood up. "Weak? How dare you?" I felt my anger burn inside my chest. I wanted to shove him, show him the strength of my rage. "You think you know me? You have no idea how hard I've tried to help her." Tears stung my eyes. "No. Idea."

"Then show me, Charlotte. Show me this determination I've heard about. Show me what you can do."

It was a strange command, but it was also a challenge to prove myself. And while part of me bristled at the idea that I had to prove myself to anyone I didn't love, another part wanted to shut him up. Maybe I'd slipped into whiner territory, but that was normal behavior after everything I'd been through. Wasn't I allowed to have a few measly moments of weakness? Why did everyone think that I had to demonstrate superhuman strength and maturity? It wasn't fair.

"Well?" Michael's eyes bored into mine. "You ready to fight for your mom? Or do you want to go back to sitting in your chair and feeling sorry for yourself?"

I stared at Mom. Her eyes were closed, her hands folded neatly on her chest. A white blanket had been tucked around her. It was as if she was lying on a morgue table.

But she was alive.

She was alive, and if she was alive, there was hope. Not much, according to the doctor, but at the moment, a shred of hope weighed more than a lifetime of certainty.

I kept staring at her, but I addressed Michael. "I'm not giving up," I said, and for the first time in a long while, I heard something in my voice, something I thought I'd lost. I held Mom's wrist.

"I'm here." I kissed her limp hand. "And I will not fail you."

fourteen

Bliss was waiting for me outside the Yerian Building the next day, her eyes wide with urgency. "I need to talk to you."

"Can it wait? Class starts in five minutes." Not that I truly cared. I was exhausted, and after the previous day's events, being late for class would be the least—and most normal—of my problems.

"Have you seen Noah recently?"

I looked at her. She was wearing a light green dress that reminded me of spring leaves, a bright contrast against the gray September sky above us.

"I haven't seen him in two days," I told her. It didn't sound like much, but it was the longest we'd gone without contact since we had begun dating. My phone showed that he had called several times the night before, but the calls had come after I'd gone to bed and he hadn't left a message.

Despite my need to talk to him, I refused to reach out. He had messed up. It was his responsibility to contact me. That's what I told myself, anyway. I couldn't decide if I was more angry or hurt.

Or scared.

Because the Noah I knew would never have lied to me or stayed away for two days. My Noah made sure my birthday was celebrated with a thoughtful piece of jewelry. He tried to defend me when we were being attacked and stood beside me when things got rough. The person I was in love with would not betray me this way. So why had he? The answer was too terrible to think about.

"I need to talk to him," Bliss said. "It's important."

"What's going on?" Bliss barely knew Noah. The three of us had shared AV class together in high school, but that was it. What could she possibly want to talk about with my boyfriend?

Or maybe, I thought miserably, my future ex-boyfriend.

"It's hard to explain." Bliss bit her lower lip. "I kind of need you to trust me on this one."

"Okay." I took out my phone. "Let me give you his number."

She seemed surprised. "Really? Just like that?"

"Right now, you're one of the few people I actually trust." I took her phone and typed in Noah's number. "If you need something, it's yours." I finished programming the number and handed back the phone. "You'll tell me later, right?"

"Of course." Bliss smiled. "Thank you, Charlotte. This helps more than you know."

"He's acting weird right now," I admitted. "If you find out what's going on with him, will you let me know?"

She bit her lip again. "I promise."

I watched as Bliss hurried away. She wasn't going to class, I realized. She was rushing in the opposite direction, toward the parking lot. I shifted my backpack from one shoulder to the other. I had no desire to go to class. I also did not want to go home and face Shane, who was working on the DVD.

There had to be someplace where I could retreat, some quiet, peaceful space that would accept me for a little while.

An hour later, I was listening to ocean waves as they cascaded through Potion's speakers. Beth was helping a customer select a calming scent of incense, but she acknowledged me with a solemn tip of her head. I ignored the selection of candles and multicolored scarves and walked directly to the back room. Then I found the door hidden between bookshelves and pushed it open.

Outside, the secret garden tucked between alleyways was alive with color and noise. Birds hopped from tree branch to tree branch while a stone fountain murmured in the corner. I sat on the bench in the center of the space and closed my eyes. I breathed in the scent of jasmine and listened to the sounds around me, allowing them to soothe my frazzled nerves.

I don't know how long I sat there. An hour, maybe less. I was aware of Beth's presence when she sat down next to me, but I was so relaxed that I didn't feel the need to say anything.

"I'm glad you're here," Beth said after a few silent minutes. "I was hoping you'd come to see me."

I took a deep breath. I had never meditated, but I could understand why so many people swore by it. A few quiet moments by yourself with a clear mind could do wonders. I felt strong and sure and ready for anything. Or almost anything.

"Michael told me about your visit to see your mom yesterday," Beth continued. "I'm so glad you went."

"Me, too."

"He said you were feeling better, stronger."

I *was* feeling stronger, but not better, exactly. My life was still a mess. You could be strong and still have crazy, unpredictable relationships. I didn't understand everything that was going on, but at least I understood myself. And what I understood was that I was a fighter, the kind of fighter who would not allow her opponent to scare her into doing nothing. I had already spent time cowering in the corner. It hadn't solved anything.

Beth took my hand in hers. Her grasp was warm and re-assuring. I held on to her tightly, imagining that she was my mom.

"What do you believe?" Beth asked. "Do you believe your mother will pull through this?"

"I believe it's possible."

So many things were possible. Doctors relied on science and research, and that made sense to me. They had to be able to provide percentages and not offer false hope. But was any hope truly false? There were always exceptions. Couldn't Mom be one of those?

"What else do you believe, Charlotte?"

I allowed myself to really think about Beth's question. I knew she wasn't trying to rush me, and I could take my time. It was time for me to start thinking about it. Until now, my parents had answered everything for me. They had shaped my world and decided what was real. Now it was time to figure out some of the answers for myself.

"I believe that my mom can get better," I said. "She might not be exactly the way she was, but she doesn't have to remain the way she is now."

I knew any possible recovery wouldn't be the kind I had seen on soap operas. There would be no fluttering of eyelids, followed by a sleepy smile and a lame joke about how long she had been out. Instead, there would be a slow return to nor-mal brain functions, and time spent in a wheelchair that we would push to rehab. It would be enough to have her look at me and know that she was actually seeing me and could reg-ister my presence.

"I also believe that I am connected to Michael somehow. But I can't figure it out." I turned to Beth. "Do you know?"

"Yes," she said. "But it's up to him to tell you."

"He's not my long-lost brother, is he?"

She laughed. "No, I can promise you that."

"But sometimes he feels like it."

"That's a good thing, Charlotte. It's your instincts telling you that he's trustworthy."

Again, there was that issue of trust. An image of the Pink Rose flashed in my mind. I could almost hear Mom's voice telling me that I could always trust family, that trust was a choice we make. I knew I could trust Beth. And Bliss and Avery and Michael.

But not Noah.

Beth pulled me in for a sideways hug. The gesture reminded me of Mom, and I dissolved into tears.

"Let it out," she murmured. "It's okay."

Except nothing was okay, and all the tears in the world would not wash away the problems that had stained my life.

After I had finished a marathon session of crying and assured Beth a hundred times that I was fine, I drove home. It was past rush hour, and traffic was sparse. I was grateful—crowded highways made me clench the steering wheel and sit up so straight that my back hurt. But the hour-long drive gave me time to think, and by the time I parked in our driveway, I determined that I needed two things: to attempt another EVP session and to see Noah in person. Both required action.

And trust.

Because despite everything, I still trusted that Noah loved me. If the Watcher was trying to take him, I would fight, just as I had the last time. When Marcus had died, I had seen his eyes. His last words were that he had tried to fight it, which meant to me that Noah would also fight being taken over. There was still time to save him. There had to be.

There also had to be time to save Mom. The whispering female voice I had captured on my EVPs was not threatening. Beth said that I had good instincts. Well, my instincts told me that the entity I had contacted meant me no harm.

Dad was reading a book at the kitchen table when I walked in. "You're home late," he said. "Did you already have dinner? Because there's leftovers in the fridge."

"I'm good."

He shut his book. "I wanted to let you know that Trisha's bringing over some of her wedding stuff tomorrow."

"Wedding stuff?"

Dad shrugged. "That's as specific as she would be. Apparently, she's run out of room in her apartment."

"Great. Well, thanks for the heads-up."

I began to make my way toward the stairs, but Dad stopped me. "Are you okay with all of this? The wedding, I mean."

I leaned against the wall. "I'm not thrilled, but it's okay. I promise to be on my best behavior and smile for all the pictures."

"I'm going to hold you to that."

I wanted to go upstairs to my room, but Dad seemed like he was in a good mood and we rarely had a chance to talk. I pulled out a chair and sat across from him at the table.

"What was your wedding like?"

I had flipped through their tiny album commemorating the event, but it consisted of formal pictures taken in a courthouse and gave few clues about the day itself.

He shook his head. "It was a total disaster. Everything went wrong."

I smiled. "Tell me."

It was a story I had only heard in bits and pieces. My parents had decided to get married on New Year's Eve at a small church in Maine, where they had been living for six months. They hadn't counted on a vicious storm front that stranded their relatives in the Midwest and crippled the entire Northeast.

"The church lost power and we had to go downtown. We were lucky to find a judge to marry us," Dad said. "We had no guests, no cake, no music."

"Why didn't you postpone it?" I wanted to know.

"We talked about it. In the end, all we wanted was to get married. Most of the details involved the reception, and that wasn't as important to us. We threw a big party a few months later, and it was great."

"A wedding with no cake? That's my favorite part."

"We improvised." He said that they found a bakery and feasted on cupcakes. Then, on the ride home through the snowy streets, Mom's favorite song came on the radio. It was one she had wanted to hear during the reception, and as soon as it came on, Dad turned up the volume, parked on the shoulder of the road, and pulled Mom close. They listened to their song as the headlights illuminated fat snowflakes that fell from the night sky.

Dad was lost in memories, but at least they weren't the painful kind. His face revealed a content happiness I hadn't seen in a long time. I listened to him for a while, letting myself be pulled into those memories. By the time he was done reminiscing, it was late.

And I still had work to do.

fifteen

The ritual was working. As soon as I sat down on my bedroom floor and arranged my equipment in front of me, I saw
results. The lights on the EMF reader flashed in an instant
rainbow of color. My digital recorder was already running,
and I didn't hesitate to ask my usual questions.

"Is someone here with me?"

The steady lights were all the proof I needed that something
was there, but I followed my standard procedure regardless.

"Can you help me? Can you help my mom?"

I waited. "What am I supposed to do?"

I sat silent for minute, hoping that my recorder was picking up answers. It was past midnight, Dad was asleep, and the
only light in my room came from my tiny desk lamp. It was
like all the other times I had done this, and there was something comfortable about it.

As I asked my questions, I realized there was one answer
I needed desperately: the Watcher's real name. After asking
it out loud, I noticed that the lights blinked wildly. I let the
recorder run for another minute. Then the EMF lights went
off, and I knew the session was over.

Grabbing my notebook and pen, I prepared to write down every syllable I could decipher from the recording.

My voice posed the familiar questions. A few seconds later, the soft female voice responded. Her answers were muffled, as if she was whispering from far away. I pulled out my earbuds so I could turn up the volume and not wake Dad.

"Can you help me? Can you help my mom?"

The answer was yes, but the voice was so weak it sounded more like *"ess."*

"Can you help Noah?"

The reply was slightly stronger this time, but hearing it made my heart sink. No. The word came out like a hoarse whisper, but the determination behind it was clear. I couldn't tell if the woman speaking was young or old. Definitely not a child, I thought.

"What am I supposed to do?"

At first, the voice began talking fast, a rush of words I could not untangle no matter how high I turned up the volume. Then it slowed down and became breathier, as if the entity was losing her energy.

I came to the question that mattered most. "Can you tell me the real name of the Watcher?"

Again, there was a rush of whispered words. I picked up on "us," but it was surrounded by other, less clear words.

Confused, I went back to the beginning of the recording. An answer was here, I knew it. I sat hunched over on my bedroom floor, scribbling down any word or part of a word that stood out. I was so engrossed in my work that I didn't register the fact that someone else was in the room with me—until I felt a tap on my shoulder.

I yelped in fear and surprise. My first thought was that I had been discovered by Dad and would have a lot of uncomfortable explaining to do. But when I turned my head slightly, a hand clamped down on my mouth. Dad would never do that. The terror that instantly flooded my senses thrust me onto the verge of a massive panic attack. I ripped out the earbuds and tried to lurch to the side, away from the intruder.

"Shh. Charlotte, please don't scream. I didn't mean to scare you."

"Noah?" My panic was only slightly diminished.

He crouched in front of me. "I'm so sorry. I tried calling, but your phone was off. I wasn't trying to scare you."

My heart was pounding, my nerves frazzled. Something wasn't right. "How did you get in here?"

"I have a spare key, remember?" He held it out as proof. I stared at the silver object in his hand as if it could explain everything to me. I had given him the key months ago, but this was the first time he'd ever used it.

I kept my teary eyes on the key. "Why are you here, Noah?"

He shifted from his crouching position so that he was sitting across from me. I pulled my knees up to my chest and wiped at a single tear that ran down my cheek. Part of me wanted to look at him, really look at him. I wanted to know that his eyes were the same, that maybe the bruise on his neck had finally faded. But I held back. What if the eyes looking back at me were not really his?

"I'm here because I haven't seen you for almost three days," he said, taking my hand in his. "I was getting worried. Are you mad at me or something?"

Now I looked at him. His green eyes were wide with concern but also appeared sunken, as if he was sleep deprived. His brown hair stood out in unwashed spikes, and the tag on his navy-blue T-shirt peeked out below his neck. It was on backward. This was not my boyfriend. This was a stressed-out shadow of my boyfriend. The betrayal I'd felt growing over the past 48 hours gave way to something else.

"Are you okay?" I reached out to touch his cheek, but he pulled away. My anger instantly resurfaced. "You lied to me." I watched his face as I made my accusation. All I saw was confusion as his brow wrinkled.

"Lied to you? About what?"

"I stopped by the school. Morley told me you dropped his class last month. So what have you been doing every time you say you're filming football games?"

Noah shook his head. "What are you talking about? I never dropped Morley's class."

He sounded incredulous, as if I'd just told him I had been abducted by purple aliens. There was something in his voice that was so genuinely confused that I hesitated, almost doubting myself. But I had spoken to Morley. And there was no reason for my former teacher to lie to me.

"I was at the school," I said again. "I spoke to Morley. He said you were no longer a student in his class."

"I was there editing footage yesterday, Charlotte. There's been a mistake." He ran a hand through his hair, creating more jagged angles. I wondered when he had last taken a shower.

"It's a mistake," he mumbled. "I would never lie to you." He took both my hands in his. "I would *never* lie to you. Not ever."

The heart is a dependable gauge of sincerity. And my heart believed him.

It was my head that couldn't make sense of the situation.

The nightstand clock showed that it was nearly two in the morning. I was tired. I wanted to return to my EVP session. I wanted to curl under my comforter and go to sleep.

I also wanted everything to make sense between me and

Noah. The list of all the things I wanted was too long to con-
template. I had to deal with what was in front of me, and what
was in front of me was my boyfriend, a person I once trusted
more than any other. My heart begged me to believe him,
that it was all a weird mistake, but my head warned me that
Noah's story did not make sense.

"You're not telling me everything." It was the only thing
I could say because it was the only thing I was sure was true.

Noah still held my hands in his, but his grip loosened a little. "I saw my dad."

"What? When?"

"A few days ago." Noah described how he was waiting for
the bus one morning, listening to his MP3 player and drinking a soda to help him wake up. The bus was turning down
the street when Noah looked up—and saw his dad standing
across the street.

"I didn't recognize him at first," he said. "He was just a guy
wearing a khaki jacket. But then he held up his hand, like a
wave to say hi. And then I knew."

"What did you do?"

He shrugged. "Nothing. I got on the bus and went to
school. I was in shock, I guess."

"That's understandable. You haven't seen him in over a decade." I thought of something. "Noah, are you absolutely sure
it was him? Maybe it was just a guy who looked like him."

"Maybe." He sighed. "Maybe I was dreaming again."

"Again? Are you still sleepwalking?" I couldn't help the
overwhelming urge to comfort him. It was so confusing. For
days I had seethed over his betrayal, but seeing him in person
changed something inside me. He denied lying and I wanted
to believe him. Part of me *did* believe him.

"I get up, I go to school." Noah was talking as if he was
trying to convince himself of something. "I eat the same

grilled cheese sandwich for lunch every day. Same classes, same everything." He looked down at his clothes. "Exactly the same."

I didn't know how to respond to his rambling. He began to stand up, but as he did he wobbled and his foot hit the EMF reader, causing it to bump into the side of my bed.

"What is all this stuff?" He picked up the reader and I cringed. My little late night secret had been exposed. I didn't want to lie, but I didn't want to explain, either. I chose a middle option.

"It's my mom's."

"Oh." He placed it on my bed. "I should go."

"Wait." Everything felt so unfinished. "Please don't leave yet. You need to rest. Why don't you crash on our couch? Even if it's just for a few hours."

He turned so that we were facing each other. He was so close that I could feel his breath when he exhaled, but all I could think of was that he looked so *sad*.

"Do you remember how we first met?" he asked.

"Of course. We met in AV class." The randomness of his question puzzled me, but I wanted him to keep talking.

"No. We met that morning, in the office."

I remembered my first day at Lincoln High. Avery and a group of cheerleaders had escorted me to the main office so I could pick up my schedule. It was crowded, and I didn't notice the other students around me.

"I was there because my locker was busted," he said. "I was waiting around, and suddenly you were there, surrounded by all those girls. But you were the first one I saw. The only one."

His voice turned husky. He leaned in, but instead of kissing, we simply let our foreheads rest against each other. "I thought, if she would only look at me, I'll be happy. And then, when you walked into class at the end of the day and helped me

with the camera wires, I thought, wow. Gorgeous *and* smart?
I was done."

The memory of that moment made me smile. At the time,
I had been struggling through my first day at a new school.
That's all I'd thought it was. If only I'd known that it was
the day I would meet Noah, the first guy I'd ever completely
fallen in love with.

"I wish that a camera had been on so we would have our
first conversation together on tape," I said, my forehead still
pressed against his. "I would watch it every day."

"I would, too. Just to remind myself of how lucky I am."
He placed both his hands on my face and kissed me, softly at
first. Then I pulled him in more tightly, wanting to remind
him of how much I loved him, how much he meant to me.
Words weren't enough—I had to show him. But as I was pulling him toward my bed, he stepped back.

"I have to go."

"No!" I needed him to stay, needed to know that he was
okay and not wandering around in the dark by himself. "You
can't leave."

I wanted us to spend the night curled around each other
in my bed, talking about everything from our first dance together on an empty beach to our picnic on campus. I wanted
to relive those moments when I'd felt truly happy, because I
had the sinking feeling that they were gone forever, erased by
an unseen hand.

Noah hugged me, and I hugged him back as firmly as I
could. "I'm not leaving you," he whispered. "Don't worry
about that."

I closed my eyes and he kissed each one of my eyelids, a kiss
that was so soft it could have been the flutter of a dragonfly's
wing.

"I'll talk to you tomorrow," he said. And then he left.

I heard him walk down the stairs and out the front door, and it wasn't until a few minutes had passed that I realized I had no idea how he had gotten to my house.

I cried for a while and tried to comprehend what had just happened. It felt important. It felt final. But it couldn't be.

My room was still littered with equipment that needed to be put away, so I busied myself with stashing the gear in its box and sliding it under my bed. The only thing I didn't put back was the digital recorder. My EVP session still needed to be transcribed, but I wasn't in the mood to do it tonight. I stored the recorder in my purse, put everything else back in its place, and went to bed without putting on my pajamas.

It was late, and despite my concern over Noah, my body begged me to let go. As I slipped into sleep, I thought about Noah, and hoped that somehow, he would find his way home.

sixteen

The next day I returned from walking Dante to discover that
our dining room had been transformed into a bridal boutique.
I stood in the entryway to the living room, baffled at first
when I saw the normally blank walls covered with dozens of
bright pictures. On closer inspection, I realized that they were
all pages ripped from magazines.

"Charlotte!" Trisha rushed into the room, her arms over-
flowing with a creamy-yellow fabric. "I'm so glad you're here.
I've narrowed down the bridesmaid dresses to three possibili-
ties."

She draped the fabric over the back of a chair. "When
Annalise gets here, you two can decide."

"Annalise is coming?"

"She'll be here tomorrow afternoon." Trisha began stacking her magazines on the table. "She's coming for the weekend to help me plan. I don't know how I can get everything
done in two weeks, and your sister is so good at organizing."

"I thought you had already decided on most of the details."

"That was for a spring or summer wedding." She pointed to
a calendar page for October taped to the wall. It was already

the first of the month, and the fifteenth had been circled in bright green highlighter. "Now that we're having a fall wedding, I have to start over completely."

I was barely paying attention as Trisha rambled about silk samples and dying our shoes the correct color. Instead, I mentally replayed my strange meeting with Noah the night before. His abrupt departure had worried me. I had called his cell phone half a dozen times since I'd woken up, but my calls went straight to voice mail.

"Charlotte?"

"Sorry. I was distracted."

Trisha nodded. "I'm sorry, too. I know I've been focused on the wedding, and I haven't had a chance to talk to you about it."

"Isn't that what you were just doing?"

She smiled. "I mean that I understand that this is something you're struggling with. I respect your feelings about wanting your mom to be there."

I did not want to get sucked into a conversation involving my mom. "It's okay. I know how important it is for Jeff and Ryan to be there."

And in a way, I *was* okay with it. Everyone was so busy with the impending ceremony that I could work with Michael and no one would notice. Maybe we could prevent something from happening without my family ever finding out that we had come close to danger.

"Things still good with you and Noah?" Trisha asked.

The question caught me off guard, and I had no answer ready for it. "Yes," I said. She picked up on the uncertainty in my voice.

"I'm not trying to pry, and I promise that anything you tell me stays between us." She was smoothing out the fabric samples hanging over the chair. "He doesn't talk to me like he used to. He's been so distant and quiet lately. All he ever seems to do is sleep." She looked up. "Should I be worried?"

Now I really had no answer. I could tell her the truth and set her off into a frenzy, potentially ruining her wedding. Or I could lie and hope I didn't regret it later.

"He's having a hard time sleeping," I said. It was a slice of the truth. "I think he has insomnia. I'm worried about it, too. Maybe he should see a doctor?"

"Insomnia." Trisha sighed. "His dad had it, too. I know how sleep problems can affect a person." She straightened her shoulders. "Thank you, Charlotte. That makes so much sense. I'll schedule an appointment for him."

She gave me a quick hug before grabbing her MP3 player and returning to her work. I left the room feeling okay. I had not lied outright. And maybe seeing a doctor would be a good thing for Noah.

Although I had been hoping to get some private computer time so I could analyze the EVPs I had recorded, it would have to wait. My laptop didn't contain the software I needed. I resolved to return later that night, after Dad was asleep.

Anxious that I might get pulled into more wedding talk or questions about Noah, I decided to hang out in my room and try calling Avery. But when I reached the second-floor hallway, I heard a noise coming from my room. It sounded like the swivel chair I kept by my desk, which squeaked when it was moved.

I paused, waiting to hear something else. I took a hesitant step forward so that I could actually see my room. To my uncomfortable surprise, the door was shut. I never shut the door unless I was actually inside. My stomach twisted a little, one of the all-too-familiar symptoms of a burgeoning panic attack. I took a deep breath and willed myself to calm down and not overreact. It was nothing. Dad or Trisha had probably closed it for some reason. Still, I felt apprehensive about taking another step forward and turning the handle.

As I put my hand on the doorknob, I heard a soft thump. Trisha hadn't mentioned anyone else being home, and Shane and Dad never entered my space without asking. Again, my stomach clenched and again, I breathed in deeply. There was a logical explanation for this.

And then I realized the simple truth: it was Noah. It had to be. School wasn't out yet, but maybe he had skipped AV and was hiding in my room so his mom wouldn't find out. I felt silly for my brief lapse into dread. There wasn't a burglar hiding in my room, and demonic forces like the Watcher didn't sit in swivel chairs.

I opened the door, prepared to hug Noah and figure out what was going on. The scene that greeted me was not at all what I had expected to find.

No one was in my room.

But someone *had* been there, and whoever it was had left behind a trail of destruction. I felt dizzy and had to lean against the bed frame. My cell phone rang. I opened it without looking at the caller ID, my eyes still sweeping the bedroom.

"Charlotte? It's Michael. Are you okay?"

"Yeah, I'm fine." I looked over to my desk, where my laptop lay split in two pieces, as if it had been sliced in half. "My room is another story."

"I had a weird feeling, like something angry was near you."

Streaks of dirt marked the carpet and my shredded comforter was bleeding tufts of white batting. "I think you're right. And I think it was in my room." I looked at the window, which was wide open. No, not wide open—it was gone. "You should probably come over," I whispered, overcome by a wave of nausea. "I think I need your help."

"I'm on my way."

I held the phone to my ear long after Michael had hung up. It felt safer that way, for some reason, as if I wasn't exactly alone in the mangled space. I went to touch my bracelet, then realized it wasn't there. I had left it on my nightstand that morning. I looked over. The lamp had been knocked to the floor and my clock blinked noon even though it wasn't. The bracelet was gone. I stepped closer, and felt something beneath my shoe. It was a single Apache tear. I bent down to pick it up and saw more scattered on the floor.

I stood up, relieved that at least the pieces of the bracelet were still there. The comforter could be replaced, the carpet cleaned. Maybe the computer could be repaired. But there would be no way to hide the missing window from my dad.

The window frame had suffered only minimal damage. Chipped paint dotted the sides and a few splinters of wood stood out like jagged fingers. Leaning forward, I tried to get a better look at the glass below. The heavy window looked as if it was intact, somehow. What had happened? Someone— or something—had entered and exited through the gaping, square hole. But how had the window been removed so completely? And why hadn't Trisha heard anything?

Slowly, I closed my phone and placed it in my pocket. Then I left my room, careful to shut the door behind me. Downstairs, Trisha was still in the dining room.

"Trisha?" Her back was to me and she was humming. "Trish?"

I tapped her on the shoulder and she spun around. "Charlotte!" She removed two earbuds, and I heard a blast of bass emanating from them. "Sorry. I had my music on."

No wonder she hadn't heard anything upstairs.

"Um, have you seen Noah today?"

She looked at her watch. "He's still in school. Oh!" She

smiled. "I forgot to tell you. He left me a note saying he doesn't need a ride home today. Some AV project."

I thanked Trisha and decided to wait on the front porch for Michael to arrive. My hands were shaking, my heart pounding with relentless fear. I remembered Beth's words from the week before, about how nothing had happened yet but we had to be prepared.

Well, something had happened.

And I definitely did not feel prepared.

TRISHA WAS STILL happily humming when Michael's black car drove down our street. I watched from the porch as he kept going and parked halfway down the hill. I appreciated his discretion: if Shane came home and saw an unfamiliar car parked in front of our house, he would get suspicious.

I walked down the steps to meet Michael—and was surprised to see that he was not alone.

"Bliss?"

"Hey, Charlotte."

I looked from Michael to Bliss. "You two know each other?"

"Sort of." Michael's gaze was fixed on my house. "Let's go inside. We'll fill you in."

"Sure." After what had happened in my room, I didn't know why seeing the two of them together should have unsettled me, but it had. As soon as we entered the foyer, though, I remembered what was waiting for us upstairs.

I led the way, feeling anxious but also stronger now that I had two people with me. I opened the door to my room and let the others go in first.

"Whoa," Bliss said. "It looks like a wild animal attacked your bed."

"And computer," Michael pointed out.

"And window," I added, stepping inside.

"Mind if I take some pictures?" Bliss held up a digital camera.

"Sure." Was she working as Michael's assistant?

He was studying the window frame. "Could you get some shots of this?"

Bliss immediately went over to him. He said something softly and she nodded. He knelt down to get a better look at the dirty marks lining the carpet. "Doesn't look like footsteps," he mused. "It's almost as if he was dragging something."

"He?" I asked.

Michael looked up. "Yes."

Bliss knelt down next to him and took a few pictures. "I'm definitely getting something."

"Getting what?" I was losing patience. "What's going on with you two? How do you know each other?"

Michael stood up, but Bliss remained where she was and continued to take pictures. It was like watching one of the investigations my family normally organized, but this time I was the distressed subject looking for assistance.

"I met Bliss a couple days ago," he said. "I ran into her on campus when you were visiting your mom. That's why I was late."

"You were late because you were socializing?"

"It's not like that," Bliss said. She was still on the floor but had moved closer to my bed. "He was helping me with something." She frowned. "What were you keeping under your bed?"

I froze. "No." I got down on the floor next to Bliss and peered under the frame. My box of cameras and paranormal tools was gone. I reached around, hoping that maybe the large box had been pushed aside, but I knew deep down that it was gone. Then I checked the rest of my room. It was a futile search.

"What was under there?" Bliss asked again. She pointed to the streaks. "It must have been heavy, because it looks like it was dragged across the floor."

I pushed back frustrated tears. "It was a box of investigative equipment. Thousands of dollars' worth."

It wasn't the monetary value of the tools that bothered me, although I knew Dad would be upset by the expensive loss. I was more concerned by the fact that it would be nearly impossible now to conduct my late-night work. At least, I thought, I still had the recorder from last night's EVP session tucked inside my purse. We had other equipment, but Dad had stored it somewhere and there was no way I could ask for it without serious questioning.

Unless it was time to tell him about what was going on. The thought had occurred to me before, but I didn't feel ready. Maybe when Annalise arrived. If I could tell Annalise everything first, we could both break the news to Dad.

"Charlotte, let's try to straighten up this room a little," Michael suggested. "Can you find some garbage bags? We'll get this comforter out of here."

I nodded, grateful for an excuse to leave my room. Downstairs, I could hear Trisha still humming in the dining room, completely oblivious to me as I went into the kitchen. As I grabbed the box of garbage bags from under the sink, I heard her phone ring. It was sitting on the counter, so I picked it up, intending to hand it to her. But when I saw the number on the screen, I answered it.

"Is this Mrs. Elliot?"

"Yes," I said, trying to make my voice sound lower and more mature.

"I'm calling from the attendance office at Lincoln High.

Noah was absent from classes today." I could hear her typing at a keyboard. "And yesterday, as well."

The night before, Noah had told me that he had been in class. *I was there editing footage.* He hadn't hesitated when he'd said it. My boyfriend was either the world's greatest liar or he truly believed he had been at school. An instinct to cover for him kicked in.

"I'm so sorry. He has the flu and I forgot to call."

"There's a lot of that going around," the secretary said in a flat voice. "I hope he gets well soon."

I deleted the call from Trisha's phone history and placed it back on the counter, then returned upstairs with the box of garbage bags. Michael was placing my broken laptop in a duffel bag. "I might be able to fix this."

Bliss took the garbage bags from me. "I'll start cleaning up your bed."

"Noah hasn't been in school for the past two days."

They stopped working. "You sure?" Michael asked.

I told him about the call from the secretary and Noah's visit the night before. "We have to find him. I'm really worried."

"Right," Michael said. "Okay, here's what we're going to do. We're going to clean up your room the best we can. I'll try to fix the window. Do you think Noah's still at school?"

For some reason, the prison popped in my mind, but I wasn't sure why. "We can start at his apartment," I decided. "Let's hurry."

We shoved the last of my destroyed bedding into garbage bags. Michael said he was going outside to retrieve the window. Before he even made it to my bedroom door, though, he stopped dead in his tracks. We all did—the noise coming from downstairs was terrifying.

Trisha was screaming.

seventeen

Before Trisha's scream had fully faded, I was halfway down the stairs. Bliss and Michael were right behind me, their footsteps pounding as fast as my heart. I didn't know what I'd find in the dining room. My brain hadn't hurdled as far ahead as my instincts, which were shrieking at me to shield Trisha no matter what. Without a weapon, the only thing I had was myself, and as I cleared the stairs and raced down the front hall, I was fully prepared, no matter what was making Trisha scream, to jump onto its back and squeeze its neck as hard as I could.

Unless it was Noah.

If I found Noah hurting his mom, I didn't know what I would do.

But it wasn't Noah standing in the middle of the dining room with his back to me. The man was taller, with the broad shoulders of a football player.

And he was lifting Trisha off the ground, his huge arms swallowing her small frame. Memories of the Watcher flooded my mind. I wanted to scream, but I was too terrified. Michael pushed past me, but he wasn't throwing punches or trying to free Trisha from the man's fierce embrace. He didn't even look scared. If he was the Protector, why wasn't he doing anything to help?

The man lowered Trisha to the ground but kept one arm around her so she couldn't run away. I could see her tear-streaked face as she turned from the man to look at Michael.

"Who are you?" she asked, wiping at her cheeks.

"He's with me," Bliss announced.

Both Trisha and the man turned around, allowing me the chance to finally see the stranger's face. He was younger than I had guessed, maybe in his early twenties. And he was smiling. So was Trisha.

"I didn't know you had friends over," Trisha said to me.

I was still recovering from the shock of hearing her scream and the instant panic it had induced. "They're from school," I explained weakly. "We're working on a project."

She wasn't listening. "Charlotte, this is my oldest son, Ryan. He has a terrible habit of scaring me."

Ryan shrugged. "I thought you'd like a surprise visit. But hey, if you want me to leave..." He pulled away a little and Trisha gave him a playful punch on the arm.

"Don't you dare. You're not going anywhere until after the wedding."

There was a mild resemblance between Noah and his big brother. I studied Ryan's face, trying to determine which features they had in common. The nose was similar, and maybe the chin. But Ryan's eyes were brown, whereas Noah's were green.

Trisha hugged her son again. "How did you know I was here?"

"I stopped by the apartment first. Noah told me where to find you."

"You saw Noah?" I gave Bliss a hopeful glance. If Noah was at home, then it was unlikely he had been the one trashing my room a half hour earlier. He didn't have a car, and there was no way he could have walked from my house to his in such a short amount of time.

"You're his girlfriend, right?" Ryan held out his hand. "Nice to meet you."

"Hi." I wanted to be polite, but I was more interested in news about Noah.

"I'm going to make some coffee," Trisha announced. "Would anyone else like some?"

Bliss declined, and Michael said he needed to go out to his car. I knew he was using the opportunity to retrieve my bedroom window.

I cornered Ryan while Trisha was in the kitchen. "So you saw Noah?"

"Yeah. I woke him up." He laughed, and it was similar to the way Noah laughed. "He was so confused to see me. Thought he was still dreaming. I got a better reaction from him than I did from Mom."

"When was this?"

"About ten minutes ago." Ryan frowned. "You always ask a lot of questions?"

"Yes. I'm very annoying that way."

He shrugged. "Mom likes you. My brother likes you. You're fine by me."

I excused myself from the room. Bliss and I grabbed some supplies from under the kitchen sink and went upstairs to continue cleaning while we waited for Michael. I sprayed carpet cleaner and scrubbed at the marks while she straightened up my books and pictures.

"You knew that Ryan wasn't the Watcher," I said.

"Actually, I didn't. But Michael seemed to know, so I didn't freak out."

I set down the spray bottle. "Why are you with Michael? I don't understand."

"He's helping me with something. Something important."

It would be nice, I thought, if people could stop being so vague. Just once, I wanted a clear, concise answer with absolutely no room for interpretation.

Michael called up to us from outside. Bliss and I went to the space where my window used to be and looked out. "I'm going to need some help! It's too big to get my arms around."

I grabbed a couple of the full garbage bags on my way downstairs, then helped Michael carry the window back to my room. Trisha and Ryan were having coffee in the kitchen, so they didn't see us come through the front door. Once in my room, I realized there was no way to put the window back without a professional. "We can't just prop it up there," I said. "And there's no way I can explain this to my dad."

But maybe, I thought, there was someone else I could explain it to. I waited until Trisha was on the phone to ask Ryan to come upstairs. "I need your help," I said. He followed me into my room. When he saw the mess, he grimaced.

"You're not going to ask me to help clean, are you?"

I showed him the window. "I need this fixed, and I don't want to worry my dad or stress out your mom. Can you help?"

He whistled. "How'd you do that?"

"Science experiment gone wrong," Bliss said.

"I'll say." Ryan inspected the window frame. "I have a buddy who can take care of this. Might be a couple days, though."

"That would be great. Thank you."

He smiled. "No problem. I'm with you—no need to get my mom any more stressed than she is." He lowered his voice. "Has she been crazy?"

"A little. Not too bad."

"Yeah, well, you've never seen her in hyperdrive. It's about to get a whole lot worse."

I almost laughed. Ryan had no idea how bad it was already. I thanked him profusely, and he said he'd check out the garage for some plastic sheeting. "Gotta keep it covered," he said. "You don't want squirrels getting in."

"Right. That would be bad."

Ryan located a thick, opaque sheet of plastic and stapled it to the frame. When everything was done, my room didn't look half-bad. Not good, but not like a tornado had ripped through it, either.

"Now what?" I asked Michael. Ryan was downstairs with Trisha, the garbage bags had been taken out to the can, and the carpet fizzed with spots of foaming cleaner.

"We need to take a little field trip. Is that okay with you?"

I wanted out of my room. "Only if it means you're going to answer every single question I ask."

Michael held out his hand and I shook it. "Deal." Then he turned to Bliss. "Is it okay with you?"

She tied up the last garbage bag full of bedding. "It's time, I guess." She looked at me. "I need you to promise not to judge me."

"I don't understand."

Bliss sighed. "You will."

THE GNOMES WERE arranged single file in a straight line that stretched from the front door of Bliss's house all the way to the street. "Wow." I tried to do a quick count. "Are there more?"

Bliss shook her head as she took out her key. "Yep. Someone brought back a dozen."

"And they set them up like that?"

"It's better than what they did last week. Our yard looked

like the set of a gnome porno." She unlocked the door, but didn't open it. Michael came up behind us. "I don't know if I want her to see this," Bliss said to him.

"It's fine. Charlotte can handle it."

I didn't know what they were talking about, but as long as the house wasn't stuffed with dead bodies or crawling with a thousand rats, I was pretty sure that yes, I could handle it. Bliss took a deep breath and pushed open the door. "Watch your step."

Despite the bright afternoon light, it was dark inside the house. The sharp smell of lemon cleaner and mothballs reminded me that this had been Bliss's grandfather's house. It definitely had that old-person aroma. I stood in the entry with Michael at my side while Bliss moved slowly forward into the next room. She bumped against something, and a second later, a lamp glowed from across the hall.

I gasped. "Oh."

Now I understood why Bliss had been so reluctant to let me inside. This wasn't a house—it was a storage facility. Nearly every inch was covered with boxes, stacked in uneven columns that grazed the ceiling. A narrow path revealed patches of carpet. I followed the path into what I guessed was the living room, where more boxes blocked out the windows and a single recliner rested in the corner, surrounded by even more stuff.

Bliss stood against one of the stacks, her face blank. She was waiting for my reaction, and I remembered what she had said about not judging her. I wasn't sure what I was supposed to say, what would be appropriate. *I'm sorry* didn't seem right. But I was sorry. I knew her living situation was not her fault. The Bliss I knew would not choose to live this way. No one I knew would choose to live this way.

"When I said I was helping Bliss with something, this is

what I meant," Michael said. "Her grandfather left a lot behind when he died."

"Okay." I wanted to make sure that I didn't say anything
that could possibly be construed as judgmental. I wanted to
be kind and supportive, the same way Bliss had been when I
had melted into a panic attack or asked to talk with her about
my problems. "So these are all your grandfather's belongings."

"Yes." Bliss ran a hand over one of the stacks. "He saved
everything, from newspapers to sugar packets. And now my
mom and I have to deal with it."

My first question—why not just throw it all away—was
answered by Michael before I could say the words out loud.

"Every time they try to remove his belongings from the
house, something happens. Something paranormal."

"About a month after he passed, we tried to get rid of all
the magazines," Bliss said. "The entire dining room is filled
with them. But as soon as we began taking them out to the
garbage, things started happening." She kept her gaze on the
boxes nearest to her. "Lights went off, piles tipped over. It was
like he was trying to block us from the room. Every time we
attempted to clean, something would happen." She paused.
"That's part of the reason I believed you when you told me
about the Watcher. I had experienced some strange things
myself."

It was a case my parents would have been interested in.
Maybe I would have tagged along and helped Shane set up
the cameras and unroll the cable. I could picture our black
van, with "Doubt" painted across it, parked in the driveway
and all of us descending on the house, dressed in our khaki
pants and matching T-shirts, ready to record and debunk the
happenings.

I missed that part of my life. Investigations had helped form my personality, defined my family. I missed it so much I could feel it within me, like bruises buried inside my bones.

I wanted to help Bliss, but I wasn't sure that I could. My fancy equipment was gone, and the Watcher was the likely thief. How many problems could I tackle in a day? Or in a lifetime, for that matter?

"We didn't bring you here to deal with this," Michael said. "Bliss and I are handling it."

"Then why *did* you bring me here?"

Bliss stepped away from the boxes. "Because it's a place Noah's never been to."

The worn recliner across the room suddenly looked very inviting. I just wanted to sit down. "He's the next Watcher." I whispered the horrible truth, but they still heard me.

"We're not sure yet." Bliss touched my arm. "He's a candidate, but that doesn't mean he's the one." She guided me to the chair and I slumped into it.

"Did he destroy my room?"

"We don't think so," Bliss said.

"Okay, you have to stop with the 'we.' I don't get it. How are you involved with this?" It came out more bitterly than I had intended. I wasn't upset with Bliss. She had been a good friend to me. But I was confused and hurt and struggling to put together the pieces of an increasingly awful puzzle.

"She's special," Michael said.

"Please be more specific." When he hesitated, I pointed at him. "You promised me answers. Now, spill."

"You already know that there are many Watchers." Michael sat on the floor by the recliner. Bliss sat on the other side. It made me feel like a queen perched on top of a shabby throne. "There are also many Protectors," he said.

"One for every Watcher, right?"

Bliss nodded. "That's right. It's the balance principle."

"Beth explained that to me. But what does it have to do with you?"

She looked at Michael, who nodded, before she spoke. "Because, Charlotte. I'm a Protector, too."

eighteen

I woke up after too little rest to the sound of yelling. Confused, I rolled over in the guest bed and squinted at my alarm clock, then groaned when I saw that it was only eight in the morning. As tired as I was, returning to sleep was impossible. The rising voices from downstairs, mixed with the unsettling events from the day before, forced me out of bed and downstairs. The chaos I found there made me wish I had stayed under the covers.

Trisha paced the dining room, her phone pressed against her ear. "But we need to have a vegetarian option!" she practically screamed. "I don't even know what a vegetable soufflé is. Can't we change it to a pasta dish?"

In the living room, Shane and Ryan were locked in a tense conversation involving the greatest college football conference of all time. They sat across from one another, arms crossed.

"Ha!" Ryan barked. "Give me the SEC over the Big Ten any day."

"The Big Ten was winning national titles long before the SEC even existed," Shane retorted. I tiptoed into the kitchen, unwilling to get trapped in a heated discussion involving field goals and championships.

Dad was at the counter, flipping through a book as he drank his morning coffee. "Welcome to the first official day of wedding madness," he said. "Get out while you can."

I slumped into a chair and put my head on the kitchen table. "Does it have to begin so early? I actually wanted to sleep today."

"At least we only have to endure two weeks of this."

Two weeks. At once, it seemed too soon and not soon enough. I had other things to think about besides my bridesmaid dress, though. Bliss's revelation that she was also a Protector wasn't exactly good news.

"Doesn't that mean there are now two Watchers?" I had asked, not really wanting to hear the answer.

"We're still figuring that out," Michael had said. "It's never happened before. But yes, that's what it would suggest."

I wanted to go the rest of my life without someone referring to my problems as something that had "never happened before." There were moments when I seriously contemplated why I had been chosen for the paranormal turmoil that seemed to engulf me. It all came back to an event in Charleston more than a year ago. I had been in the wrong place at the wrong time—and I wondered how long I would have to pay for that innocent, accidental moment.

One Watcher was bad enough, but two? They could team up. One could come after me while the other went after my parents. I had stayed awake most of the night, staring at the plastic stretched across the window frame. Every time there was even the slightest breeze, the plastic rippled and my heart had started beating faster as I had braced myself for something to come tearing through it. Unable to stay in my room, I had grabbed my pillow and slipped into the guest room across the hall, which felt marginally safer.

Trisha walked into the kitchen, the phone balanced between her ear and her shoulder. "I'm on hold. Again," she said to us. "Noah should be here later. I let him sleep in. Actually, I couldn't even wake him. He must have been up talking to Ryan all night." She offered me a wry smile, then turned back to the phone. "Hello? Yes, I've been on hold. No, I don't want you to transfer me." She returned to the dining room.

Dad closed his book. "You want to go out to breakfast?"

I was already standing. "Give me five minutes."

Shane and Ryan's voices began to rise. Dad gave a wary look in the direction of the living room. "I think I'll wait in the car."

I ran upstairs to throw on some clothes. A quick glance in the mirror told me I would require a hat, as well, but I couldn't find one in my room. I headed to the laundry room downstairs, where I knew Mom had stored a box of winter and outdoor gear.

Shane was sitting alone in the living room, angrily punching buttons on the remote control. Trisha was still yelling into her phone. So far, the wedding wasn't doing a whole lot to bring the happy couple closer. If anything, it was making their relationship worse.

I was about to step into the laundry room when Ryan's voice stopped me.

"What do you mean, you're already here?"

He was in the laundry room, which made sense. It was away from the bedlam reigning in the other rooms downstairs. I figured he was talking to Jeff, who wasn't due to arrive for another week. I decided to forget the hat and hope that at this hour only senior citizens were dining on pancakes, and any critical fashionistas would still be asleep.

"Yes, it's a problem," Ryan said. He sounded mad. I began to walk away, but his next sentence made me freeze.

"Because you haven't seen her in fourteen years, that's why!"

He wasn't talking to his brother. He was talking to his father.

"Stay away from her. I'll come to you, okay? But you can't do this."

I slunk away from the laundry room and left the house. Dad was sitting in his car. "Everything okay?" he asked as he backed out of the driveway.

"I think Trisha's ex is planning on crashing the wedding."

"I see." We drove to the end of our street. "In that case, I think we're going to need more than just breakfast."

Twenty minutes later we were sitting in a booth, waiting for our waffles to arrive. I recited everything I had overheard Ryan saying while Dad listened. I was worried for Shane and Trisha, but there was something about the problem that was so normal, so human. Maybe it bordered on talk-show territory, but at least it didn't involve an evil paranormal force. That alone made it seem manageable to me.

"So what do we do?" I asked.

"We keep him away from the wedding," Dad replied. "It sounds like we can count on Ryan for help, and probably Jeff, as well. Do you know how Noah feels about his father?"

"He thought he saw his dad hanging around the bus stop a few days ago. It shook him up." I sighed. "I thought it was a mistake. He hasn't seen the guy since he was little."

"That's got to be tough for him."

"He hasn't talked about it much, but yeah, I think it bothers him more than he lets on."

"Are you two okay? I noticed that he hasn't been coming around as often."

"We're fine."

It wasn't the truth, but Dad didn't need to know that. I wasn't going to tell him about Noah's late-night visit to my room or the fact that he was skipping school and suffering from a case of major sleep problems. I wondered if this was the right moment to reveal what was really going on, but I felt that I couldn't do it alone. I needed my sister with me. I needed us to be united when we broke the horrible news that the Watcher was not done with our family.

Our waffles arrived and I drowned mine in warm syrup. I was digging in when I noticed that Dad hadn't touched his food yet. "Aren't you hungry?"

"I was just thinking about you and Noah."

I tried not to choke on my waffle. The idea that Dad had contemplated my relationship was an uncomfortable one. "Um, what about us?"

"You two had a rough start. Not many couples can get through the kind of trauma that you both went through, especially at your age. It says something about your bond."

It may have said something then, when our first kiss was immediately followed by a night of terror, but I wasn't sure what it said about us now. I was losing him. I blinked back my tears and tried to focus on my waffles. I would not melt down in front of Dad.

"Did I ever tell you how proud I was of you? You were so strong that night."

This was not a conversation I wanted to have in a diner. We hadn't talked about the night Mom was hurt since right after it had happened and Dad was still recovering in the hospital.

"I don't feel strong now," I mumbled.

"Strength is not a light switch, Charlotte. It doesn't flick on one moment and stay on for the rest of your life. You have to work at it." He began to cut his waffles. "But now you know that it's there. You know what you can do."

We finished our breakfast in comfortable silence. I thought about Dad's words. Maybe I knew what I could do, but what about the things I *needed* to do? Where did I even start?

On the ride home, Dad reminded me that Annalise would be arriving later. "She's going to stop by and see your mom first, but she should be here after lunch."

"If she knew what she was walking into, she never would have left Charleston."

We pulled into the driveway and Dad turned off the ignition. "I'm going to talk to Ryan about his dad, but I don't want to alarm Shane. He's got enough going on right now."

I assured Dad I wouldn't say anything. It was strange, though, how we were all keeping secrets from one another. Everyone was afraid of hurting everyone else. Would it really be that bad if everything was out in the open? If all our weird secrets were peeled back and revealed?

Then I walked inside the house and remembered exactly why I was keeping so much to myself.

It was as if we'd never left. Trisha was still pacing the dining room with her phone. Shane and Ryan sat in the exact same spots in the living room, arguing about football. Tensions were high. But in two weeks, they wouldn't be. That was when I would come clean, I decided. I would tell Annalise before then, but we could wait until after the wedding to introduce the paranormal problems to everyone.

As I debated a new escape plan from my house, the doorbell rang. "I'll get it!" I yelled over my shoulder. I was hoping it would be Annalise. But when I opened the door, it wasn't my sister looking back at me.

It was the police.

nineteen

Opening the door and finding two uniformed police officers standing on the front porch sent an instant, horrifying jolt through my system, which was immediately followed by a hundred frantic questions. Had something happened to Mom? Had Annalise been in a car accident on her way to see us? Or was it Noah? I knew only one thing: the police were at my house for a reason, and it wasn't good.

One of the officers stepped forward. "Is Patrick Silver here?"

"What's wrong?" I clutched the doorknob so my hand wouldn't shake so badly.

"Who's at the door?" Dad called from the kitchen. When I didn't answer, he walked into the foyer, wiping his hands on a dish towel. Shane and Ryan left their athletic dispute behind and joined us.

"Mr. Silver?" the first officer asked.

"Yes, that's me."

I didn't have to turn around to know that everyone held the same frozen expression. We could hear Trisha in the din-

ing room, still talking on her phone, oblivious to what was
going on a few feet away.

Dad cleared his throat. "Is there a problem?"

The officer didn't answer. "May we come in?"

"Of course, of course."

We took a collective step backward to allow the two po-
licemen inside. It had been only a few seconds since their arrival, but it felt like an hour. Was their news so bad that they
couldn't just say it? Did they need us to sit down in case one
of us fainted and fell to the floor?

Trisha finally poked her head in. "I have to go," she said
to the person on the other end of the phone. "I'll call back
later."

Once the five of us were gathered in the living room, the
first officer began to speak. "We were contacted today by a
Mr. Wilbur Pate."

"Who?" Dad was genuinely baffled. The name was lost
on him. He had met Pate only once, more than a year earlier
when we'd filmed the original footage at the prison. Dad had
no idea that Shane, Noah and I had been back to the place.
I was just as confused as everyone else. What had happened?
How was Pate involved?

"Is everything okay with my mom and sister?" I asked.

They ignored my question, but the second officer stepped
forward. I noticed for the first time that he held a box in his
arms.

"Sir, is this your property?"

I immediately recognized the box as the one that had been
taken from my room. It was full of equipment, and I could
see the EMF reader sitting on top of everything else.

Dad stepped closer to inspect the items. "Well, yes, these
look like mine." He reached to pick up a digital camera, but
the officer stopped him with a simple shake of his head.

"Where did you find this?" Dad asked.

"Can you verify that these items belong to you?"

Dad nodded. "Yes. Yes, they do. But I haven't seen them in months. They're supposed to be in storage."

"Well, they're not." The first officer took over again. "These items were found inside the Southern State Penitentiary this morning."

"I haven't been there in over a year."

Dad was still struggling to understand, but I knew what was happening. Shane looked at me, and I wasn't sure which one of us was supposed to say something. Fortunately, he took over.

"Um, actually, we were there a couple months ago."

"You were?" Dad turned to Shane. "Why would you go there?"

"We were finishing the DVD, getting some more footage."

"We?"

Shane's face was red and he avoided Dad's glare. I stepped in, hoping to save him from the uncomfortable moment. "I was there, too. I was helping."

Dad glanced at me, then turned back to Shane. "You took my daughter on an investigation? After all that's happened, you decided to take her there? Behind my back?"

"It wasn't an investigation," I protested. "We were only there for a couple hours, and it was just to film a scene. That's it."

"I'm sorry," Shane said to Dad. "I should have told you."

"You're damn right you should have told me!"

Sensing the beginning of a volatile situation, the first officer spoke up. "We need to get back to the issue at hand. This equipment was discovered at the penitentiary, which is private property. Mr. Pate wants to file charges for trespassing and harassment. We need to ask you some questions at the station."

Dad was fuming, but he agreed. In the end, he and Shane went with the officers. Since they weren't under arrest, they were able to drive—separately—to the police station. Trisha, Ryan and I stayed behind. The house was unnaturally quiet.

"What was that all about?" Ryan asked. "Is Shane some sort of criminal?"

"No!" Trisha and I exclaimed at the same time.

"It's all my fault," Trisha moaned. "I was the one who encouraged him to finish that DVD."

"It's not your fault," I said. "It was work that needed to get done."

I wished Avery was here. She would swoop in, take charge and figure out how to make things better. And then I remembered what Dad had said about strength, how I had it and could use it when I needed to. He said it wasn't a light switch, but I disagreed. It was—and it was up to me to flick it on. And even though this wasn't a life-or-death situation, it was emotional and required a clear head. Trisha was crying and Ryan clenched his fists as if he was ready to punch a wall.

"Okay," I announced. "Here's what we're going to do while we wait for them to get back."

I told Ryan that his job was to call back the caterer, say he was the groom, and demand a pasta dish. "I'm on it," he said, determined to help his mom. Then I told Trisha to go through Shane's computer and pull up any and all correspondence that Pate had sent us. She knew about the lawsuit and how to get the information. Dad would return from the police station wanting answers, and this would help.

While Ryan and Trisha worked, I tackled the kitchen, which needed a good cleaning. As I loaded the dishwasher and wiped down the countertops, I couldn't help but feel pleased with myself for taking charge. When Annalise arrived an hour later, the kitchen was clean, the caterer had agreed to a new entrée and pages of emails had been organized and printed out. After a round of hugs and introducing Annalise to Ryan, Trisha explained what was happening.

"Dad and Shane are at the police station?" My sister sat down in the dining room, surrounded by piles of wedding plans. "I thought I was coming here to help with bridesmaid dresses and centerpieces."

"You are." I sat down next to her. "But now we have to deal with a little unexpected problem, as well."

To keep our minds off the image of Dad and Shane being interrogated, we focused on wedding details. Phone calls were made to the bakery and the reception hall. Tuxedo fittings were scheduled, reservations confirmed for the rehearsal dinner. We accomplished in a few hours the work Trisha had thought would take all weekend.

I found a moment to slip away to my room. A breeze from outside pushed against the plastic serving as my temporary window, causing it to bulge. Ryan had told me earlier that it would be repaired by the next day. I hoped the work could be done without Dad finding out, and I wondered how bad his mood would be when he came home with Shane. They'd been gone about two hours. Not a good sign.

A soft knock at my door pulled me away from my worrying. "Charlotte?"

"Hey, Annalise. Come in." There was no way to conceal my missing window, but I didn't care. I was tired of hiding things all the time. "Welcome home," I joked.

She gave me a rueful smile. "Why is it that every time I come back, something big has happened? I swear you plan it that way."

Annalise pulled out my squeaky desk chair while I plopped

down on my bed, which I had covered in a beige blanket from the hall closet. It wasn't as fluffy or as colorful as my old comforter. It was funny how I missed such a simple thing.

"So I saw Mom today," my sister said. "She's basically the same. A nurse told me that there's been some brain activity at night. Not much, but it's something."

I nodded. Maybe it was good news, but how much of "something" did it require to amount to a positive development in her condition? As badly as I wanted to feel hopeful that Mom was turning a corner, it didn't sound like much. If she was coming out of her vegetative state, the doctors would call us. Until that happened, it was hard for me to accept any news with joyful optimism. My promise to her still stood—I would not give up. But I would also be careful not to get too excited.

"I ran into Beth while I was there. She was visiting at the same time as me. She was placing these crystals all over Mom." Annalise shook her head. "I'm not sure if I buy into the idea of healing rocks, but then again, experience has taught me to be a lot more open."

I picked at the tiny balls of fuzz poking up from my blanket. It was something I had done when I was a little kid and we stayed at hotels all the time. After plucking as many of the little "fuzz nubs" as I could, I would wad them into one big ball and leave them in the nightstand drawer for the next person to find. I always wondered if other people did that, and I would check each new nightstand when we moved on to a new hotel. The only things I ever found in the drawers were notepads and Bibles.

"Beth filled me in on everything," Annalise said. "I know about Michael and Bliss. I know why there's a big hole in your wall. And I know that you're concerned about Noah."

"Yes." It was actually nice that I didn't have to explain everything. There was too much—I wouldn't know how to begin. Beth had saved me from a lengthy and difficult conversation.

"So." Annalise slapped her hands on her knees. "We have two weeks to plan a wedding, destroy two Watchers and return Noah to normal. And if we can work some additional magic to make Mom all better, that would be a bonus."

A smile pulled at the side of her face. I started to giggle, which morphed into laughter and grew into the kind of body-shaking bellows that could not be controlled. Tears streamed down both of our faces, but it was the best I'd felt in weeks, a much-needed release of a hundred different emotions that had been clawing to get out.

When we were finally able to catch our breath, Annalise had a question for me.

"I'm caught up on everything but this whole lawsuit business," she said, wiping at her eyes. "When did all that happen?"

She knew that Shane, Noah and I had made a visit to the penitentiary, but that was all. I told her about Pate's claims that someone was breaking in, and how he was certain it was one of us.

"Do you think it's possible that he framed us?" I looked toward my plastic window. "What if he was the one who broke in and took the cameras? Then he could have taken the stuff back, called the police, and claimed we were trespassing."

"But why would Pate break into your room and look under your bed? Of all the rooms in the house, why a second-floor bedroom? It doesn't make sense."

No, it didn't. And it was also physically impossible. But it was easier to conjure up theories rather than face the one thing I was sure of: only Noah knew that I kept equipment in my bedroom.

But it couldn't have been him. He'd been asleep in his apartment miles away when the break-in had occurred. And even if he possessed Watcher-induced superstrength, there was no way he could have run across town in the middle of the afternoon, unnoticed and carrying a heavy box of equipment.

While Annalise and I pondered every scenario possible, Dad and Shane returned home. The front door slammed shut and angry voices drifted up the stairs.

"I shouldn't have had to tell you!" Dad yelled. "You knew my position on this."

"No, actually, I didn't!" Shane yelled back. "Everything stopped. Everything. I knew you needed a break. I never thought it would be permanent!"

It sounded as if they were in the kitchen. Trisha's voice joined the others. "This is my fault, too. Patrick, I was the one who said Shane should finish the work. Don't be mad at him. Be mad at me."

Annalise and I went downstairs, but we didn't go directly to the kitchen. Instead, we stood with Ryan in the dining room, listening to the heated conversation.

"It's over, Shane." The anger in Dad's voice had been replaced with defeat. "It was over the moment Karen was hurt. You know that. I'm sorry if I wasn't clear, and I've tried to make sure that you'll receive a good share of royalties, but if you need to move on, I understand.".

"This isn't about me finding a new job," Shane said. "This is about finishing the work we started. This is about what she would want us to be doing."

"She would want us to keep her daughters safe, not drag them to haunted prisons!"

Shane was quiet for a second. "That's the first time I've heard you use the word *haunted* that way."

"What way?"

"Like you thought it was true."

I wanted to walk into the kitchen and be a part of their discussion, but it was important for Dad and Shane to get it all out. If they knew that we were eavesdropping, they might not say the things they needed to say. Trisha sensed this, too. She backed out of the kitchen and joined the rest of us in the dining room.

"I don't know what's true anymore," Dad said. "Nothing prepared me for this."

"I know."

"And I don't understand it. All I know is that I can't let something else hurt my family. I can't, Shane."

There was a strangled sob, a sound so unfamiliar and heart-breaking that I wanted to cover my ears and disappear.

"This way," Trisha whispered. "Let's give them a moment."

We quietly crossed the dining room and went out the front door. We gathered on the porch. I was surprised at how dark it was outside. Streetlights were slowly coming on, glowing with their unnatural orange radiance.

Trisha sat down on the steps. "They need to work this out."

"Do you know what happened at the police station?" Annalise asked.

She did. Shane had called her before leaving the station and given her a quick rundown. Pate had not been present, but his lawyer was there with a briefcase full of new complaints. The ancient electric chair had been destroyed, and the room where it had once stood had suffered extensive damage, as if someone had taken a sledgehammer to the cinder-block walls. It was the same room where the box of equipment had been discovered.

"Fortunately, they both had alibis. But your Dad had to re-port the equipment as stolen, and Pate is livid." Trisha sighed.

"According to the lawyer, Pate claims to hear voices inside the building all the time now and says that we are responsible."

"No judge is going to take that seriously," Ryan said.

"I know, and that's part of the problem."

Annalise sat down next to Trisha. "What do you mean?"

"He's desperate to be taken seriously. Desperate people do strange things sometimes."

She told us about printing out the emails Pate had sent to Shane. There were dozens of them, and according to Trisha, their content grew progressively weirder and angrier. "One of them was a three-page rant. It was ridiculous."

"Don't worry, Mom." Ryan crossed his arms. "If some whack job decides to start causing problems, you've got me and Jeff. He's not getting anywhere near you." He paused. "He won't get near any of you. We're family now."

Annalise beamed, then stood up and hugged him. "I always wanted a big brother," she said. Her sudden show of affection made Ryan blush and look down at his feet. Trisha laughed and joined in. I held back, but when Annalise reached for me, I let them pull me into their little circle.

"Think they're done talking in there?" Ryan asked, releasing us. "Because I'm starving."

Trisha decided to pick up pizzas for dinner and asked Ryan to go back to the apartment and get Noah. "I feel like I haven't seen him in ages," she said. I tried not to show my delighted relief.

After they left, Annalise and I remained on the porch. We gazed out at the empty street and watched the sky grow darker. When we were able to see a sprinkling of stars, Annalise spoke. "Everything with Dad and Shane will be fine, I know it. Shane's family."

We got up. "You're right," I said. "And you can always trust family."

twenty

The red numbers on my bedside clock seemed to mock me. It was 3:14. I should have been asleep, deep inside the caverns of a meandering dream. But all I could think about was Noah.

Dad and Shane had resolved their issues by the time Annalise and I came back inside the house. They were sitting at the kitchen table, immersed in a quiet discussion. They smiled when we walked in, and that's how I knew things were okay. Not because they were smiling, but because of the way those smiles looked. There was no forced sincerity, no overly toothy grins. They just looked at us, and their natural reaction shone through. Annalise saw it, too. She squeezed my hand before announcing that dinner was on its way.

The pizzas arrived, but Noah did not. Ryan returned with a hastily scribbled note he'd found on the counter in which Noah had said he had to film a football game for AV class. A quick search on Lincoln High's website showed that there was no game scheduled. My heart sank. He wasn't deceiving me directly, but he had intentionally lied to his family. I knew why. How much proof did I need that he was being taken over by the Watcher?

I turned my attention from the exasperating numbers on the clock to the billowing plastic on my window. Ryan had scheduled someone to replace it, but the work wouldn't be done until the next day. Annalise was asleep in the guest room, so I couldn't retreat there for a sense of safety. The cloudy plastic sheet blocked any view I might have had of the half-moon perched in the sky. The moon would have been nicer to stare at than the clock.

Thoughts of Noah weren't the only things fueling my insomnia. I had finally been able to process the EVP session I had taped before my room was trashed. Using our voice analysis software, I isolated a few seconds of the digital recording, cleaned it up, and heard much clearer answers to some of the questions I had asked.

"What am I supposed to do?" my voice asked.

The jumbled response was difficult to decipher. It took me a half dozen tries before I was able make out the response.

"Close the gate."

It was little more than a murmur, but there was an undeniable urgency behind the command. I replayed it several times, hoping I had heard it wrong, but the words were unmistakable, and I knew they were directly connected to the creepy graffiti sprayed inside the penitentiary: *The gate is now open.*

I copied some of the DVD footage so I could show Michael and Bliss what the EVP meant. Then I worked on understanding the answer to the final question I had asked.

"Can you tell me the real name of the Watcher?"

Again, the word "us" stood out to me, but it wasn't until I cleaned up the audio that I realized my otherworldly guide was giving me a real name, a name with which I was already familiar. I wrote it down, packed up all the evidence I needed and stored everything inside my backpack.

Hours later, and I was still struggling to sleep. Every little

noise startled me. The ice maker in the kitchen rumbled, causing my tired eyes to fly open in a panic. Down the hall Dad
grumbled in his sleep, and I almost ran to his room to make
sure he was okay.

I sighed and turned over in my bed, desperate for even a
few minutes of rest. The plastic stretched with another breeze,
and the crinkling sound it made grated on my nerves so badly
that I got out of bed, stomped over to the window, and ripped
off the covering.

There was now nothing separating me from the night. But
did it matter? Was a sheet of plastic really going to keep the
Watcher out of my room? The only thing it was protecting
me from was the possible presence of a misdirected squirrel.

The plastic fell to the floor. I rose out of bed and leaned
out the window, breathing in deeply. There was nothing like
nighttime air. It felt purer to me, like cool water. I stood there,
my eyes closed and my breath slow and even, trying not to
think of all the things pulling at my mind.

A dog barked somewhere nearby and I opened my eyes,
immediately scanning the yard for Dante in case he had escaped. But it wasn't Dante I saw below my window.

It was Noah.

His back was to the house, but I knew it was him. He stood
perfectly still, his head tilted up as if he was gazing at the half-
moon glowing in the sky. It was unnatural, and the bizarre
image froze my heart. I watched him for a while, waiting to
see if he would move.

A memory of Marcus hit me like a sudden headache. I had
seen him months earlier, crawling down the middle of our
dark street. He had been possessed by the Watcher, and that
possession had given him superhuman speed and strength. I
shuddered. Noah could not become that creature. I could not
allow him to become that creature.

I backed away from the window but kept my eyes on Noah. He hadn't moved from his place in the yard. It was like looking at a statue.

My robe lay in a heap on the floor. I put it on and tied it tight. Then, still watching Noah, I moved away from the window until my back was pressed against the bedroom door and I could no longer see him.

A decision had to be made. Should I go outside and try to talk to him, or should I wake Dad and tell him something was wrong? I stared at the window, half expecting Noah to suddenly appear there, crouched like a gargoyle in the open window frame.

No, I thought. I would not be afraid of my boyfriend. He was not a demon. He was someone who needed help, and he would never hurt me. I tiptoed down the stairs as quickly as I could and made my way to the kitchen door, flicking on the back porch light. My hand trembled over the dead bolt, but I made myself turn it and open the door. Then I took a tentative step outside, into the chilly night.

Noah was still standing in the exact same spot, in the exact same position. The porch light illuminated his back, but the glare made it difficult for me to see him. I stayed near the back door.

"Noah?" I was afraid to get too close. Marcus was still in my head, his eyes filled with an inky blackness. If I saw the same thing in Noah's gaze, I would know it was too late.

Another step forward, and I was almost within range of being able to touch him.

"Noah? It's me."

My voice didn't provoke any reaction from him. It was as if he was an ice sculpture frozen to the spot. I waited, wondering how long we could stay out here. I needed to see his face.

I carefully walked around him, keeping a few feet between

us. Finally I was standing in front of him, about an arm's length away.

His eyes were closed. Was he asleep? If he was sleepwalking, I was pretty sure I wasn't supposed to startle him or even try to wake him. But he couldn't stand outside all night, either.

"Do you know where you are?" I asked. Maybe he would react to my voice and I could bring him out of his sleepwalking trance that way.

"I followed it here." His voice was hoarse.

"What did you follow?"

"The burgundy car."

Immediately, I spun around to face the street. It was empty as far as I could see. There was no car. I turned back to face Noah, ready to ask him more questions.

His eyes were open.

I thought of Mom's vacant stare. This was similar. He wasn't looking at me—he was looking through me. But his eyes were green. Pure green, with no hint of the darkness I'd seen in Marcus. My relief gave me the courage to step closer and touch his shoulder.

"Time to wake up," I whispered.

He blinked once, then turned his head so he was looking at me. "Charlotte?" He noticed our surroundings. "What are we doing out here?"

"I think you were sleepwalking. Do you remember anything?"

He shivered. "What time is it?"

"Time to go inside. Come on." I tugged lightly at his arm. At first, it was like trying to move stone. He was fixed in place. But then he relented, and I led him across the yard and into my house.

Once we were inside, I bolted the back door shut and had Noah sit down in a kitchen chair while I got him a glass of water. "My head hurts," he murmured, so I got him a couple aspirin, as well. He was shaking and, although I hated to admit it, smelled bad. He was wearing the same shirt I'd seen him in last time, and his hair was matted down.

"You need rest," I said softly. "I'm going to get some blankets, and you're going to sleep on the sofa. I'll be right back. Don't go anywhere, okay?"

He nodded, his eyes glassy. I ran upstairs, grabbed blankets and a pillow from the hall closet as quietly as I could, and came back downstairs. It was a relief to find Noah still sitting at the kitchen table, drinking his water. I had almost thought he would disappear into the night when my back was turned.

I made up the sofa and helped him lie down. He was burning up but shivering at the same time. I tucked the blankets around him, then sat down on the floor.

"Thanks," he mumbled. "So tired."

"I'm going to stay right here," I said. "If you need anything, I'll be right here."

He fell asleep almost immediately. For the next hour, I held his hand and occasionally pressed my scarred palm to his fiery forehead. Then I fell asleep, my hand still wrapped in his, my head on his arm.

When I woke up, he was gone.

twenty-one

The gnomes were playing a football game when I pulled up to Bliss's house the next morning. Statues with red hats stood on one side, green on the other. I guessed the ones in the middle were the players. Someone was having way too much fun messing with the ceramic dwarves.

I rang the doorbell and gulped down the last of my jumbo cup of coffee while I waited. I didn't like the bitter taste, but after yet another night with not enough sleep, I needed the jolt of caffeine. If I could have injected the stuff directly into my veins, I would have.

Waking up on the floor hadn't been the best way to start my day. I had no memory of Noah leaving, but the front door was unlocked and Dad, who was usually up before seven, hadn't seen him. I called Noah's cell phone and left a message asking him to call me back. He was sick, he was sleepwalking and his comment about the burgundy car had left me rattled.

Trisha had arrived as I'd poured my first cup of coffee in the kitchen. She had planned a busy Saturday for all of us. The guys would be getting fitted for their tuxedos, while Anna-lise and I were to accompany Trisha for a bridal gown fitting,

followed by finalizing our own bridesmaid dresses. Ryan had
arranged for his friend to fix my window while we were away.
I asked Trisha about Noah and she told me that he hadn't gone
to school. "I think he's catching a cold," she said, shaking her
head. "He's still in bed, but Ryan promised to wake him in
time for the tuxedo fitting."

At least he had found his way home. It was something, but
I knew he was sinking, being pulled down into a murky abyss
by forces I didn't want to think about. We needed to do something soon. And we would. That's why I was at Bliss's house.
I had an hour before I needed to be back, and I wanted Bliss
and Michael to listen to the EVPs I had transcribed.

Bliss answered the door wearing jeans and a pink T-shirt.
Her hair was pulled back into a ponytail. It was the most casual I'd ever seen her.

"Hey. I didn't think you'd be here until later."

I shifted my backpack. "Couldn't wait. I figured out those
EVPs, and I need you to listen to them now."

She let me in. The hallway seemed less narrow, and when
she led me into the living room, I saw that one entire wall
was clear of boxes.

"Wow. Bliss, this is fantastic."

"Yeah? My mom's away at a conference, so Michael and I
worked on it yesterday."

I placed my backpack on the recliner. "Would your mom
be upset if you cleaned? I thought she was trying to help."

"It's not the cleaning that upsets her," Bliss said. "It's what
happens when we try."

She had mentioned before how attempting to remove anything from the house resulted in items being thrown against
the walls and lights turning on and off. Of course they were
scared.

"So how has Michael helped?" One way was obvious: significant progress had been made in both the front hallway and living room.

"We started working after lunch yesterday." Bliss looked at the wall that was no longer blocked with towers of stuff. "As soon as we moved the first box, there was a reaction."

Boxes had opened, releasing a geyser of old papers. A lamp had flicked on before tipping sideways and falling to the floor. Bliss had been ready to run screaming from the house, but Michael had stood his ground. He had ignored the chaos and methodically picked up boxes, taken them outside and placed them in a Dumpster he had rented. Bliss had calmed down and did the same, and they'd been able to fill the Dumpster within a few hours.

"The entire time we were dodging newspapers and falling cardboard," she said. "But neither one of us was directly hit with anything. It was like we were inside a snow globe and it was all shaken up, but the snow wasn't falling on us." She shook her head. "And when we were too tired to do more?" She snapped her fingers. "Everything stopped, just like that. It was like someone had turned off a tornado."

I noticed a trail of papers leading to the front door, as if a wind had blown from the corner of the room and pushed them to that point. From the living room I could see into the dining room. Boxes had tipped toward the windows. Again, it looked like everything was being shoved forward.

"It sounds terrifying," I said. "Do you think you were able to handle it because you're a Protector now?"

"No." Bliss sat down on the floor while I took the recliner. "I haven't been a Protector for very long, you know? There's so much I have to learn." She frowned. "But it's more than that. I have a hard time accepting that my grandfather is now some angry spirit who refuses to let us move on. It doesn't make sense."

It didn't make sense to me, either. Bliss had adored him and they had shared a close relationship. Why would his energy be so angry?

"Enough about me." Bliss adopted her no-nonsense tone. "What's going on with you?"

I filled her in on Noah's sleepwalking episode outside my house. "He's getting worse," I said. "We have to do something for him." I unzipped my backpack and pulled out the DVD and digital recorder. "And I think this is the first step to finding an answer."

I gave her a brief rundown of what was on the DVD, as well as the EVP I had captured telling me to "close the gate." Then there was the name. I didn't understand why, but the voice had said Marcus was the real name of the Watcher. It was confusing, because Marcus had also been the name of the last person possessed by the Watcher.

Bliss looked as puzzled as I felt. "Are you sure?"

"It took me a while, but yeah, I'm sure."

"Charlotte, I have to tell you—"

She stopped speaking and looked toward the staircase. Someone was coming downstairs. A moment later, Michael stood in the doorway.

"Good morning."

"Morning." I was surprised to see him. "Late night?"

"Yeah." He yawned. "Bliss, you mind if I take a quick shower?"

"Sure." Her cheeks were as pink as her T-shirt. Michael went back upstairs. We could hear the slide of the shower door, followed by the water running.

I raised an eyebrow at Bliss. "Your mom's away and Michael spent the night?"

She shook her head and turned an even darker shade of pink. "You know it's not like that."

"If you say so." I was teasing her, but from her embarrassed reaction I could tell that she was starting to develop a little crush on her mentor. Her normally polished appearance contrasted with Michael's more informal take on fashion, but somehow I could see them together.

She cleared her throat. "Didn't you say you had a dress fitting today?"

I got up. "I'm going, I'm going."

"Michael and I will look everything over and talk to you later, okay?" Bliss walked me to the door. "Thanks for bringing this over. I know it will help."

"Good." I paused at the door. "What were you going to tell me earlier?"

"Right." She glanced toward the stairs. "Nothing much, just that we have the list of names narrowed down to less than a dozen."

"Great. Oh, and Bliss?" I smiled. "Maybe you should take a towel upstairs to Michael. You know, for after his shower."

Her eyes widened. I began laughing and she shoved me out the door, trying to suppress a smile.

When I got home, Annalise was waiting. "We're going to be late. You have everything you need?"

"It's a dress fitting. What do I need besides myself?"

I wondered how much of my day would be spent riding in the car. It seemed like a waste of energy. There were real problems that needed to be handled, and I was off to try on dresses? It seemed stupid, but I knew I needed to keep going. The wedding was important. It was a fixed date, and it helped me focus on the fact that Noah needed to be better by then.

Annalise drove and I closed my eyes, relaxing a little as she chatted. Jeff had arrived late the night before. All the guys, including Shane and Dad, were now at the tuxedo place.

"Noah's there, right?" I asked.

"Of course he's there. Where else would he be?"

I didn't know. Following the mysterious burgundy car? Hanging around the Southern State Penitentiary? Sound asleep in his bed? At least he was surrounded by his family. Now that Jeff was home, Trisha had all her sons together. I doubted they would let Noah slip away, no matter what his excuse might be.

Trisha was already wearing her wedding dress when Annalise and I arrived at the bridal boutique. "What do you think?" she asked.

"Gorgeous," Annalise breathed.

I agreed. It was an understated, cream-colored gown with capped sleeves made of lace. Its simplicity made it elegant. Trisha looked beautiful. And seeing her like that, happy and nervous and so eager for her big day, made me want to be there. I wanted her and Shane to celebrate a perfect day and I wanted to be a part of it.

The saleswoman brought in our bridesmaid dresses. Annalise and I put on the butter-yellow gowns. The empire waist looked good on me, but the color was not my favorite. Annalise looked great, though, and Trisha beamed at us. "It's just what I wanted," she said. "This is turning out to be such a wonderful day."

I wouldn't go so far as to call it wonderful, but I had to admit it was shaping up to be a pretty good day despite everything. Bliss and Michael were close to finding the Watcher's real name, which would be a vital tool in conquering the entity. Noah would be spending all day with his family, so I didn't have to worry too much about him. But when things were going well, I tended to stop myself from getting excited. Based on my experiences over the past year, I was beginning to believe that I had to pay for every good moment with an onslaught of bad ones. Although, I reasoned, wasn't I due for a day without drama, paranormal or otherwise?

With the fitting finally over, Annalise and I prepared to head back home. Trisha was meeting "her boys" for a special lunch, and Dad had called Annalise to suggest that the three of us do the same.

Maybe it was time to tell Dad about the Watcher. I brought it up on the ride back, ready to go with whatever Annalise decided would be best.

"Yes," she said. "I know the timing is weird with the wedding, but that might be a good thing. Maybe he won't focus so much on the negative when something so positive is about to happen." She nodded. "We should tell him today, Charlotte. During lunch. You ready?"

"No." I stared out the passenger window. "But I won't ever be ready. So let's do this and get it over with."

Dad was on the phone when we got back. I ran up to my room to check on my window, and was happy to find that Ryan's friend had completed the work. My window looked like nothing had ever happened to it. I changed my shirt and went back downstairs, prepared for an uncomfortable lunch. Maybe it wouldn't be so bad. Maybe this would all work out.

Then I saw Dad.

He emerged from the kitchen, still holding the phone.

"Where do you want to have lunch?" Annalise asked. "How about someplace new?"

He looked as if he was surprised to see us standing in the hall. "I got a call," he said. His eyes were wet with tears. "I got a call from one of the nurses."

Annalise put her hand on Dad's arm. "What happened?" she whispered.

"She needs us there. We have to go right now." Dad

sounded like a zombie. His eyes were wide with shock. Annalise had started crying, so I grabbed the car keys.

"Let's go," I said, trying to sound stronger than I felt. Something had happened, and Mom needed us. As we left the house, I caught a glimpse of her slippers, still tucked beneath the computer desk. Part of me wanted to grab the blue shoes so we could bring them to her.

And part of me knew that it didn't matter.

twenty-two

It was silent inside the car. Dad and Annalise sat in the back, lost in their thoughts and apprehensions. I tried not to think about what we would be told once we arrived at the care facility, focusing instead on getting us there as quickly as possible. I drove fifteen miles over the speed limit and wished for the first time that the police would pull us over. If they did, I would insist on an escort with flashing lights. It didn't happen.

The lobby was empty. We ignored the elevator and ran up the stairs. I almost didn't quite understand our collective rush. If Mom was gone, getting to her a minute sooner wouldn't mean anything.

The young nurse sitting behind the desk looked up at us with a smile. "Can I help you?"

I explained who we were.

"You'll need to wait here for the doctor," she said. Her good-natured smile didn't waver.

"How long will that take?" There was no way I was going to take a seat and twiddle my thumbs while Mom's condition was so uncertain. The nurse seemed to notice our stricken faces for the first time.

"You haven't been told yet, have you?"

Behind me, Annalise sucked in her breath. My stomach clenched, and I felt seconds away from falling to the floor.

The nurse took pity on us. She got up from her chair and leaned across the desk. "It's against policy for me to tell you anything because that's the doctor's job," she said, her voice low. I nodded, hoping it was enough to encourage her to break policy and give us the information we had raced here to get.

She glanced down the hall. "The doctor is in there with her now."

"She's not dead?" I blurted out.

The nurse's smile returned. "Far from it. She's awake."

"What?" I'd heard wrong. My hopeful imagination had twisted the nurse's words. I couldn't trust what she was saying. She had the wrong patient and it would turn out to be a horrible mix-up and our hearts would be smashed when the truth was revealed.

"She regained consciousness this morning." The nurse put a finger to her lips. "But you didn't hear that from me."

If she was right and this was real, I vowed to send the nurse a huge bouquet of flowers to keep on her desk.

I turned around to face Dad and Annalise. They looked as shocked as I felt, and just as wary. We weren't ready for this. All along, the doctors had told us that change would be gradual, the road to improvement slow. At no time did anyone suggest that she would simply wake up.

Annalise reached out and hugged both me and Dad. We squeezed her back. Still, we said nothing. The nurse suggested we sit down, but we were too wound up. Finally, a doctor emerged from the end of the hallway.

Dad practically pounced on him. "What's going on?"

I recognized the doctor as the same one who had explained

Mom's vegetative state without glancing at me. "Mr. Silver, we have good news."

That was all we needed to hear. Dad charged down the hallway. Annalise and I were close behind.

"Wait!" the doctor shouted.

But we weren't waiting any longer. Dad pushed open the door to Mom's room. And for the first time in five months, she was sitting up in her hospital bed. I knew right away that she was not completely healed. She didn't turn her head when we came in, but she did begin blinking rapidly.

"We're here," Dad said. He knelt by her bedside and hugged her carefully. Annalise and I did the same, lightly embracing her and then standing back to wait for her reaction.

"She has limited movement and hasn't regained her capacity to speak," the doctor said. He was standing behind us. "If you'd allowed me a minute to explain before you came in here I could have prepared you better."

"But she's out of the vegetative state," Annalise said. "And she can see us and hear us, right?"

"Yes, but it's more complicated than that."

Maybe it was complicated to the doctor, but it was simple to us: Mom was awake. And, we discovered, she could communicate with us. She could answer yes or no questions by blinking. One blink meant yes, two meant no. While the doctor droned on about the need for additional tests, we stood on one side of Mom so she could see all of us and we could talk to her.

There was so much to say and we had no idea how to begin. After telling her that we missed her and loved her, we wanted to give her only good news.

"Shane and Trisha are getting married next week," Annalise said. "Isn't that great?"

One blink.

"And now you can be there!"

"No, she can't." The doctor stepped forward. "I'm sorry, but your mother's condition is still delicate. She'll be here for a few more weeks, at least."

"Then we'll bring the wedding to her," Dad decided. "I'll set up a live feed and you can watch it from your room. How does that sound?"

One blink.

Dad beamed. "And I'll be here with you. We can watch it together."

Two blinks.

"I think she wants you to be at the wedding," I said.

One blink.

"All right, but I'm coming here immediately afterwards. Is that okay?"

One blink.

Annalise clapped her hands together. "Shane and Trish are going to be so happy! We have to call them."

A blink from Mom confirmed that yes, we should. The doctor left to complete his rounds but promised to return within an hour. Annalise went out into the hall to call Mills and Beth. Dad followed so he could call Shane. I stayed behind.

"We've missed you so much," I said. "And I have so much to tell you."

Her eyes were focused on mine. She was trying to squeeze my hand, but it was a very light pressure. There was something urgent about her gaze. "Are you trying to tell me something?"

One blink.

"Is something wrong?"

One blink.

"Are you okay?"

One blink. I wasn't sure how I could ask yes-or-no questions when I had no idea what my mom wanted me to know. Something popped in my head and I asked it before really thinking.

"Am I okay?"

Two blinks.

"Is it the Watcher?"

One blink.

"You don't have to worry about that," I said. "He's gone."

Two blinks.

She was still stuck in the memories of that night so many months ago. She had been attacked and had no idea what had happened afterward. Maybe to her it was still that same night and no time had passed. And even though now there was a new threat, she didn't need to know that.

"He's gone," I said again. "You don't have to worry about it. The only thing you need to do is get better."

Two blinks.

I didn't have the words to reassure her, so I continued to hold her hand. Annalise came back in and announced that Beth would be visiting the next day and that Mills was thrilled with the good news. After Dad returned, I went outside to make my own calls.

Noah was the first person I dialed. "My mom just told me," he said. "It's such great news, Charlotte. Everyone here is thrilled."

There was no trace of the sick and exhausted guy I had discovered in my yard the night before. "You sound good," I said. "How are you feeling?"

"Great." He paused. "I'm sorry about last night. I don't know what happened."

"Don't be sorry." I wanted to ask him more, such as how he had gotten home and if he remembered following the burgundy car to my house, but I needed to call Avery and get back to my mom. I was satisfied that Noah sounded better and was safe with his family. I told him we'd talk later when I had more time, then I called Avery.

She squealed with joy when I told her about Mom. "Charlotte, this is wonderful! Will we get to see her at the wedding?"

"You're coming to the wedding?" I hadn't been a part of the invitation mailing. All I knew was that the guest list hovered right around fifty.

"I'm holding the invitation in my hand right now," Avery said. "Jared and I are both coming and we're so excited."

My day was getting better by the minute. I missed my best friend, and knowing that I would be seeing her in a little over a week was an unexpected slice of good news.

The last person I called was Michael. He was with Bliss, and when he repeated my message, she cheered in the background. I laughed. It was an amazing feeling not only to receive good news, but to be able to share it with others.

With all of my calls made, I returned to Mom's room. The nice nurse was there, unfolding a cot. "I figured you would all want to spend the night," she explained. "These aren't the most comfortable things, but they're better than sleeping in a chair."

I learned that the nurse's name was Mary Ruth. She was officially my most favorite person in the world, and I told her that. She smiled. "I've been here six years," she said. "And I can count on one hand the number of times we've had this kind of reunion. Anything I can do, you let me know."

The doctor said we had to keep Mom awake for as long as possible. It wasn't a problem. We had five months' worth of stories to tell her. When I got tired, I curled up in my cot.

I closed my eyes and listened to Dad talking to Mom, and Annalise laughing softly.

It was the best sleep I'd had in months.

twenty-three

"Feel like finishing the DVD today?" Shane was looking at me in his rearview mirror. Annalise and I sat in the backseat of the Doubt van. Trisha was in the passenger seat.

"Absolutely," I replied.

I had woken up hours earlier curled in the fetal position, with no idea where I was. Then I'd opened my eyes. Dad was awake and sitting next to Mom, holding her hand and speaking softly. Annalise was still asleep on her cot. Everything from the day before came rushing back to me, and I smiled.

Nurse Mary Ruth came in to check on Mom. She handed Dad a cup of coffee, then went about inspecting the IV and checking things off on Mom's chart. It was a surreal scene, but I didn't want it to end. I wanted all of us to remain in this room until Mom was completely healed and could walk out the doors on her own two feet. It wasn't realistic, though, and I reminded myself to be grateful for the miracle we had been given.

Shane and Trisha arrived. Shane hugged Mom for a long time, unwilling to let her go. Trisha placed a bouquet of purple irises on the table. "I know they're your favorite," she said.

We spent a few hours chatting and asking Mom simple questions. Her eyes kept finding mine, and I smiled every time, trying to reassure her that I was fine.

A team of doctors had descended on the room before lunch. They had scheduled a day full of tests for Mom and suggested we go home. Dad wasn't going anywhere. While I'd wanted to stay, I knew there wasn't much I could do at the care facility except wait. Shane had offered to drive me and Annalise home.

"I can help with the DVD," Annalise offered, sitting next to me in the van's backseat.

Trisha turned around in her seat. "I'd love some help with wedding plans today, if that's okay with you."

"Sure. Whatever you guys need."

"Thanks." Trisha smiled. "We have to finalize songs for the reception."

"That's my job!" Shane protested.

Trisha turned back to him. "That *was* your job. Then I saw your playlist."

"What's wrong with my playlist?"

She sighed. "There is no way we're playing a song called 'War Pigs' at the wedding reception!"

"It's Ozzy! It's a classic tune!"

"Fine. We'll take a vote." She turned back to us. "Who thinks 'War Pigs' is an appropriate song to play after a wedding?"

Annalise and I kept our hands down. Shane shook his head. "Don't vote until you've heard my rationale," he said.

"It better be good," I muttered.

"I picked that song because it was playing in this van when we met," he said to Trisha. "Do you remember that?"

I remembered their first meeting. My family had been signing books and Silver Spirits DVDs outside of Giuseppe's. Noah had arrived with Trisha, and she'd immediately gone over to the van for autographs. She and Shane hit it off right away. They'd been together ever since.

"That is kind of romantic," I admitted, "even if the song isn't."

Trisha softened. "Okay, we can play it. Toward the end, though."

Shane nodded. "Deal."

Once we got home, I ran upstairs to take a much-needed shower. Then I tried calling Noah, but it went straight to voice mail. I was about to go downstairs and help Shane with the DVD when there was a knock at my bedroom door. It was Ryan.

"Just wanted to check on your window," he said. "And tell you how glad I am that your mom's doing better."

"Thanks, Ryan. And the window looks great."

I let him in to inspect the work while I sat at my desk. "Have you seen Noah today?" I asked. "I tried calling him, but there was no answer."

Ryan bumped the sides of the window frame with his closed fist. "He was up really early this morning. Said he had to run some errands." Satisfied that the window had been installed correctly, he looked at me. "We had a great day yesterday, once he finally woke up and I convinced him to take a shower."

I wondered what errands Noah needed to get done. But I was optimistic that he was turning around. From our brief conversation the day before, I could tell that spending time with his family had a positive effect on him.

"I wanted to ask you something," I said.

"Sure."

"It's about your dad."

"Oh." Ryan crossed his arms over his chest. "What about him?"

I didn't want to reveal that I had overheard his conversation in the laundry room. "Noah mentioned seeing him last week."

"He did? He didn't say anything to me."

"It's not like they talked or anything," I rushed to add. "Noah thought he saw him across the street one morning."

"Dad's in town," Ryan said. "Jeff and I aren't happy about it. We're worried he might try to ruin the wedding, so we've been giving him false information."

"Good. That's good."

"I love my dad, but my mom is the one who's been there for us. She deserves a perfect wedding day."

"Yeah, she does."

"I'll let you know if anything comes up, though, okay?"

"Thanks, Ryan."

He began to leave my room, but stopped when he reached the door. "Shane's a good guy, isn't he?"

"He's the best. Your mom couldn't ask for a better husband."

"Yeah, that's what I thought. I mean, just because his taste in football is questionable doesn't mean that he's a jerk." He winked at me.

Downstairs, Shane was already at a computer working on the DVD. Everyone else had left to complete the day's wedding errands. Trisha and Annalise were picking up the dresses and Ryan was going with Jeff to get the tuxes. Soon, Shane and Trisha would be married.

"Not much left to do," Shane said as I pulled up a chair next to him. "I think we can get this done in an hour."

"Let's do it."

I turned off my phone so I could focus on the project in

front of me. We worked fast but thoroughly. When we were done, Shane high-fived me. "I want to make a copy and get this mailed today." He glanced at his watch. "I still have time to overnight it, which would be perfect."

After the copy was made and Shane had left for the post office, I checked my phone. Five messages were waiting, all from Michael. Instead of listening to every voice mail, I called him back.

"What's up?"

"I've been trying to reach you!"

I shut down one of the computers. "I've been busy. What's wrong?"

"Bliss figured out the name. We need you over here."

"Sure. Give me a couple minutes."

"No. Charlotte, please. Get here *now*."

I didn't like the urgency in his voice. "I'm on my way."

I left a note for Shane explaining that I would be back later, then grabbed my purse. My phone rang while I was searching for my car keys.

"I'm leaving right now!" I said.

"Charlotte?"

"Hi, Beth. Sorry. I'm kind of in a rush. Michael needs me for something."

"I'm here with your mom," Beth said.

I stopped rummaging in my purse. "How is she?"

"She's good. She just got back from a CAT scan. Charlotte, she has a message for you."

"A message?"

"Yes. This may sound strange, but I brought a Ouija board with me today." Beth knew about Mom's ability to blink yes or no, but figured she would want to communicate with words, as well. She had brought the board because the alphabet was printed on it. Beth pointed to each letter, and if the letter was part of the message, Mom blinked once. "It took a while," Beth said, "but she needed to tell you this."

"Okay," I said slowly. "What's the message?"

"One second." Beth's voice got softer. She was asking Mom a question. It sounded like, "Are you sure about this?"

"Charlotte, your mom wants me to tell you one thing. It's very important."

"Tell me." It came out as a whisper. I knew that whatever Beth was about to say was not going to be something I wanted to hear, and when she finally spoke, I felt my heart drop.

"Close the gate."

twenty-four

How had I missed it? How many times had I studied the EVPs and heard the whispered voice and not realized that it was my own mother?

As I made my way to Bliss's house, I played the recordings. Even with the volume turned up all the way, it was difficult to hear. Mom's words weren't clear, and even though she spoke in a hoarse murmur, I knew it was her. The doctor had mentioned once that there had been an increase in her brain activity at night. She had been communicating with me. But how was that even possible?

I had too many questions and not nearly enough answers. I pulled up to Bliss's house, where both she and Michael were waiting for me. Before I could count the gnomes, Bliss and Michael were getting into my car.

"Drive," Michael instructed.

Bliss sat in the back. She rifled through an oversize canvas bag that appeared to be stuffed full of papers. "My house isn't safe anymore. We have to get away from here."

That was all I needed to know. "Where to?"

"Get on the highway," Michael said. "We're going to Potion."

"Beth's not there," I said. "She's with my mom right now."

"I can get us in."

As I navigated the familiar route to Potion, Bliss filled me in. They had been cleaning out the dining room, she said. Papers whirled around them as they hauled away boxes full of old wire hangers and empty medicine bottles. Bliss was carrying an armful of tattered sheets across the foyer when the front door slammed shut, preventing her from leaving the house. Then the dead bolt clicked into place.

"Michael tried to help me, but we couldn't open the door," she said. "Then we looked out the window and saw it."

I didn't ask what they'd seen. I was too busy trying to merge onto the highway without getting flattened by a semi-truck.

"It was the burgundy car," Michael said. "It was right in front of Bliss's house."

"How do you know it was the same one I saw?"

"We knew," Bliss said. "We both felt something at the exact same time. And it wasn't good."

"A man was behind the wheel, but we didn't get a clear look at him," Michael added.

"But you think it was the Watcher?" I asked. "That he's some guy driving around town?"

"Yes," Michael confirmed. "He's our guy."

"I thought you said there were two of them. Was he with anyone?"

"We have a new theory," Bliss said. She seemed hesitant to share it with me, so Michael took over.

"There's only one, but he's strong enough that defeating him will require two of us."

"So Bliss is also my Protector?"

"No." She cleared her throat. "I'm here for Noah."

I remembered her asking me for his number and how she had said she really needed to talk to him. "At first, I thought he could be the Watcher, but we've figured out that isn't the case."

"Then what's happening to him?" I asked. We were approaching the exit that would take us to Potion. "He's not right."

An uncomfortable silence followed my question. Michael finally spoke. "Charlotte, do you understand why the Watcher has targeted your family?"

"He's trying to punish me," I replied. "He thinks I've seen too much of the other side."

"Yes, but it was never only about you." Michael's voice was calm, like a kindergarten teacher's as she patiently explained a story to her students. "It's about your family and what they do. This thing has been monitoring your family for a long time, since before you were even born. It came after you as a way to hurt your parents, to make them stop their investigations."

Bliss spoke up from the backseat. "And he was unsuccessful. So now he's after Noah as a way to hurt you."

I almost turned the car around. "So let's go get Noah! We have to protect him!"

"He's gone," Bliss said softly. "I failed."

"You didn't fail," Michael said. "Don't say that. We still have a chance."

"Where is he?" I yelled.

"We're not sure." Bliss sounded close to crying. "But we know the Watcher has him. We saw him get in the burgundy car."

I was close to tears myself. Michael placed his hand over mine. "Just drive," he said. "I have a plan."

When we arrived at Potion, Michael pulled out a key and let us in. "Beth has some emergency stuff stored here for me," he said as he turned on the lights. "Bliss, will you show Charlotte what we found?"

While Michael went to the back room, Bliss and I sat on the floor between racks of dresses. She opened up her canvas bag and pulled out a manila file folder.

"We figured out the name using old inmate records and cross-checking them with names from the prison you visited in Ohio last year," she said. "Since the Watcher first came into power there, we figured there was a connection between the prison and the penitentiary here." She opened the file. "We were right."

"Was his name Marcus?"

"Marcus was his middle name." She handed me a photocopy of an old newspaper article. "Meet Lloyd Marcus Greene."

The article was a hundred years old, and it was a bad copy. The letters were smudged together into a blurry black mess. The only thing I could read clearly was the headline: Bloody Baker Convicted on Thirteen Counts.

"Bloody Baker? Please don't tell me he stuffed his victims into an oven."

"He didn't." Bliss took out another paper. "They called him that in reference to the thirteen murders. You know, a baker's dozen?"

"That's bad." I took the next paper, which was an article announcing that Greene had been sentenced to death.

"Let me guess. The electric chair?"

"Yes," Bliss confirmed. "But there was a problem."

The night of Greene's scheduled execution was also the night of one of the county's worst thunderstorms. I could almost picture the flickering lights and slashes of lightning illuminating the dark interior of the penitentiary. Greene had been strapped into the electric chair, but when the switch was thrown, it didn't work. Despite several attempts, the warden had been unable to execute the Bloody Baker.

Greene had escaped death and then had become a kind of cult figure among the other inmates. He'd said he couldn't die, that he'd sold his soul to the devil. He'd cultivated a large following of men eager to escape death. But another inmate had taken Greene's boasting as a challenge and stabbed him during lunch one day. Greene died on the floor.

"While he was on trial in South Carolina, he was also under investigation for murder in Ohio," Bliss said. "He spent time at the prison there before being extradited."

"This is our guy." I handed back the proof to Bliss. "You did great work."

"Thanks. But there's something else you need to know."

"Right." It was time to get down to business. We had the name, but now what? How did we use that information to close the gate?

Bliss glanced toward the back room, where Michael was gathering materials. "The thing is, this Marcus connection? It's more important than you might think."

"What do you mean?"

She set aside her papers. "Tell me what you remember about him. Tell me about the Marcus you knew."

It was a painful memory, one I had avoided for a long time. I had only met Marcus a few times. The first time had been on Christmas, when he was assisting his boss in a paranormal investigation at the same time as my family. The last time I'd seen him was when he had been fully taken over by the Watcher.

"His eyes were black," I said. "A dull black, like someone had drawn over his eyes with permanent marker."

He had tried to kill me. He had tried to kill my parents and almost succeeded. He had lifted Noah by the neck and left a permanent bruise. He had done all of these things, but it wasn't really him. His body was basically a puppet for the Watcher. And I had ended it—temporarily, at least—with a blow to the chest.

"Before he died, his eyes went back to normal." I had trouble getting out the words. "He was lying on the floor. He looked at me, and I knew it was him, not the Watcher."

I hadn't known what to do. Marcus was mortally wounded, and all I could do was watch as his life slipped away.

Bliss took my hands. "It wasn't your fault. You know that, right?"

My friends had said the same thing after it had happened, but I needed to hear it again. Maybe I needed to hear it for the rest of my life.

"The Watcher attaches itself to a person," Bliss said. "And once it does, that's it. There is no way out. The person can't live without the Watcher."

I nodded. "Marcus said that he tried to fight it. Those were his last words, that he tried to fight it."

I looked at Bliss, hoping she would offer more comforting words, but her eyes were looking beyond me. I turned my head and saw Michael standing a few feet away.

"Those were his last words?" His voice sounded strained and distant.

I turned around so I could face Michael. His eyes held tears. And that's when it clicked. I understood the connection we shared, why he had seemed familiar to me.

Marcus was his brother.

"I'm so sorry." I stood up, but I couldn't look at Michael. "You have no idea how sorry I am."

"You were the last person to see my brother alive."

I bit my bottom lip and tried to keep from crumbling. Even if Marcus's death wasn't my fault, I felt diminished in the presence of such pure grief. They had been brothers. They had kept sleds in their bedroom so they could slide down the snowdrifts outside their window. Marcus had been loved, and he had taken his last breath on the floor of a strange house.

And my eyes were the last he'd seen.

Michael placed his hands on my shoulders. "I don't blame you. Please don't think that. I blame *it*. The thing that destroyed him." He hugged me, and I felt a wave of calm pass through me. "Now it's time to fight back," he said.

I was done with living in fear. I would not allow it to chase me anymore.

It was time to close the gate. For good.

twenty-five

Close the gate.

That was our three-word plan, but I had no idea what it meant or how to accomplish it. I was still stunned by the fact that Michael and Marcus were brothers.

It explained why Michael hadn't been there when the Watcher had attacked my family. He'd been halfway across the world, trying to save Marcus. But he'd gotten there too late.

"We're not going to the penitentiary right now, are we?" Bliss asked.

Michael was busy packing a duffel bag. "I have the tools Beth said we'd need and we're less than twenty minutes away. I want to end this now."

"So do I. But it's almost dark and Beth said we should wait for her." Bliss frowned. "Do you really think we're prepared to go storming in there?"

I was torn. As much as I wanted to pull Noah away from danger, Bliss made sense. Were we ready for this? I knew I wasn't, but if we were going to save Noah, we definitely didn't have a lot of time.

"Pate probably has the police checking on the place at night," I said. "Noah might not even be there yet. And if we get caught, there's no way we'll be able to go back later. Maybe we should wait until morning."

Creeping into the potential portal to a demonic realm was bad enough, but sneaking in at night? It wasn't paralyzing fear that told me that was a bad decision—it was pure logic.

"You're not coming with us, Charlotte."

I looked at Michael, confused. "Of course I am. Noah needs me."

"He needs you to be safe and so do I. You're staying here."

"No. I'm not." I held up my hand before he could begin arguing with me. "I'm a part of this, too. I can help. I'm the only one here who's actually faced a Watcher. And I'm incredibly stubborn, so there's no point in fighting me on this."

He didn't like my answer, so he looked to Bliss for support. She didn't give him any. "I say she comes with us. At the very least, she can drag Noah out of there." She turned to me. "But if things get really bad, I want you to get out, understand?"

"I understand." We looked at Michael. He sighed but gave in. We also convinced him that rushing to the penitentiary at night and without Beth's help might not be the best idea.

"You two really know how to gang up on someone," he muttered. "But I don't want to drive back home tonight. We need to stay close by."

"Then we stay here." I was already forming a plan. "We spend the night in the store. It's safe, right? And Beth can meet us at first light."

"Sounds good to me," Bliss said.

Michael finally agreed. While he called Beth to let her know what we were doing, I called my sister.

"Is Noah with you?" she asked.

I froze. I didn't want her to know that there was a problem. "No, he's not with me."

"I'm here with Trisha," she continued. "The high school called and said he's been absent all week. We can't get ahold of him. No one knows where he is."

"Annalise, I need you to tell Trisha that everything's fine and Noah will be home tomorrow," I said.

"What's going on? Where are you?"

I explained that I was at Potion with Michael and Bliss and wouldn't be back until the next day. "Cover for me, okay? I don't want Dad to worry."

"I don't like this."

"Please trust me."

"How can I trust you when I don't know what's going on? You're scaring me, Charlotte." She took a breath. "We just got Mom back. I don't want you to put yourself in a situation where you could get hurt."

"I'm safe," I assured her. A thought occurred to me. Maybe I was secure inside Potion, but what about the rest of my family? How could I be sure that the Watcher wouldn't make a surprise stop at my house?

"Can you and Dad spend the night at the care facility?" I asked. It was one place I felt my family would be out of harm's way, especially with Beth still there.

"Dad's already there," she said. "Do you think I need to leave the house, too?"

"Yes. Just in case. And Annalise, I'll be home tomorrow, okay? This will all be over tomorrow."

"I'm holding you to that. If I don't hear from you by noon, I'm calling in a SWAT team."

"Deal."

We got off the phone. Through the store windows I could see that it was nearly night. Bliss had made tea in the back room and offered me a cup. Michael wanted to go over our plan, so we gathered in the middle of the front room. Potion featured shelves of brightly colored blankets. We each took a few and made comfortable little nests on the floor. We turned off the overhead lights and Bliss lit a candle and placed it in the middle of our circle. She gave us a wry smile. "It's supposed to be a stress relief candle," she said. "I figured we could use some of that."

"Tell me about what we're doing tomorrow," I said. "Are we really going to walk in there and start shouting this guy's name?"

"It's not that simple," Michael said. "And it's going to be dangerous."

"I know. I've kind of been through this before." And I did not want to go through it again, but it felt like something I was supposed to do, as if I'd been chosen. It made me think about the other time I'd been selected for a paranormal errand. I told Bliss and Michael about the other Charlotte, a girl who had been dead for more than a hundred years, and the spirits of her parents, who had followed me because I shared their only daughter's name.

"Is that why the Watcher chose your brother?" I asked. "Because they shared the same name?"

"It may have been a factor," Michael said. "Or simply an evil coincidence. Names have power, more than we realize."

Michael said we would use some of that power when we called out the Watcher by name. He was attached to the name he had used during his lifetime. It was like a string that lightly tied him to the sliver of self that remained human.

"After we call him out, Bliss and I will try to force him back through the gate."

"We think it's inside the electrocution chamber," Bliss

added. "Not a real gate, but some sort of entry he uses to cross into our world."

I remembered the way both Pate and Noah had suddenly jerked their heads to the left. The action suddenly made sense. "That's where the gate is," I said. "It will be on the left side of the room."

"Good to know," Michael said. "Let us handle it. Your main job will be to get Noah out of there."

I wondered if Noah was there now, scared and trapped by something immensely powerful. Maybe we should have gone to the prison instead of camping out in Potion for the night.

"I think he's okay," Bliss said softly. She was looking at me. "He's not dead. I would know—I would feel it."

"What if we don't get there in time? What if we're too late?"

She didn't have an answer for that. We watched the candle flicker inside its glass holder. "I've been thinking about something," I said. "About what's happening inside Bliss's house."

I had noticed the way that most of the boxes leaned toward the front windows and door, as if someone was pushing them. The front door had locked so no one could go outside when the Watcher was there. The clutter never hit Bliss directly. And I knew how much she had loved her grandfather and been loved in return.

"He's not angry," I said. "I think he's trying to help. It's just coming out wrong."

Bliss considered this. "His energy is trying to move all the stuff he held on to. Maybe he wants us to start over?"

"I think so, I really do."

"That's a nice thought." Bliss smiled. "That would fit in with his personality, actually. He could be very determined."

Sleep came eventually, but it felt more like a light nap than deep rest. It was still dark when we left Potion. A ribbon of pink curled across the horizon. Sunrise was approaching.

Michael drove my car. Bliss and I sat in the backseat. She talked me through some of the rituals she wanted to try, rites I was already somewhat familiar with. A circle of salt to offer protection, candles for light, and some prayers in a little notebook, written in Bliss's neat handwriting.

We parked a few blocks from the penitentiary and walked the rest of the way, cutting through backyards and avoiding the main roads. It didn't matter—the town was still asleep.

We approached the building from the back, where there was a delivery entrance. It was locked with a rusty metal chain, but Michael pulled out a pair of bolt cutters from inside his duffel bag. The chain fell to the ground with a clang.

"Ready?"

"I thought we were going to wait for Beth," Bliss whispered.

"She'll be here soon," Michael said. "I don't want anyone to see us standing out here."

My heart was a loud hammer as we stepped inside the windowless hallway. The cement floor sloped upward and I realized it had not been used simply for deliveries. It had also been used to wheel out the bodies of dead inmates.

The hallway ended in a massive kitchen. Dusty windows allowed a shard of light into the dank room. A rat scurried across the floor, startling us. We followed Michael out of the kitchen. He seemed to know exactly where he was going, whereas I had no idea. My two previous visits had begun at the front door, so I was turned around and confused by the layout.

As we ventured farther into the belly of the building, it became darker. Our footsteps echoed as we climbed dirty stairs and came to the main floor. Michael pulled open a heavy door, which led to yet another hallway. This one was lined with empty cells, their doors pushed open as if inviting us to sit down on one of the metal bed frames. It was slightly easier to see because each of the cells had its own tiny window. Pink sunlight glowed behind the glass.

We came to the end of the hallway. I was beginning to recognize my surroundings. To the left was the hallway that would end at the front doors. Taking the right would lead us to the execution chamber.

And in front of us there was a body.

Michael crouched down next to the person spread out on the floor and pressed two fingers to his neck. From his size I knew the man wasn't Noah.

"He's cold," Michael announced. "I think he's been here awhile."

I didn't want to be near the body, but I needed to know if he was someone I could identify. I took a step closer and looked down. I immediately recognized him.

It was Pate.

twenty-six

My stomach churned and I tried not to vomit. I looked away from Pate's body. "How did he die?" I asked Michael. "Can you tell?"

"There's a lot of blood," he replied. He was still crouched down next to Pate. Bliss stood off to the side, averting her gaze. "Looks like he was stabbed in the neck."

"Should we call the police?" Bliss asked.

"Not yet." Michael stood up. "We can't do anything for him. We need to keep going."

To keep going meant we needed to step around a shiny puddle of blood. I tried not to look down as I passed the heap on the floor. Bliss had a harder time than I did, as if she was afraid to go anywhere near the corpse. I held out my hand and she took it.

"Be strong," I whispered.

"I'm trying," she replied.

Michael turned right, toward the execution chamber. He walked with angry purpose. He was on a mission, I realized. It wasn't so much his duty to protect me or banish the

Watcher, though. He was determined to punish the thing that had killed his brother.

We reached the execution chamber. Before Michael could storm through the doors, I stopped him. "Do you know what you're doing?" I asked. "Because I don't want to see any more dead bodies today."

He shrugged me off. "He's in there. He's in there right now, and I'm going to make him wish he wasn't."

"I need to get my supplies," Bliss said. "Give me a moment, okay?"

"Michael, think about this!" I hissed. "You can't go in there yet! Calm down and think."

He looked at me with eyes filled with rage. "I *have* thought about this. Stay back, Charlotte." He pushed open the door with both hands. "Lloyd Marcus Greene!" he yelled. "Come out here and face me!"

Bliss was behind me, holding a lit candle. As Michael charged forward, we stepped into the room carefully, scanning the corners.

"Noah." She pointed to a dark corner with the candle. "Look. There he is."

At first, all I could see was debris. Chunks of wood from the shattered electric chair still lay scattered on the hard floor. It was too dark to see much in the murky corners, but the light from Bliss's candle helped direct my gaze until I finally saw him.

Noah was hunched in the corner, his back against the cement wall and his head between his knees. I wanted immediately to run to him, but Bliss held me back.

"Wait," she whispered. "I think it's a trap. Help me make the circle of salt."

Every instinct inside me screamed to go running to Noah, but I listened to Bliss. The fear was gone from her voice and had been replaced by determined confidence. It was like a light switch had flicked on, and the Protector in her was now at full force. We worked quickly to pour a thick circle of salt on the floor. I didn't know where the Watcher was, but I could feel his presence, somehow. I knew he was nearby, that he could see us.

"Stay close to me," Bliss whispered when we finished. "No matter what, stay where I can see you."

"We have to save Noah." I took a step forward, but Bliss pulled me back so hard that I lost my balance.

"Sorry," she said. "Guess I'm stronger than I realized."

Michael stood in the middle of the room. "Where are you?" he screamed. "Come out here!"

I could only stare at Noah. He flinched at the sound of Michael's screams but did not look up. My eyes were still adjusting to the darkness of the room. Light seeped in through cracks in the cement blocks, but it wasn't enough to illuminate the space. Bliss lit more candles, placing them around the circle.

"I am here." The voice came from another corner of the room. It was a voice I had heard before, one that had lingered in my nightmares. It was neither male nor female.

But it was definitely evil.

Even though Bliss and Michael had never heard it before, they recognized the unmistakable sound of the Watcher and froze.

A wicked cackle filled the room. The laughter had no discernable source. It came from everywhere, hanging all around us. But there was no one else in the room. Michael began pulling objects out of his duffel bag.

"I'm going to get Noah," Bliss said. "You keep him in the circle and stay there. And take this." It was a shard of wood from the electric chair. The sharp point at one end made it an ideal weapon.

She darted across the room, running fast in a straight line for the corner. Just as she reached Noah, something came shooting out from the opposite corner of the room. Arms outstretched and moving so fast it was little more than a black blur, the thing resembled a huge bat. It was on top of Bliss within a second, pulling her away from Noah and wrapping its long arms around her. She gasped in terrified shock.

I couldn't see the face of the Watcher. He was over six feet tall and the black trench coat he wore was ripped at the armpits, as if he was bulging out from its confines. Bliss struggled, but the Watcher's eerie hug kept her in place. He leaned down and whispered something into her ear.

Then he bit it off.

Bliss screamed. Michael was already standing, something clenched in his hand. He shot me a quick glance. "Stay there," he ordered.

Then he was running forward, his hand out. He stabbed the Watcher in the lower back with the object, forcing him to release Bliss. She crumpled to the floor, breathing hard and holding one hand to her ear. I could see flesh hanging off the side of her face and wanted so badly to run to her. I peeled off my jacket, knowing that she would need it to stop the bleeding.

The Watcher quickly regained his strength and turned on Michael, who stepped backward. He was drawing the Watcher away from Bliss and Noah. I could pull one of them away, into the protective circle of salt. Noah sat in the corner, his knees drawn up to his chest and his head down. Bliss was struggling to get up, but she was on her hands and knees, blood running down the side of her face.

Michael was chanting something. With every backward

step he took, I saw a half second of time in which I could pull Bliss or Noah to a safer place. I still couldn't see the Watcher's face. He had one arm raised as if to strike down Michael and was matching him step for step. When they were more than halfway across the execution chamber, I made my choice.

Sprinting forward, I reached Bliss. She was in pain and needed help. I put my arms under hers and dragged her into the circle, smearing the salt. I gave her my jacket, then tried to repair the circle, cupping the salt with my hands and re-forming it.

"Noah," Bliss croaked. "I have to save him."

I gingerly held the jacket to the bloody hole where her ear had been. "You need medical attention," I said softly. "I'll get Noah."

She tried to sit up but a rush of pain forced her back down. "My notebook," she gasped.

I scanned the floor, searching for what Bliss needed. I saw it lying just outside the circle. Kneeling down so that half my body was still within the perimeter, I stretched out my arms to grab the book. My fingers barely grazed it.

A few feet away, Michael was battling the Watcher. And, from a brief look in their direction, I could tell Michael was losing.

He stumbled as the Watcher brought both fists down on his shoulders. He tried to hit back, but the Watcher was too fast and easily stepped out the way. I wanted to help, but I knew that Bliss's notebook was more important at the moment. I dove for the book and pulled it back into the circle with me.

"Here." I placed the open book in her hands. "I need to get Noah."

"No," she moaned. "It's not safe."

"Neither is sitting here and hoping Michael can defeat that thing."

The Watcher had him cornered. Michael was on the ground, looking up at his attacker. It was almost exactly like what had happened to my mother. Only the location was different. I knew what was about to happen, and a tidal wave of fear crashed into me and pulled me into the first stages of a panic attack. I felt lightheaded and tried to breathe deeply.

The Watcher's voice echoed throughout the room. "I had fun with your brother," he said to Michael. Then he laughed. "So much fun."

Michael closed his eyes. I turned away from the scene. I fought against the dizziness. A panic attack would not kill me. The Watcher might, but not this. I had to crawl to the corner in order to get to Noah. I had to ignore the sickening thump that erupted from the area where Michael was. I focused on my one goal: to pull Noah into the circle of protection. He was still hunched in the corner, but as I got nearer, he looked up.

I locked my eyes on his. "Charlotte?" he whispered.

I made it to him. I tried to smile, but I was having trouble breathing. "We have to go," I wheezed.

"I think I like having you right here." The Watcher's voice was directly behind me.

I bowed my head, trying not to cry. This was it. I had tried and I had failed. A peculiar thought flittered across my mind. I wondered what time it was, and knew I wouldn't be calling Annalise at noon as I had promised.

I slowly turned around so I could finally see the face of the thing that had left Pate's body in a hallway. I did not want to see what had been done to Michael, and the Watcher blocked my view of Bliss.

The Watcher gazed down at me. He was smiling. I knew

that smile. It reminded me of Ryan, for some reason. And then I knew who it was, and why he had chosen Noah.

The creature in front of me was Noah's father.

twenty-seven

I sucked in my breath as the realization of what had been happening struck me. Noah's father had not arrived in town to crash a wedding. He had been lured here by the Watcher and had been meticulously stalking his prey for weeks, gradually infecting Noah until he had all of us right where he wanted us to be.

We were in his lair. The gate was open, and something within me understood that the Watcher intended to take us through that gate with him. We would disappear, and no one would ever know our fate.

I was past panic attacks. I was past anything remotely rational, and somehow, that gave me a curious kind of strength. When you know it's over, what is there left to lose?

"You can't have him," I croaked, huddling closer to Noah.

The Watcher grinned. He had too many teeth, I thought. His skin stretched like rubber across his mouth. "He's already mine." He squatted in front of me, the way an adult might do if he was speaking to a small child.

"You're all coming with me." His breath hit my face and I turned away, trying not to breathe in the foul odor of decaying flesh. "You're my special sacrifice." He reached out and curled a tendril of my hair between his fingers. "My *very* special sacrifice."

I swallowed a sob. I thought of my parents and my sister and the wedding I would never attend. And I thought of Noah, who felt like a rock, cold and unmoving. This wasn't fair. I had not chosen any of this. It had chosen me.

Then Noah's hand found mine. I felt his fingers searching for my own, but slowly, as if he didn't want the Watcher to notice. He squeezed my hand lightly, and I knew that he was out of his trance. I also knew that if I could turn around and see him, he would still have that glassy look in his eyes. He needed the Watcher to believe that he was still under his control.

Feeling Noah's grasp gave me a burst of energy. "I'm not going anywhere with you," I said.

This earned me another cackle. "Princess, you don't have a choice."

But I did. I could choose to accept this conquest or go out fighting. Bliss was still in the circle, chanting softly. In the opposite corner, Michael was stirring. I needed to keep the Watcher focused on me.

"I defeated you once," I said, making my voice loud. "I can do it again."

The Watcher pulled at the curl of my hair still entwined between his fingers. It came out—along with a piece of my scalp. Blood trickled down my forehead and tears stung at my eyes, but I refused to let him see the pain he'd caused. It was nothing compared to what Bliss and Michael had endured.

"You did not defeat me. You simply prolonged the inevitable." The Watcher licked the blood at the end of my clump of hair. He closed his eyes in delight.

And that was the precise moment Michael made his move.

Armed with the bolt cutters he had used earlier, my Protector sprang forward, clasping the tool around the Watcher's right ankle. Even though the Watcher was part demon, he was still using a human body. When the bolt cutters made contact, the Watcher howled in pain.

He spun around. Noah leapt up, grabbing my hand. We ran toward the doors leading out of the execution chamber. I wanted to take Bliss with us, but Noah pulled me forward and out of the room.

We raced down the hallway lined with jail cells, passing Pate's body. The doorway leading to the stairwell was nearby, but I was having trouble remembering exactly where it was located—halfway down the hallway or all the way at the end? Behind us, the doors of the execution chamber flung open, hitting the cement walls with a bang that reverberated throughout the penitentiary.

"Hide." Noah panted.

I ducked into the next cell and without thinking pulled the door shut. Metal clanged against metal and I winced. An unlocked jail cell was no place to hide, especially with the sunlight streaming in through the grime-streaked window.

I could hear the Watcher as he approached my cell. His labored breathing was loud, his heavy footsteps sluggish. Michael had wounded him. Maybe Bliss's prayers were working, as well. He was not the fast-flying thing that had come out of nowhere. His power had diminished, but that didn't mean he was weak enough to subdue.

He was also a few feet away from me. I didn't know where Noah was. I was defenseless. Trapped in a cage. I had no way out.

As the Watcher's footsteps got closer, I backed myself into the farthest corner of the cell. My heart pounded so loudly I was sure it could be heard throughout the entire building. I took a deep breath and kept my eyes on the entrance to the cell. I had nothing, and something bad was coming for me.

I braced myself for the Watcher's appearance. And when I saw him, I tried to keep breathing, to focus my mind. Even if all I could do was stall him from reaching Noah, it was something. The Watcher's black eyes found mine. "I'll be back for you," he snarled. His words seemed to sizzle in the air. He lurched forward, down the hall. I wanted him to keep going, to put some distance between my cell and wherever Noah was. I wasn't going to remain here. But again I reminded myself that there was little I could do. I had no weapon. How could I hurt this thing without one?

But even when you think you have nothing, you still have yourself.

As the Watcher's footsteps grew more distant, I let myself out of the cell, carefully sliding open the door so it didn't make too much noise. He was almost to the end of the hallway and, I assumed, near Noah.

I could do only one thing: run to the end of the hall and leap onto the Watcher's back. Maybe it would give Noah enough time to escape to the stairwell. But as I began to run, I heard something. My first thought was that it sounded a lot like horses stampeding in my direction. I stopped, confused. Then a doorway flung open, and Beth emerged from the stairwell. Behind her were Ryan and Jeff.

"Over there!" I screamed, pointing to the end of the hall.

Ryan and Jeff immediately charged forward. Did they know the Watcher was their father? Beth looked at me. "Annalise is waiting in the van outside," she said. "Get out of here. Now!"

She took off down the hallway after Jeff and Ryan. The door to the stairwell—to my escape—was only a few feet away from me. But Bliss was wounded. Michael might be dead. I had to go back for them.

I ran in the opposite direction, jumping over Pate's body like a track star completing hurdles. Inside the execution chamber, Bliss was kneeling inside the circle. Her right hand pressed my jacket to her ear. Her left hand held her open notebook.

"Let's go!" I yelled. "Beth is here. Come on!"

"I have to finish this." Her voice was oddly calm. "I can't leave yet."

I was already at her side. "Yes, you can. Help has arrived. You don't have to do this." I got her to her feet, then looked around the room. Michael lay on his back in the other corner. I could see dark liquid surrounding his head.

"Check on him," Bliss said. "I need to complete this."

I left her inside the circle and rushed over to Michael. I was afraid to look at him, afraid to touch him and discover that he was dead. But I did it anyway, stepping in the blood and holding his hand in mine. It wasn't cold, but it wasn't exactly warm.

"Can you hear me?" I asked.

His eyes fluttered open. "Close the gate," he groaned.

I felt relief that he was still alive. "I don't know how to do that," I said. "But Beth is here. We can get you out and she can close the gate." Even as I said it, I knew it was not going to be possible for me to help both Michael and Bliss escape. Michael was too injured to sit up, much less run.

"Only blood will do it," Michael murmured.

"Right. Blood." There was enough of that all over the floor. I took a breath, then cupped my hands together and collected some of his blood.

"Over there!" Bliss shouted. I looked in the direction she was pointing. One wall glowed with a faint red outline. The gate. I approached it with the sticky blood covering my hands. The red light glowed dark and formed a kind of arch. I thrust my hands forward, wiping the blood in the middle of the arch. Immediately, a howl erupted from the hallway beyond the execution chamber, followed by a chorus of yelling.

I returned to Michael. Needing more blood than my hands could hold, I took off my shoe and used it to scoop at the congealing puddle. "Sorry," I said to Michael. "I know this is gross." He didn't respond, but I could see that he was still breathing.

I carried my shoe back to the gate and poured the little blood I had collected onto the wall. As soon as it touched the cement, another howl exploded. But this time it was much, much closer.

Turning around, I saw the Watcher leaning against the doorway, panting heavily. He limped toward me. A knife protruded from his neck. I frantically smeared the blood from the bottom of my shoe onto the wall. The Watcher staggered back.

Suddenly, Beth appeared. As she raised her hand to strike the Watcher with another blade, he sensed her presence, spun around and grabbed both her arms. The cracking sound that followed made me instantly sick to my stomach. Beth didn't scream, though. She simply slumped to the floor, her useless arms bent at unnatural angles.

I needed more blood, but there was no way for me to get to Michael. The Watcher was blocking him. I could see Bliss pulling an unconscious Beth into the circle. She had let go of my blood-soaked jacket.

Ryan and Noah burst through the doors next. Ryan tackled the Watcher from behind. Noah was about to, as well, but I caught his eye. "My jacket!" I screamed. Bliss tossed it to him, and Noah sprinted over to me. I pressed it into the wall, which started to give way. The cement blocks moved back as if they were being inhaled. The Watcher shrieked and bucked Ryan off his shoulders. The Watcher came right for us. I looked at Noah.

"I have never loved anyone more than I love you," he said, taking my hand. He bowed his head to kiss it. And that's when I saw the deep gash across the side of his face, a jagged line that ran from near his left eye and all the way down to his chin.

"I love you, too." I wiped the blood from his face. Then I pressed my hand into the wall with all the force I had in me.

The cement bricks dissolved and ruby-red light poured through. The Watcher screeched as he fell to the floor. Invisible hands seemed to pull at him, dragging him toward the gate. He clawed at the cement floor, but there was nothing to hold on to. He was being sucked into the gate. Noah wrapped his arms around me and began to move me away from the wall. The Watcher's legs were no longer visible, but his arms still clawed at the air—and fastened onto my arm.

I was too shocked to feel the pain as the Watcher's clawlike fingers dug into my skin. I was aware of a ripping sensation, but it was only afterward, when Noah had hauled me away and used his shirt to try and stop the bleeding, did I realize what had happened.

We all stared as the Watcher disappeared down into the gaping red hole. His screams became more distant, until finally there were only a painful whisper. The bricks slowly reassembled themselves. The red light flashed even more brightly, then dimmed and faded until it was gone, leaving the wall as it had been before, with no trace of the gate. Sirens wailed in the distance. I held on to Noah, and he hugged me tightly to his chest.

Footsteps pounded down the hall. Annalise stood in the doorway, her eyes wild with fear. "I waited," she said, out of breath. "Then I called the police." She took in the scene, the battlefield of bodies. Ryan was coughing, Beth was still unconscious. It wasn't okay, but it was over.

The gate was closed.

twenty-eight

Most people would say that it wasn't a perfect wedding. Heavy rain forced the outdoor plans inside, so the vows were said within a wood-paneled courthouse instead of a gazebo decorated with roses. The groomsmen sported black eyes and arm slings. The bridesmaids wore dresses that didn't quite match: one was in long sleeves, one in short sleeves. And it may have seemed odd that at one point, everyone in attendance, including the bride and groom, turned toward a video camera and yelled, "Hi, Karen!"

It was a ceremony filled with imperfections. But the vows were recited with the kind of love and sincerity that made guests reach for their tissues, and the applause that followed drowned out the thunder rumbling overhead.

There was no way to explain what had happened to the mystified police when they'd arrived at the penitentiary. Our attacker had vanished. Ryan was the one who had identified his father as the assailant. Later, he told me that Beth had explained everything during the ride to the prison. He and Jeff hadn't believed her, but they had believed Noah was in trouble. Beth had told them they would understand when they got there. "And the instant I saw him, I knew what she said was true," Ryan had told me later that day. "I knew it wasn't really my dad."

Jeff had been knocked unconscious and suffered a concussion. I met him for the first time in the hospital, where I received a dozen stitches to my arm. He looked just like Ryan, with slightly lighter hair. All he said was, "This is one tough family my mom's marrying into." But I think he knew we made up for it with heart.

Noah and his brothers weren't exactly acknowledging the death of their father, because who knew what happened after he went through the gate? For now, they were focused on recovering from their injuries and moving forward with the wedding. There would be more than enough time later to come to terms with the fact that the father they barely knew had disappeared from their lives permanently.

Two days before the wedding, we'd made a trip to see Mom. She still couldn't talk, but her eyes had lit up when we walked in, despite our bandages. I'd worn long sleeves to cover my arm, which was wrapped in gauze. There would be a permanent scar, the doctor had warned me, but it really didn't bother me. It was my scar. I had earned it.

After the ceremony, we left for the reception under a canopy of umbrellas. Inside the reception hall, strings of little white lights blinked from behind the leaves of tall topiaries, and candles glowed from inside pumpkins that had been carved with Shane and Trisha's initials. The music began, toasts were made, and pictures were taken. We clapped when Shane and Trisha kissed. I had never seen them look so happy.

Noah and I sat at a table with Avery and Jared, who was thrilled to discover that the pasta dish was vegan. "Look who I brought with me," Avery said. She opened her oversize purse and Dante peeked out. I laughed and fed him a piece of my steak.

"Is that your dog?" Bliss came up to our table and smiled down at Dante. "He's cute."

"Thanks." Avery beamed. "You look great, Bliss."

She was dressed in a pale green gown. Her ear was bandaged, but she had styled her hair so it fell to one side, covering the injury. Doctors had been able to reattach most of the ear, but Bliss would require at least one more surgery. I noticed that the color of her gown matched the color of Michael's tie perfectly. He had been released from the hospital that morning and leaned on a cane as he limped over to our table.

"I'd ask you to dance, but I don't think I can," he said to Bliss.

She kissed his cheek. "We can just watch, then."

"How's Beth doing?" I asked Michael.

"Not too bad, considering both her arms are broken. I'll be helping out at Potion while she recovers."

Dad came over to say that he was leaving to see Mom. "And you're staying at Avery's tonight, correct?"

Annalise had told him everything before she joined Beth and had headed for the penitentiary. Dad had contacted the police and arrived with them moments after the gate had sealed itself. And while he was upset that I hadn't come to him, and shaken over having to see me in the hospital again, he was trying to stay positive. We were alive, and that was what mattered. And although he did not see the Watcher, he believed my story without question.

"The next time you think there's even a chance that something might possibly be after you, I expect you to talk to me immediately," he had said.

I promised I would. It was an easy promise to make. For the first time in over a year, I felt safe. Really, truly safe.

"Could you take these to Mary Ruth?" I handed him one of the centerpieces. "Trisha said it would be okay." I wanted to keep the promise I had made to myself when Mom woke up. My favorite nurse would find the floral arrangement on her desk the next day. Dad kissed my forehead and left with the flowers.

A new song started. "Is this 'War Pigs'?" Jared asked. He grabbed Avery's hand. "We are *so* dancing to this."

"It's not really a dancing song," she protested, but Jared was already halfway to the dance floor.

"Can I talk to you?" Noah asked.

"Sure. Bliss, will you keep an eye on Dante?"

She patted the dog and fed him more steak. "I'd love to."

Outside, the rain had slowed to a light drizzle and the sun was setting. Already, the full moon was visible in the darkest part of the sky. Noah and I stood under an awning. He looked amazing in his tux, and the bruise that I had once thought was permanent was finally beginning to fade from his neck. A pink line was etched across his face where he had been cut by the Watcher, but I knew that would lighten with time, too.

"I've barely seen you," Noah began, his eyes focused on the sky. "And so much has happened. We haven't had a chance to really talk."

I looped my arm through his. "But things are better now and settling down. We can be together more."

He inhaled deeply. "I broke my promise to you."

"What promise?" I didn't know what he was talking about.

"On your birthday, when I gave you the bracelet. I said I wouldn't be the cause of your tears." He looked away from the sky and into my eyes. "I broke my promise so many times over the past few weeks."

"It wasn't your fault. I know that."

And I knew that he had believed he was going to school and completing his daily routines. In reality, he'd drifted through the days in a kind of walking coma as he was sucked into the Watcher's control.

"I should have been stronger. I should have been able to stop it."

I put my hand on his cheek and he closed his eyes. "It took all of us to stop it. You couldn't have done it alone, and not because you're weak in any way, but because it was a force beyond your control. You have to let it go, Noah. For both of us."

He put his hand over mine. "Do you think you can ever trust me again?"

Like so many things, I had realized that trust is a choice we make. I kissed him lightly on the lips. "I already do."

"Thank you." He pulled away and reached into his pocket. "I know your bracelet was broken, so I got you this."

He held out a long, black velvet box. I opened it. Inside was a necklace. A single Apache tear was attached to the end of a long silver chain.

"I love it."

I turned around so Noah could put the necklace on me. Once it was fastened, he kissed the back of my neck.

"So we can start over?" he whispered.

"No," I said, turning to face him. "But we can keep going."

We choose what we leave behind. For some, it is anger and grief and a hurt so deep it echoes for centuries. For others, it is joy and wonder and gratitude.

I reached for Noah. He smiled and took my hand.

I made my choice.

★ ★ ★ ★ ★

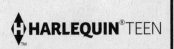